MESSIAH

MESSIAH

JUDGE, JURY, & EXECUTIONER™ BOOK TWENTY-ONE

CRAIG MARTELLE

MICHAEL ANDERLE

We can't write without those who support us
On the home front, we thank you for being there for us

We wouldn't be able to do this for a living if it weren't for our
readers
We thank you for reading our books

FROM LAST TIME (JJE20—FRENZIK)

Wyatt Earp, in Orbit over Jilk

"We have identified four different military training areas that are populated with cutting-edge weaponry: ground assault vehicles, attack skimmers, artillery, and personnel carriers. This is for a planet that allegedly doesn't have a military, which is required to be registered with the Federation," Clevarious reported with a hint of pride.

Rivka smirked. "Are you angling for a SCAMP body, C? I think you deserve one, but make sure one of your reprobate buddies is schooled up in how to run my ship for when you pull out."

There was silence, the length of which would have been a lifetime for an SI. Finally, Clevarious answered, "I'm not sure a simple thank you is enough. Not for what you're willing to do for me, but what you've done for all of my kind."

"It was the right thing to do, C. Just like letting you go.

That's the right thing, too. If Grainger gets *Wyatt Earp*, make sure you train him properly."

"My replacement will be trained well, I assure you," Clevarious replied.

"I have no doubt. I was talking about Grainger. Train *him*. I'm sure he'll mess things up."

"Unacceptable," a small voice stated from the corridor. "The embassy of the Singularity is on Rivka's ship, not Grainger's ship."

"Ankh, nothing is confirmed yet, but after we drop off a few of our charges at Jhiordaan, we'll go straight to Yoll and get some answers. I've been given leave to contact Lance Reynolds directly."

"We've already sent a formal message via diplomatic channels."

"Moving at the speed of light," Rivka replied. "Maybe we can upgrade the comm channels on all twelve planets of the Barrier Nebula to reestablish direct contact with Yoll."

Ankh asserted, "We shall subcontract the work. There is a team of traveling technicians working under the embassy. We'll have them deploy here immediately. Do you have more work to do with Frenzik?"

Rivka sighed and smacked her lips. "After consultating with his lawyer, he refused to answer any more questions."

"Chaz is supremely competent," Ankh replied in his emotionless voice.

"We have enough to put him away for a long time. Well, we already judged him and delivered the sentence. Thirty years for sedition. Ahsooleyman and Belloward are taking over Rising Sun Industries to maintain the lucrative elements, eliminate the universe-shaping elements, and continue to deliver the philanthropy. Rising Sun Industries has become the organization it appeared to be."

Rivka realized she was talking to an empty corridor. Ankh had left.

"How are you going to ensure that?" Clodagh asked.

"I'm the CEO. Unpaid, of course, but I have to approve expenditures. I have full access to everything, which means the entire operation will be viewed by our friends in the Singularity."

"You mean one of the reprobates," Clodagh quipped. "Abeldour will do a great job in that role. Good thing you left him behind in the computer system. He's already setting things up."

"I know," Rivka replied. They had inserted one of the SIs the second they had access. It made searching the system for the diplomatic communications easier. Abeldour had found them behind a multi-layered firewall. "It's nice having evidence in hand. I better follow up with Frenzik."

Rivka left the bridge. She found Chaz outside the conference room. "Is there anything you can tell me?"

"No, sorry. Attorney-client privilege. I know there's no appeal, but thirty years seems light for sedition."

"Counsel for the defense thinks the sentence is too lenient. That's a great headline. To be honest, it was his friends in high places who swayed me from life without chance of parole. I checked his age versus the actuarial tables for his race. He's got twenty years left on average. Thirty years in Jhiordaan is a life sentence for him."

"Well played, Magistrate," Chaz conceded.

Red snorted. "I wanted to pound him. I still do, even

though he's pathetic and sniveling. Big baddies aren't so big and bad when the Magistrate has them in cuffs."

"The different levels of evil. I keep thinking of Nefas. He was evil to the end, over and over when his clones kept popping up. And the creature that was Jack the Ripper." Rivka bowed her head, and her shoulders sagged. "Frenzik isn't evil, but he *is* a bad man. His days of freedom are over. Let's see if we can keep Rising Sun doing the good things they've done without any of the bad stuff. They might make more credits on the right side of the law. In any case, set course for Efrahim. We need to find their governmental leaders or help them with the process of new elections."

Red put his hand on her shoulder. "Why does that have to be us? We can look for them, but elections are a Federation thing. Tell them to bring their embassy team. Get off their fat asses and get to work!"

"Vered the Mighty, father of the Glazoron Messiah, lays down the hard truth."

Red frowned. "I saw that. I'm not sure I like it."

"I'll be in my quarters. Clevarious, use the team to find those ministers."

"Magistrate!" Sahved called from down the corridor.

Rivka looked at him, her eyes half-lidded. She was almost too tired to make it to her quarters, which were only a few steps away.

"I have no questions, only my compliments. Putting Ahsooleyman and Belloward in charge of the good work that Rising Sun does while being their overseer was genius, and installing an SI in the Rising Sun corporate tower will ensure continued compliance despite their proclivity to be, well, Albions."

Rivka chuckled. "Yes. We must protect the Albions from being Albions. Thanks, Sahved. We'll be looking for the missing people on Efrahim. Can you take care of that for me? I'm going to grab a short nap."

"Of course. It would be my honor." Sahved tried to salute in the Bad Company's style but ended up jamming his fingers into the overhead.

Rivka waved and stumbled to her quarters. Red opened the door for her and waved Tyler over to help her into bed. "Make sure she stays there until she's had enough sleep."

Red gripped Tyler's arm, and they held each other's gaze for an impactful moment. Then Red left, closing the door on his way out.

<u>Two Days Later</u>

"Why did no one wake me?" Rivka bellowed.

Tyler shrugged and paused the movie he was watching. "Take a shower. Drink a mocha. Then get briefed on where we are. Yell at me all you want, but they've been working their asses off to find the missing Efrahimi."

Rivka jumped into the shower, yelling, "What'd they find?"

Tyler moved into the bathroom to continue the conversation. "Sahved decided to put Ahsooleyman to work. He asked questions and got answers. I suspect he already knew, but it gave him plausible deniability. The missing had been killed. We have found the single grave they were dumped into. The Efrahimi are recovering them. The Federation is on its way to oversee new elections."

"Then what are we doing still here?"

"We're not here. We're there," Tyler replied.

The shower stopped, and Rivka held her hand out for a towel. "Are you speaking in tongues?"

"We're in orbit over Yoll. Grainger is waiting patiently for you, and I'm not being sarcastic. He ordered us to make sure you got all the rest you needed. The SI team is installing direct comms from the Barrier Nebula on the remaining eight planets. Abeldour took care of Albion's direct link, which was already in place. Did you know that the Albion government moved its offices into the Rising Sun tower?"

"I should have figured. So, good news all the way around. Do we still have a stack of Albions on board the ship? I almost feel sorry for those three in the brig."

"We dropped them off at Jhiordaan on our way here."

Rivka grunted and ground her teeth. She headed for the closet to get her clothes. "I would have liked to see the look on Frenzik's face one last time as he disappeared into prison, but then again, that would have been more gloating than I should do. My job was done once he was sentenced."

"We have video of the whole thing. He looked like a shell of his former self. There was nothing to gloat over. We need to celebrate the liberation of the Barrier Nebula. I think they're holding a thing at the council for you."

"I think you know more than you're letting on."

"Like, Lance Reynolds is waiting for you and is the host of the event? I knew that and didn't tell you."

Rivka nodded. "When is it?"

"When do you think?" Tyler jousted.

"Probably as soon as we can get there. We headed down as soon as I woke up, didn't we? Never mind. Business as usual while being completely different. Can I tell him I'm not doing the High Chancellor thing?"

"No. You know you're going to do it."

Rivka smirked and nodded. "Damn Grainger. Payback is going to be a bitch."

"No one doubts that."

When they reached the airlock, the entire crew was waiting. First in line to head out the hatch was Wenceslaus, the big orange cat.

Rivka looked at Tyler. "This isn't going to go well, is it?"

"Not at all. Business as usual, Magistrate."

CHAPTER ONE

<u>Yoll Capital City, Governmental Offices</u>

"Your Supremeliness, command me," Vered joked. Lindy elbowed him in the ribs.

"Red, I'm going to kick you right in the nuts." Rivka paced behind the High Chancellor's desk. Her nameplate was already there, declaring her the senior interpreter of the Federation's laws. She now ran the Magistrates. She had been one a day prior.

Wyatt Earp was on the lawn in front of the building, cloaked since spacecraft weren't allowed in undesignated areas. It was Rivka's way of flouting the very laws she was supposed to support.

Incessant meowing declared Wenceslaus was hungry. Or thirsty. Maybe bored, or maybe none of the above. One never knew with big orange cats.

"Get him some water." Rivka waved Red away, but he only shook his head.

"I don't work for that cat. You know that."

"Then go get Floyd, so our little girl can keep the big

orange company." Floyd the wombat. She had an implant that allowed her to talk to others, but she had the intelligence of a toddler and spoke in simple language. Wenceslaus tolerated her.

Red stared.

"She's still on board *Wyatt Earp*," Rivka explained, trying to sound normal and in control before the fire seized her soul. "What a bunch of shit. They're making noises like they're going to transfer my combat team."

"Aren't you the person who makes those decisions?" Lindy wondered. Red tapped his nose and nodded at his wife.

"Those fuckers!" She stomped her foot. "Grainger put this stuff in place before he handed over the reins." She smiled with an evil twinkle in her eye. "Watch this."

She took a seat behind her desk and logged into her new account.

Red and Lindy looked at each other, wondering if they were going to be transferred, too. With the Magistrate being promoted to High Chancellor, everything was changing. She'd spent the last few years building her team so that they could handle any situations that arose during the difficult cases Grainger assigned to her.

She also had the biggest ship, a heavy frigate that also carried the embassy of the Singularity. It was a unique situation.

"Get me Grainger, please."

A strange SI replied, "This is not the optimal time to call Magistrate Grainger. It's the middle of his night."

"Who in the holy jump the fuck up and down are you?" Rivka demanded.

"I'm Cyrus, your personal assistant."

"Listen, Clippy, I appreciate that you're here and doing a bang-up job, but I'm going to replace you with one of my own people." Rivka paused her computer to use her comm chip. *Clevarious, you magnificent bastard. I need your help. Lots of help. All the help you and my team can muster.*

Is there an emergency, Magistrate? I mean, High Chancellor? the sentient intelligence from *Wyatt Earp* replied.

The SI assigned here told me I couldn't call Grainger because it's the middle of his night. Do you believe that? Rivka groused.

That's bullshit, Clevarious replied. *Let me work through the Singularity to put one of your people in place. He really said that? Doesn't he know that Grainger serves best when Grainger is in his place?*

I'm not sure I'd put it that way, but since you said it, damn straight! How long is it going to take to remove all these landmines Grainger put in my way?

"Not long at all," Clevarious said from the sound system attached to the computer on Rivka's new desk. "Cyrus has been moved to waste disposal management, where he'll have a great deal of time to contemplate the errors of his ways. Give me a moment, and we'll have Grainger roused appropriately from a deep slumber so he can have a candid conversation with his new boss."

Rivka leaned back in her chair with her hands laced behind her head. Red raised his eyebrows at her. "What?"

Red sat down across from her. "The hardest thing to do is not let power go to your head. Petty doesn't suit you, Rivka."

She lost her smile. "Cancel that call, C."

"Already done, High Chancellor."

Rivka leaned forward. Red was right. "I hate this."

Red and Lindy nodded. "We know. What can we do to help?"

"Get Floyd up here, and Dery and Tyler. Where's Hamlet? Also, I need a live video with my ship. Put it on a screen in the corner where I can see it. I want an open door with my team surrounding me. Set a schedule where we can have a couple in the outer office at all times. The animals have free run of this floor. Make sure everyone knows, and make sure everyone on this floor plays with Floyd if she stops by. If they don't, there will be hell to pay!"

"There you go, HC! We're on it."

Lindy pointed at the floor. "I'll stay here."

Red kissed her and rushed out.

"I love that man," Lindy said.

"Me, too. As odd as that sounds. I wouldn't be me without you guys."

"We wouldn't be us without you. We might not have a direct hand in serving up a full buffet of Justice, but that doesn't mean we can't keep dishing it out. Your new role will be more of the same but on a grand scale."

Rivka leaned back and rolled her shoulders, trying to relieve some of her tension. "The vision of Justice throughout the Federation is important." She laughed. "Well, it's what I live for. We can influence the entirety of our member planets and beyond."

She looked at her computer screen, unsure of where to start.

"May I suggest potential cases?" Clevarious offered.

"That's why you're in this steaming-hot box, C. Work your magic. Let's see what needs to be addressed."

A list of short briefs appeared on her screen, and she scrolled down. "This isn't too bad." She reached the bottom, where it showed it was the first of seventy-four pages. "Oh." Her face fell.

She stared at the screen while scrolling back to the top of the first page. "C, sort the cases by number of people impacted by the transgressions, giving extra consideration to violent crimes and potential crimes committed by planetary leadership or representatives."

"Of course," the SI replied. A new list appeared, showing few of the cases from the first list. Rivka now had four pages. Only forty cases remained. She read the briefs, holding back from designating cases for action until she reached the end of the list.

Rivka got lost in the briefs. When she finally looked up, she found Dery watching her from where he perched on his mother's shoulder, wings tucked behind him. Red was sitting in a chair by the wall. Floyd snuffled at his feet. A cry of surprise from down the hall suggested the cat was making himself at home.

Tyler sat next to Red. "Good morning, sunshine."

"I need a food processor so I can have what I want when I want," Rivka ordered. "Just because the engine's idling doesn't mean we're not burning fuel."

"What do you want? I'll get it from the ship," Tyler offered. Rivka told him, and he hurried away.

Rivka frowned. "I don't want a bunch of servants." She had to rethink her team's presence and objectives.

"I'll submit a requisition to get one installed or at least

put a cantina on the first floor where everyone can benefit," Clevarious suggested.

"Cantina. We need a go-to place for everybody. C, have a dumbwaiter installed." Rivka pounded her fist on the desk as if hammering the gavel to declare her ruling complete.

"Why wouldn't you want a smart waiter?" the SI asked.

"Expand your horizons, Clevarious! There's more to Buck Rogers than the twenty-fifth century."

"Do we have a case?" Red asked.

"I'm supposed to give cases to the Magistrates, along with the new crop of field judges. Not quite Magistrates in their authority, but they can expand our reach. Make sure we get the biggest bang for our judgely credit. But I'm in charge, aren't I? I can give myself a case every now and then. Remote work from *Wyatt Earp*!" Rivka lowered the timbre of her voice. "Make it so, Number One."

Tyler reappeared with a large mocha. She smiled, and her eyes sparkled as she took it from him. They held each other's gaze for a moment. Rivka turned her attention back to the cases, and a new window popped up.

"You might want to look at this one, High Chancellor," Clevarious suggested.

Rivka read it. Her expression turned contemplative since she refused to descend into darkness in front of those who were being so supportive. She crooked a finger at Lindy. "Take a look at this."

The group glanced at each other. Lindy pointed at herself, and Rivka nodded vigorously and spun the screen around.

The future of the past, Dery told them all.

Rivka briefly wondered what he meant, but she didn't dwell on it since that always ended in her wasting time. She'd understand when the time was right or not at all. There were no other options.

Civil Unrest in the Barrier Nebula. Starting on planet Glazoron with the announcement of the return of the Messiah in the flesh, the provisional governments are increasingly under pressure to restore theocratic rule. The descent into a civil war on the planets of Glazoron, Jilk, and Lewbamar threatens to engulf neighboring systems until all the Barrier Nebula worlds are involved.

"What Messiah?" Red asked.

Lindy gave him the side-eye.

"No," Red replied when the truth dawned on him. He spun the monitor back to face Rivka. He didn't want to see the report.

"As much as it chaps my ass, we need to consult with the faeries." Rivka chewed her lip, staring at the screen but not reading. "I'm sure they never intended the deification of their progeny. Maybe I'm not sure, and that's why I feel the need to ask, and what the hell we do about it."

Dery unfurled his wings and took to the air. He made a slow circle around the office, then landed on Rivka's desk.

"What say you, little man?" she asked.

He pointed at the ceiling. *Peace rides a golden chariot.*

"That's oddly specific while remaining obtuse, which is perfect for anything you might tell us," Rivka replied. "Do we need to go to Glazoron?"

He looked at her with his big eyes. He leaned close and kissed her forehead.

Rivka vaulted upright and twirled her finger. "Time to

go, people. We have to return to the interstellar highway in the back of *Wyatt Earp's* chariot."

"Shouldn't you assign some cases?" Clevarious asked.

Rivka sat back down. She nodded at Red. "Prepare the ship. We're out of here as soon as I finish this." She prioritized the first page of cases one through ten. She gave three to Grainger and two each to the other Magistrates: Buster Crabbe, Cheese Blintz, and Jael. Rivka took the case that wasn't a case. She racked the next ten for the following week, which gave the Magistrates a week to finish their current caseload.

She smiled at her computer. "That's how it's done. Stop goofing off and get to work. Shut it down, C, and get back to the ship. We're out of here."

"What about the twelve meetings on your schedule over the next three days?"

Rivka sat down once more. "C, I swear, you're trying to kill me. Death by a thousand cuts. Thank you, sir. May I have another?"

"The High Chancellor's time is in great demand among diplomats and government officials alike."

Rivka leaned close to the monitor. "Fuck those people. I'll tell them what they need to know in an email."

"You don't even know the people or the questions," Clevarious countered.

"Why does it look like you're leaving?" a familiar voice asked from the open doorway.

Rivka stood when she saw who it was.

General Lance Reynolds.

"Duty calls, General," Rivka replied, walking around her desk to lean against its front.

"Are you sure?" The question wasn't open to misinterpretation.

"I feel like I don't need to answer that because you're going to tell me where I've already gone wrong."

"Not yet, but you were about to." He took a seat in the chair across from Rivka's desk. Red chased everyone out, including Floyd, and shut the door. Rivka was alone with the leader of the free universe.

"Not all cases can be resolved from here," Rivka started.

Lance held his hand up to head off further excuses. "Why do you think you're the High Chancellor? Be honest."

"Be honest, you say. It would only be my opinion. You can tell me why I'm here, and it would be factual."

"I would like to hear your opinion."

"I'll call it speculation, but since you insist... I'm here because Grainger wanted out of this chair. I respect Grainger, and I'd like to think I understand him. After being in this chair for an hour, I know he didn't like it. Tag, you're it. I'll pass it to Chi Siblinz, and he'll pass it to Buster Crabbe."

"You won't," Lance stated matter-of-factly.

That gave Rivka pause. Her shoulders slumped under the burden.

"My daughter wanted you in that seat from the second she met you."

"Bethany Anne? I'm better out there." Rivka pointed at the window.

"Are you?"

"You're asking questions that are really hard to answer because they aren't questions at all."

"When you get to be my age, you find it's better to ask

questions than just give answers. People need to arrive at the right answer in order to embrace it."

"I think I'm better out there." Rivka stared at the window.

"Maybe right now, but eventually, you'll be better here. To do that, you need to be here and do the job from here."

"A civil war is brewing, and it's going to be a religious war, which means it won't be pretty. Too many people will die if I don't act. They want the Messiah, and as weird as it sounds, his parents work for me. I won't send them in there without me flying cover." She gave an analogy the General could sink his teeth into. "I have to go to prevent a war among ten different worlds. The theocracy versus the aristocracy versus democracy."

"They think Dery is the Messiah?" General Reynolds asked.

"Glazoron. They bowed and scraped when he passed. They believe it with all their hearts. I think starting a war in his name will be detrimental to the boy's psyche, not to mention those who get killed."

"What if he *is* their Messiah?"

Rivka stared blankly. "He's not..." Her voice trailed off. He was making her question what she knew. The faeries had helped Lindy and Red conceive. That was all. No different from what nanocytes did for those who carried them in their bloodstream, like Rivka and the man before her.

"I've seen too much that I couldn't explain. Sometimes, you have to accept what you don't know and take it on faith. The people of Azfelius might be the gods we've lost.

They successfully hid from the Kurtherians. That's no easy thing."

Rivka decided that not answering his earlier question would protect what was left of what she believed.

"They kicked me and my bodyguard off their planet."

"I know. They told me that you shouldn't take it personally."

"It was hard not to."

"You're not ready for what they offer. That's all. Back to you. I want you in that chair because Bethany Anne wants you there. I trust her judgment, and I've formed my own opinion, too. Do you want to hear it?"

Rivka kept getting set up. She smiled. A man who wasn't a barrister was two steps ahead of her. She was glad that he wasn't across the aisle from her in a court of law. "If I say no, will you tell me anyway?"

"No."

Rivka nodded. "Then yes. I'd like to hear your opinion because it matters very much to me. I want to know where I stand and, more importantly, where I'm going."

"I trust you. There are many worlds out there that trust you, too, and there are those who fear you, but they know you are not vindictive. If they pay the price, it's because they crossed the line. They're mad that they were caught, not that they disagreed with the law or the crime."

Rivka stood so she could pace behind her desk. She held her hands behind her back and walked back and forth. "Keeping the peace among the member planets of the Federation may seem like a Foreign Affairs responsibility, like the Council of Ministers, but not in this case. Frenzik's empire had a soft landing, but it left a void in guidance.

"I don't want to say leadership since he didn't lead. He dictated a strategic future that benefitted him alone. The economies didn't crash. The downtrodden are looked after. I'm pleased with the outcome, but this new development arose rather quickly, within days. I feel like I have to handle it. Then I'll return and give the High Chancellor's seat one hundred percent of my attention."

General Reynolds stood.

Rivka stopped pacing.

"Deal. Hurry back. You know that none of your workload will change while you're gone."

Her face fell.

He laughed on his way out the door.

Red returned and looked at her, expecting their guidance to change.

"Let's go fix those people in the Barrier Nebula. They're raining on my parade, and I don't like it."

He looked surprised. "The General isn't making you stay?"

"I got me an approval to work remotely. I get to go while still doing the job here. Clevarious, tell me how I can handle those meetings while not being here."

"By doing them remotely," the SI answered.

"Sounds like a video call. Everyone to the ship. We've got places to go and people to see." Rivka strode out the door. A big orange cat ran between her feet, almost tripping her. Floyd cheered and bounced ahead until she ran out of gas. Tyler scooped the wombat up on his way past. Rivka leaned close to Red and whispered, "When we return, I fear that I'm going to be stuck here for the duration. You should start looking for another job, my friend."

"Fuck that," Red replied and hurried to the front of the group so he wouldn't have to hear any more.

CHAPTER TWO

<u>In Orbit over Glazoron</u>

"I know this may come as a complete surprise, but we're cleared to the stadium where they await the Messiah's arrival," Clodagh reported from the captain's seat.

Rivka gripped Clodagh's shoulder as a sign of camaraderie. Rivka was out of her element, so she got the opinions and ideas of others. "C, all hands to the cargo hold for a BOGSAT."

"'BOGSAT,' High Chancellor?" Clevarious wondered.

"Bunch of guys sitting around talking."

"Should I have them set out chairs?"

Rivka laughed. "We're far too cultured to sit on the deck. Have it done by the time I get there." She took off running.

Cole popped out of the airlock leading to the cargo bay as Rivka reached it three seconds later. She tried to dodge past him, but he blocked her.

"Can I help you?" he innocently asked.

"This is cheating, C," Rivka declared.

"I'm sorry you feel that way. I am working within the loose parameters I was given," the SI replied.

Rivka crossed her arms and tapped her foot, staring at Cole. Banging and scraping came from within the cargo bay. One of the Bad Company squad cursed. Cole looked away but didn't move until after his team called that they were ready.

He casually stepped aside. "High Chancellor." He ushered her through the airlock, and unsurprisingly, she found the chairs set up in a rough circle.

Rivka nodded at the warriors, Lewis, Russell, and Furny, who grinned at their complicity in something they didn't fully understand: the old Magistrate's mental chess matches with the ship's sentient intelligence. They suspected a bet of some sort was behind it, and they supported Cole when he decided on one second's notice to play the role of spoiler.

Rivka took her seat and waited. The other members of her team filtered in. The SIs Chaz and Dennicron, in their self-contained artificial mobility platform SCAMP bodies, opted to stand after politely nodding at the group. They had been working on their motion subroutines, which they shared with SCAMPs throughout the Singularity. It was inevitable that they would all have identical movements and gestures.

Sahved was the next to arrive. He ducked to get through the airlock, having smashed his head into the frame on more occasions than could be counted. The Pod-doc, the device that used nanocytes to repair damage to flesh and blood creatures, had finally reinforced his skull rather than deal with yet another concussion. He was one of the very few Yemilorians who had left their homeworld, a ring planet with the habitable region in the interior. The change to a globe-type planet or artificial gravity was too extreme. It had taken Sahved months to get over his nausea, in addition to a few Pod-doc treatments.

Tyler moseyed in like he owned the place. Rivka gave him a Look.

"What's up with you?" she asked when he handed her a large mocha fresh from the food processor.

"I just realized I'm now the First High Chancellor Man. Possibly the First Man. First High Man? Or maybe it's just the Hymen."

"Stop it," Rivka warned with a tight smile to keep from laughing.

Red and Lindy strolled in. Dery flew in behind them, chirping and singing without using words. The parents beamed at their child as he took a spin around the cargo bay. All eyes were on him.

Carrying her daughter Alanna, Clodagh entered. Ankh and Chrysanthemum walked hand in hand behind her.

"Now that we're all here, you're probably wondering why I summoned you," someone said on the ship's speakers. Erasmus was not bothering to use Ankh's voice box.

"Funny one, Mister Ambassador." Rivka motioned for everyone to take seats. Ankh stared unemotionally until Chrys took her seat, even though she was in her SCAMP body and could stand with ease. Ankh was Crenellian and had a chip in his head that contained part of the SI called Erasmus, one of Plato's stepchildren. Plato was Ted's SI from his original programming. Ankh and Erasmus were a couple and were married to Chrys.

Some things Rivka didn't question. If they worked, they worked.

Red and Lindy's son was part-faerie. That was why he had wings. He had all the knowledge of the faeries and was highly honored on Azfelius.

Floyd bounced through the first door and fell over the second. She hung on the coaming until Tyler picked her up and held her. She was asleep before he returned to his seat.

"Do you need the pilots, Magistrate? I mean, High Chancellor?" Clodagh asked.

"If they can make it," Rivka replied.

Clodagh pointed at the ceiling. Within a minute, all three pilots arrived—Aurora, Ryleigh, and Kennedy.

Rivka nodded at the assembled group and took a sip from her cup. "Everything has changed, but we've been given one last chance to do what we do best. We're heading back to the Barrier Nebula to prevent civil war. In this case, it's not necessarily the void left by Frenzik's machinations but the absence of something greater that has left their souls begging. Our last trip through, and most importantly, Dery's appearance, convinced them that he was what they'd been missing. They think Dery is their Messiah."

The crew knew that.

"He's not," Red stated with conviction, then softened. "As far as we know."

Lindy shrugged.

Dery landed on her arm and giggled. *It is what is,* he told them all.

"It is," Rivka agreed. "We can't have the natives fighting over it, between themselves as well as between planets. Ten of the twelve worlds seem ready to go to war over this issue. Ypswych and, oddly, Albion, aren't. The others are gearing up for a fight. We can't allow that."

"Are we going in ready to make war? We did last time and eliminated a couple vessels that you declared as the enemy," Aurora asked.

"They were the enemy. They were pirates carrying no planet's flag. Lawless mercenaries, unlike the Bad Company, that acts as lawful mercenaries when required, always with the approval of the affected planetary government..." Rivka stopped and frowned as she thought about her engagements using the Bad Company. "Or requested by lawful authority, as in, me."

"Are we going to bring them in on this?" Clodagh wondered.

Rivka wanted to resolve this case without the threat of force, but with that many planets ready to go to war, *Wyatt Earp* could quickly be overwhelmed. She stood.

"All those tasty warriors going to waste in the Dren Cluster," Kennedy joked to get a rise from her boyfriend Lewis.

"You have all the warrior you can handle right here, babe." He winked at her and took her hand.

"Probably not a bad idea," Rivka agreed to the earlier question. "Clevarious, can you check the current status of the Bad Company? I thought they were leaving assets at the shipyard in the Jilk system to assist with Gate drive production and installation on Bad Company ships. After I voided the pending contracts, that is."

"I'll report when I have something," the SI replied.

"It never hurts to have reinforcements, but please understand my guidance on this case." Rivka hesitated.

Red coughed. "Mission." He did it twice so there would be no mistake.

"Case." Rivka glared at him.

Red said, "We're out here to put ourselves between eight planets getting ready to throw down. What law are they breaking?"

"Red, you're being intransigent. The law in question revolves around 'Love thy neighbor.'" Rivka kept a straight face.

Red looked at Sahved and then at Chaz and Dennicron for confirmation.

The Yemilorian raised his hand. "I don't know of such a law. Oh, if only there were! Can you imagine how much love there would be?"

Red recoiled. "You're kidding."

"You cannot legislate love, Vered the Mighty," Chaz explained.

Sahved touched his nose with the tip of one of his three fingers.

"I think the High Chancellor is having us on," Chaz continued.

"I hate to say it, but we are going for the sole reason that we have their Messiah on board. No one can resolve the concerns in the Barrier Nebula without him. Dery can make quick work of this with the right words to the right people. Tell them it is against his wishes that they fight and they will receive immediate condemnation from on high for crossing their savior."

"I thought we determined he's not their Messiah? I'm

not sure my one-year-old son is going to, heaven forbid, play God. Pun intended," Lindy added.

"Hang on." Red waved his arms to get everyone's attention. "Did no one hear the High Chancellor admit that this is a mission and…wait for it…Red was right?"

Lindy backhanded his arm. Dery hugged her neck, and she apologized to her son but not to Red.

"Ballsack!" Red blurted. "Are the bets in already? Rivka's last case. People will be throwing a lot of credits around on this one. We're going to have a huge bistok roast if anyone is on the receiving end of our good fortune." Red stabbed a finger at Rivka.

"Why me? I already pay for everything. I think I do, anyway." She looked at Ankh for confirmation.

He shook his head.

"The rules," Red continued. "Half the take has been going into a pot for the no-no case that has never materialized. The case that closes without hitting key lines."

"I don't expect to be running or punching people in the face on this one, swearing at them or blood," Rivka countered. She looked at the deck. "Then again, I *never* intend that. I'll try to be better on this *case*. After all, I *am* the High Chancellor, Grainger be damned for all eternity."

"Rolling a no-no. We might never have to work again." Red raised one eyebrow, eyeing Rivka. Then he faced the group and made a terrifying face. "Any of you fuckers let her fall off the no-no bandwagon, I'll beat you into last week, then drag you forward in time to pummel you into next week."

He raised his chin toward Rivka. "And don't make me tackle you. No swearing. No arresting people. No bullshit.

We stop the war and go home rich. Right, little buddy?" He smiled at his son.

Dery giggled and launched himself from his mother's shoulder into his father's arms without bothering to unfold his wings. Red caught him and lifted him over his head before cradling him in his arms.

"Being a father has turned you into a pussycat," Rivka purred.

Red pointed at his eyes with two fingers, then stabbed them at Rivka. *I'm watching you.*

"Where was I before getting so rudely interrupted by talk of dirty credits?" Rivka ran through the issues again. "Bad Company might be at Jilk, but we need to go to Glazoron and talk them down off their mountain of inspired deification."

"We're already in orbit over Glazoron and cleared for immediate landing," Clodagh explained.

"And they're getting impatient," Clevarious added. "*War Axe* is at the shipyard in the Jilk system as the sole Bad Company asset."

Rivka ordered, "Untether *Destiny's Vengeance* and leave it in orbit. It's going to be a tight squeeze on the planet. Take us down. All we'll concede is letting them see the little man, but we will not grant access. This isn't an airing of grievances or a worship session. We only want to hear what they think they want, and then we'll refine that to what they'll accept.

"Under no circumstances will they have direct contact with Dery. As Lindy so rightly pointed out, and it is easy to forget, Dery is a one-year-old. He might have the knowledge of the universe, but he's a child. Overzealous worshippers could unintentionally harm him. We will not allow the conditions where that could happen.

"No access. You four, Cole, Lewis, Furny, and Russell, get your suits on in case we need to protect our little man with all the firepower at our command. I hope you're not needed, but there will be hell to pay if you are."

No booms, Dery stated.

Rivka grimaced. "You don't want us to go in armed? It would be to protect you."

No need, the boy explained. He extricated himself from Red's embrace and flew to Rivka. She held out her arm, and he landed. He touched his forehead to hers.

Calmness threatened to overwhelm her, so she sat down. "Please! I can't allow anything to happen to you," Rivka pleaded as her agitation rose anew.

Dery's influence took the edge from her angst. There was no fighting it. "I take full responsibility for you, little man."

No. Dery's rebuke wasn't harsh, but it was firm. It felt like a crushing blow.

"Where you go, I will go. Don't fly away because I can't do that. *Promise me.*" Rivka caressed his cheek with one finger. "My authority and your visibility."

He hugged her face. She glanced at Red and Lindy. She had their full support, but concern filled their faces. They wouldn't be far from the boy either.

"No suits," Rivka told the warriors.

CHAPTER THREE

<u>Glazoron, Planetary Sports Stadium, Meeting of the Faithful</u>

The warriors had realized they weren't going to suit up and hadn't moved since being given the order.

Wyatt Earp flared for a landing. "Be prepared to see every citizen of Glazoron pack tightly around the ship," Clevarious warned. "Also, we're approaching a closer pass to the first star in the system, which means they're losing their fur and fat as temperatures ratchet upward. They might look patchy."

"Thanks for that." Rivka approached the cargo bay ramp as it descended. A hot wind blew into the bay, carrying the stench of the million bodies in and around the biggest stadium on the planet. Rivka snorted and coughed.

Dery unfolded his wings and gently flapped them to hover. *Peace,* the boy sent to every mind in the crowd.

Rivka, Red, and Lindy followed him out as he left the cargo bay. Those gathered knelt, then bowed as well as they could, considering there was barely enough space to stand. The wave continued from the ship through the field into the stands and beyond. Rivka didn't have to see to know that crowds beyond the walls were bowing in homage to the one they considered to be the Messiah.

"Fuck me," Red mumbled.

"With one word, the good people of Glazoron have stopped arguing, stopped fighting," Rivka whispered. In the silence, Red and Lindy heard her.

The others trailed down the ramp after them to a narrow cleared path. They could only pass in single file. Red clicked his tongue, and Dery rose to allow Red to pass beneath and lead the way. Rivka moved in directly behind the boy, and Lindy tucked in close to Rivka. At a gesture, the others stayed with the ship. Rivka requested, *Clodagh, get a drone into the air. I want to see what's happening outside the stadium.*

On it. The chief engineer bolted into the ship, although they both knew Clevarious was already taking care of it.

Rivka didn't want it to happen, but Dery ascended and flew a circuit around the field. Red tried to follow, high-stepping through the bodies, but they were too tightly packed. He fell, got tangled up, and was unable to follow. Helpless, he watched from where he lay.

Rivka also watched.

People of the twin stars, hear me! someone boomed: Dery, but not Dery. It sounded like an all-faerie chorus. *Your prayers do you honor, but your violence destroys what you seek. Put away your weapons and embrace the trilogy of food, family, and friends.*

Rivka looked at Lindy. She shook her head.

Red carefully stepped through the bodies to get back to the path.

"Your enemies will not give us peace. We do not seek violence. It seeks us. We cannot die at its hand while doing your bidding," someone cried over the loudspeakers.

Rivka, Red, and Lindy looked to see who was speaking but couldn't locate anyone who wasn't prostrate.

Clodagh? Find me that speaker, Rivka requested.

Right in front of the ship. There's a grandstand with a podium and microphone. There's some roly-poly in a cloak standing there.

Roly-poly. The Glazoron. It wasn't the nicest term, but it was clear who Clodagh was talking about.

Rivka tomahawked an arm in that direction, and she and Red and Lindy squeezed under the ship to get to the speaker. They only had to work their way through a few rows of worshippers, who obediently bowed. Rivka climbed the small stage and squeezed in next to the Glazoron.

She covered the microphone with her hand. "Would you join me on my ship so we can talk in private?"

He shook his head with great vigor while pointing skyward. "Flee before the Messiah? Never!"

"You're not leaving him behind," Rivka explained. "Didn't we just arrive with him on board our ship? He lives there. You are entering his domain, not fleeing from it." Rivka had to avoid calling him the Messiah, even though that was how they knew him. It would have given her more leverage, but it wasn't the right thing to do.

"What a shitshow," Red grumbled, not taking his eyes off his boy.

Peace, Dery again boomed through their collected minds. He completed his circuit and descended.

Lindy rushed under the ship to wait for him on the other side.

"Please, come with us, and let's talk. I assume you're the leader here."

"I am."

"I'm High Chancellor Rivka Anoa. I'm from the Federation, and I'm here to help. Come with me." Rivka lowered her voice, but there could be no mistaking what she wanted and that she wouldn't be refused.

Red was torn. Stay with Rivka or go to the cargo ramp? Family and friends. He had both on the other side of the ship waiting for Dery. That was what the boy had said. Food, family, and friends. It seemed too simple to be a messianic prophecy. Maybe it was a simple formula for happiness. In any case, Red liked it. Maybe he could convince Ankh to order an All Guns Blazing delivery.

The religious leader resisted until Dery was out of sight. Then Rivka waved for him to follow. If he didn't, she'd have the warriors grab him. He had no authority while Dery was there, and maybe he didn't like it. It depended on whether he was a true believer. The only choice she was giving him was to come willingly or be dragged into the ship.

Come, Dery requested in his normal voice, which was light and happy.

The religious leader followed as if in a trance. Rivka crouched to get under the ship, then jumped onto the ramp and entered. Dery flew in behind her. Red stayed between the religious leader and his son.

"What's your name?" Rivka asked from the top of the ramp.

"I am His Humble Servant Maggus." Rivka had expected a more awe-inspiring title like the Preeminent Supremeness of All Religious Matters on Glazoron and Beyond. She was pleasantly surprised by the simplicity.

"Maggus, follow me to my conference room." Rivka took a step, but Dery hovered nearby, facing His Humble Servant. The Glazoron bowed to the deck and stayed that way.

Rivka stepped over next to Dery and encouraged the boy to land on her arm. "Could we retire to the conference room? Let's try to settle this as soon as possible. We can prevent a shooting war. We can save all their lives. *You* can save all their lives."

A tear escaped Dery's eye and trailed down his face. He hugged Rivka's neck while she carried him to the conference room and took a seat. Profound sadness threatened to send her to the pit of despair, and her confidence evaporated.

"Maggus. We need you to stop the call to arms, either to defend Glazoron or to project His word beyond this system. There can be no holy war."

"It is in the best interest of the non-believers that they be given a chance to see the light," Maggus replied.

"Your mind is already made up, sounds like, yet you have him right here and reject that he's telling you to find peace. Food, family, and friends are the three pillars of a stable society. Focus on that, and the rest will fall into place."

The Glazoron stared at Dery, but not with the worship in the others' eyes.

"This isn't about him but about you," Rivka stated. She shifted Dery away from Maggus. Red stepped in and took the boy, cradling him while glaring at the becloaked religious leader. Rivka touched Maggus on the arm and gripped it when he tried to pull away. "I need you to order all Glazoron forces to stand down."

The Glazoron were the technical developers of the Barrier Nebula. They ran the high-tech factories that were responsible for building Frenzik's Gate drives. They'd also been building drone ships. Push a button and fight a war. He'd ordered them to Jilk to destroy the shipyard.

Rivka leaned in. "Recall those drones!"

"No Glazoron will be hurt. We only remove the enemy's ability to attack us."

"That won't do it." Rivka stood. Red put a hand on her shoulder.

No punching people. No swearing. Rivka didn't care about the credit stockpile or the fortune it would bring to her crew. She wasn't even sure there were any betting lines since this wasn't a real case, but the Singularity and the Federation gamblers would come up with something. She didn't care. She had to stop a war.

"You don't believe he's the Messiah, do you?"

Maggus didn't answer, but Rivka saw the answer clearly in his mind. *Of course he isn't. There is no Messiah.*

"That's a rough admission for the religious leader. You see Dery as a challenge to your power. I think I might have to detain you while we continue our negotiations. In the meantime, I'm going to let our people know that they need to deploy some serious firepower to protect the shipyard. We'll blast your drones into clouds of debris. Clevarious, rally the Bad Company. As many ships as they can spare. There are drones headed toward the shipyard at Jilk using faster-than-light. There won't be much time to engage them when they arrive."

"I'm talking with Smedley right now. Relaying the information you've shared. I've emphasized that time is of the essence," Clevarious replied.

"Put Maggus in the brig," Rivka flicked her fingers. She didn't even want to look at the religious leader.

Maggus smiled as if he'd won a great victory. Rivka tried to grab his arm again, but he threw himself away from the table. She followed him down with her hand outstretched. He hit the floor with a thud and a single huge exhale and stopped breathing. When Rivka touched him, he was lifeless.

She looked at Red and Lindy. "What the fuck was that? Tyler!"

Lindy ran from the room, almost bowling over the good doctor. She dodged out of the way so he could enter.

He checked the Glazoron, but he wasn't familiar with that species' physiology. "I'd guess poison."

"I refuse to let him be a martyr. Put him in the Pod-doc. Revive him, and then put him on ice." On ice, as in unconscious in the brig.

Tyler and Lindy struggled to move Maggus, who was half their height but round and difficult to get a grip on.

Rivka flopped back into the chair. "Is there anything worse than zealots?" It was a rhetorical question.

"Nefas was pretty bad," Red suggested while stroking Dery's hair.

"He didn't kill millions like this knothead is fixing to do, but Nefas *was* pretty bad. I hate that guy and his AI clones. He doesn't get to be called an SI." Rivka stared at the table. "C, what's going on outside the ship?"

The image from outside the ship appeared above the conference table. With a swipe of her hand, Rivka spun the image through three hundred and sixty degrees. The mob had compressed even more tightly around the ship. Crowds outside the stadium were tightening up against the walls, acting as if they would batter their way through the hatch.

"Get us airborne. Hover five hundred meters above the fray. That'll put us out of range of that surly mob." Rivka slouched in her chair. "Can you check on the Pod-doc's progress?"

Red nodded and walked out. The feeling of doom passed, replaced by a gentle touch on her mind, as soft as a feather's caress.

"Dery," she called, realizing after she had spoken that she hadn't needed to. "Thank you, little man. Whether Messiah or not, we couldn't love you more."

I know, came the unambiguous reply.

Fifteen seconds later, Red stuck his face in the door. "You better come." He didn't explain further.

Rivka jumped up even though she felt tired enough to remain seated for hours. She followed Red into the cargo bay. A red light flashed on the Pod-doc's control panel.

Tyler lifted his chin to her with his lips tightly pressed together.

She sighed. "I'm guessing you have bad news." There was no mistaking what the panel was showing.

"He's got some kind of anti-nanocyte technology. There's nothing we can do for him. His nanocytes killed him as surely as ours would have saved him."

"We got ourselves a martyr," Rivka mumbled. She looked for the nearest chair and sat. "Options?"

Tyler shook his head. "He's dead, and we can't revive him. He's going to stay dead."

She closed her eyes. "Think propaganda. What message can we send on his behalf to allay the masses until the situation is defused? His death right now is much worse than his death later. C, can you do up an artificial construct to fool his followers?"

"Fake videos! We can do that. I'll pull every video resource showing him speaking to catch the nuances he uses and the particular turn of phrase. It'll take us a little while to come up with something convincing. Say, fifteen or twenty minutes? What do you want his message to be?"

"Exactly what Dery told them. Food, family, and friends. Focus on the good in life that's right here on Glazoron. And find out if he told them anything about attacking Jilk. What an asshat!" Rivka was very frustrated. "I'll be in my quarters. By the way, how long did it take for this case to go south on us?"

"About twelve seconds," Red admitted. "It's gone downhill from the second we got here."

"Dery is special, aren't you, little man? What if he *is*

their Messiah?" Rivka wondered. Dery seemed oblivious to the conversation. He stared into the distance.

"It's hard not to think that way. If he is, do we lose him to worshippers? I'd rather let him stay on Azfelius, and you know how much Lindy and I are against that."

"I don't like the no-win situations. Dery, we need you on this one, buddy," Rivka prompted. The boy didn't respond.

"You'll get the word when it's the right time," Red told her.

There was no doubt about that, and it would be plenty ambiguous.

Tyler opened the Pod-doc. "What do you want us to do with the body?"

Rivka scowled at the Glazoron. "Since we can't admit he's dead, or not yet, anyway, we're going to have to freeze him and thaw him out later when he's ready to be returned. This guy was a predator, though. I'd say airlock the remains, but we're not in space. Him making a big splat in the stadium wouldn't be best for our position, but he needs to deliver a message to the worshippers and soon."

"Dery's message to them wasn't good enough?" Red wondered.

"No. This guy had them under his spell, but since he was so quick to martyr himself, there's someone else down there calling the shots. Another Humble Servant. My ass. We'll need to root out that person and stop them before they make too much noise. How could they not listen to their Messiah after demanding that he show up? This guy probably assumed we wouldn't come since he didn't think

Dery was the Messiah any more than we do. That threw a wrench in his gearbox."

"Monitoring the airwaves for the new player to appear," Clevarious announced.

"What would we do without you, C?"

"I don't know. Wander aimlessly through the cosmos in a pitiful and worthless existence?"

Rivka cocked her head and made a face. "I'll be in my quarters. Call me when you have a convincing message from the Grand Poobah."

CHAPTER FOUR

<u>Glazoron, Planetary Sports Stadium, Meeting of the Faithful</u>

Rivka was reclining on her couch when Clevarious interrupted her. "The video is ready to be projected to all screens throughout Glazoron. You can view it using your hologrid."

Rivka moved to her desk and raised the grid. When she was surrounded by information screens, she selected the video and expanded it. His Humble Servant Maggus appeared in an appropriately pious posture. "Today, you heard the Messiah speak directly to every one of you. Food, family, and friends. Those are the three pillars of our stability as a society.

"Faith in the Almighty has delivered a new role for all of us. Provide and be provided for. Find peace in service to your family and friends. Enjoy the bounty of your tables. Be thankful for these each day. I am honored to be in His presence and will return if He wills it." The figure on the screen bowed deeply. The video cut off before he straightened.

"Are you sure that looks and sounds like him?" Rivka asked. He sounded more pious than the raging asshole she'd encountered earlier, who had made little pretense of his lack of piety.

"It is him, taken from numerous videos. The gaps were filled using enhanced techniques."

"What's the worst thing that can happen?" Rivka asked. Then she stopped trying to envision it since the perps in her cases always strived to exceed worst-case projections. "Don't answer that, C. Go ahead. Transmit it on behalf of His Humble Servant."

"There it goes," the SI confirmed.

"How long before they start screeching?" Rivka asked.

"We're five hundred meters up. We won't hear any wailing or gnashing of teeth," Clevarious replied.

Tyler's fingers dug into Rivka's shoulders. She relaxed into his grip. "I heard. It's not looking good for the home team. How are they going to react to the death of their boy? I figure his associates might already know about it since it seemed to be the plan. He relished it."

Rivka moaned as a knot in the gap between her neck and shoulder socket was pummeled into submission. "He was going to take one for the team. Gauge the so-called Messiah's response by trying to establish an alternative path to enlightenment, righteousness, mindfulness, higher consciousness, or whatever the hell they want. C, what is the goal of their religion?"

"Higher state of being," Clevarious instantly replied. "As in, they aspire to break the bonds lashing them to their planet. To be free and soar. Dery made the perfect idol for them. Speaking directly into their minds sealed their faith."

"Then they duly ignore what he tells them. Is that what it's like to be religious?" Rivka waited, but the SI had no answer for her. The question was unanswerable. Faith demanded belief without facts and, when challenged, it caused internal strife. Rivka and her team were up against the greatest challenge known to sentient races, where faith challenged those without for primacy. In modern societies, citizens tended to stray from faith-based leaders, opting to put their trust in those with math and science supporting technical solutions to hard problems.

That didn't always work because of the soft science of leadership and dealing with people. That was where lines crossed. The hard problems could only be solved through faith.

Rivka added, "Convoluted logic is pervasive. To preserve our faith, we have to attack the shipyard of our greatest trading neighbor." She shook her head. "It is insanity."

"That's the argument that's launched a thousand wars, High Chancellor."

"Call me Rivka. I'm not sure how long it will take me to embrace the new title. I never thought of Grainger as the High Chancellor, only Wyatt."

"No can do, HC."

"You're killing me, C," Rivka quipped. "Back to the war. I couldn't see into his mind enough to determine what his goals were, only the short-term actions. What do they expect to get out of this? He wasn't a believer in the Messiah. I will consider that odd for a high priest or whatever that thing was called beyond Humble Servant, which was a lot of smoke and mirrors since he was neither humble nor a servant. He liked yanking the masses around by their nose rings."

"I didn't see any rings," Tyler muttered.

"Euphemistically speaking," Rivka clarified. "Manipulation. I'm sure there are plenty of faithful among the masses, as evidenced by how they responded when we entered their stadium, but the leaders need a greater level of scrutiny. The kind that only I can give since they are never going to reveal that their agenda is far removed from the precepts of their religion."

"Put the faithful in charge. Then Dery's influence will deliver what he wants. Peace," Tyler replied.

"You make it sound so simple," Rivka countered. "But that sounds like the right answer. Do we need to know their motivations? Because without the means and opportunity, their motivations don't matter. We remove the faithful from their clutches, they become powerless to act, and the good guys win!"

Tyler chuckled. "Make it that easy so we can go home."

Rivka sighed. "I'm home right now. Anywhere else is not home."

"You know what I mean," he argued. "I don't want to keep coming back to the Barrier Nebula. We've not explored Yoll at all. The General said it's a beautiful place once you get outside the Royal City of Khn'Chik. Even the city has a beauty all its own. There's also the diner, Steak in the Heart. You like that place."

"I do, but I also like All Guns Blazing. Is Terry Henry's

franchise open yet? Sorry, I guess it's Marcie and Kaeden's franchise now."

Tyler didn't know. He didn't know anything that would change Rivka's resistance to her new position or the move into her new office. He didn't ask about getting a place to live in the city. He knew she'd sleep on her ship for as long as the powers that be tolerated it. Then she'd move the ship and keep doing it.

She was the power.

"Resistance is futile," he muttered.

"Stop it. Resistance is nothing more than voltage divided by power." Rivka smiled at Tyler. "Thanks for trying. I know. It's unavoidable. I don't see how I can make the position my own. Not yet, anyway. I want to make a difference, like I know we've made out here. It'll take time, but we don't have much of that, do we?"

"Rivka!" Red bellowed from the corridor.

"You mean like that?" Tyler quipped and stepped back.

The masses had not reacted to the SI-generated video, so Rivka dropped the hologrid. She stood and stretched. "Thanks, you big husky hunk of man candy."

Before he could reply, Red pounded on the door to her quarters.

"Yes?" she called, crossing her arms to prepare for whatever onslaught of drama and doom that Red was bringing with him.

The door flew open. "Dery's gone."

The humor drained from Rivka's face. "Clevarious! All cameras outside the ship. Find when Dery left and where he went."

Red stepped out of the doorway. Rivka ran for the

bridge. When they arrived seconds later, Clevarious had Dery's departure tagged and tracked.

"Why did no one stop him?" Rivka barked at the screen. The boy had left via the main airlock. He had opened the hatch, stepped out, and glided down. "Follow him." Rivka gestured wildly at the deck.

The ship banked, and the image on the screen leaned, but the artificial gravity kept everyone in place as if there was no movement. Rivka subconsciously leaned into the turn and back as the ship's nose pointed at the ground. They did not accelerate as Rivka expected.

"Clodagh?"

"Don't want to mow down the boy while we're trying to get in front of him."

"Good point." Rivka was embarrassed. Dery had a five-minute head start. He was probably already on the ground, but since they had lost sight of him, it was much better to be safe.

Red moved close to the front screen. He caressed the image with a light touch.

Lindy tried using her chip. *Dery?*

"Clevarious, intercom, please." Rivka waited the obligatory three seconds, and the overhead speakers crackled to tell Rivka she could speak to the whole ship. "Cole. Suit up and prepare to go out via the cargo ramp. Quick as you can. Dery is flying around down there. We need to send our flyers after him."

"Consider it done. We'll be out the door in three," Cole promised.

Rivka studied the screen, looking for Dery's wings over

the crowd below. The SI was looking, too. Probably more SIs than just Clevarious.

"Scans?" Clodagh requested.

"Nothing," Clevarious replied. He hadn't sugar-coated his answer. It was brutally honest in a departure from his usual.

Lindy tried again. *Dery?* Red also sent a message to their son, but Dery didn't have a chip; he had telepathy. They needed to dig deeper. Lindy closed her eyes and concentrated. She furrowed her brow, and sweat beaded until it trailed down her face.

Red swooped in to grab her shoulders before she could fall. She continued her efforts until a sob escaped her lips. She collapsed in Red's arms. "I can't reach him."

Rivka's breath caught in her throat. They all felt helpless.

"On our way," Cole reported as the four warriors left the ship. The feed on the main screen showed the men dropping through the air. They activated their pneumatic jets to slow their descent and separated. Spreading out gave them a better chance of putting eyes on the boy.

They scanned and circled until they had to land. The faithful barely took note of their presence. "Have you seen a little boy with wings?" they repeatedly asked, but no one responded.

Cole tried a different approach. "Where is the Messiah?"

All nearby eyes glanced in one direction.

"That way," Cole told his team, hatcheting his arm in the direction they needed to go. The four shot into the air and angled toward the end of the stadium, circled once, and landed.

"Where is the Messiah?" they asked the Glazoron worshippers, but that bullet had been fired. They were no longer responsive. They stood, heads angled back, eyes turned to the sky.

There was no one up there. The boy had come down. He had to be here somewhere.

Had he been kidnapped? That was the question Cole was struggling with. He didn't want to raise it with Red and Lindy. "Keep looking," Cole directed. "Next place we look is under the stadium. See if someone brought him down there."

"No fear, Corporal," Lewis responded. "We won't stop until he's found."

CHAPTER FIVE

War Axe, Illicit Shipyard, Jilk System

Charumati couldn't shake the feeling that they were missing something. The Glazoron drones were due to arrive in ten minutes. The tension grated on their nerves, though they'd seen much worse.

Terry Henry Walton breathed like a stallion ready to be loosed on a hard track. "I got a bad feeling about this, Char."

Captain Micky San Marino sat in the captain's seat overlooking the bridge. "Ruzfell, power all weapons. TH, get your fighters into space, and I recommend you preemptively load your personnel into the Pods just in case."

"We would, except all my people are going to be in space, ready to shoot down those drones. The last line of defense, Micky. I don't want this shipyard destroyed. We can advance the Bad Company's fleet by ten years if all the ships have Gate drives. They'd be only one jump away from a conflict. They'd avoid any delay from using system Gates."

"Do you think that'll be effective?" Micky wondered.

"It'll be better than hiding in the Pods, waiting for *War Axe* to get killed so we can save ourselves. That's bullshit, Micky. I'm surprised you suggested it."

"The Pods have been configured with railguns."

"You don't need Bad Company warriors on board to fire them. Launch the Pods, and put them in position."

"Fighters launching," Ruzfell announced.

"*Get some!*" Terry bellowed.

Char chuckled while shaking her head. "Tactical." The display showed the interlocking fields of fire and the number of munitions and energy weapons designated to defend the shipyard. "Nice plan, TH."

"It's not the size of the dog in the fight. It's the volume of fire he can bring to bear in case those drones can defeat normal targeting systems," Terry explained.

"Counting down," Ruzfell announced. "Any time now."

On cue, the first wave of drones appeared as blips on the screen. Terry scanned the live feed but saw nothing. *War Axe* hummed as the defensive systems fired into the void, filling it with projectiles, plasma, and energy. The defensive line of warriors in powered armor unleashed volley after volley from their railguns, putting shrapnel in the way of the incoming drones.

The Pods swooped away from the shipyard as the first line of engagement. Small flashes on the main screen signaled the destruction of drone after drone. The fighters hovered, waiting for more.

One drone broke through, raced past the gauntlet, and angled toward the shipyard. The fighters accelerated at a crushing pace, firing everything they had, both ship-to-ship missiles and railguns. They followed the drone, dialing in their attack until fire poured directly into the engines. Finally, the drone jinked sideways, split, and exploded in an enormous fireball. The momentum carried the fragments to the shipyard, peppering it and the hulls in the berths.

"Hopefully, the particles were small enough and not going too fast," Terry muttered. He wasn't a fan of hope as a plan, but only one drone had gotten through. "Regroup and prepare to fire."

The second wave was inbound. They expected three waves and stragglers that couldn't keep pace. Not every engine put forth identical output.

"Damage report," Char requested from the shipyard.

"Small impacts have penetrated multiple support arms in Berths Six, Seven, and Eight. Automated systems have filled the penetrations. Ships' armor on the hulls in Six and Seven was sufficient to prevent loss of atmosphere. No casualties," someone reported over the comm.

"Firing," Ruzfell announced. The heavy destroyer thrummed with the energy it expended in defense of the shipyard.

War Axe maneuvered closer to put itself between the incoming drones and the spindly arms and berths of the shipyard. Micky had waited until the inbound vectors were pinpointed, and they now had the tracks. The other ships adjusted. The warriors arrayed perpendicular to the inbound drones, focusing more firepower in a smaller area. It gave them a better chance of defeating the drones.

"We could use more ships. This *little* engagement confirms we need the fleet able to Gate anywhere at any time. I could be miffed to the nth degree about it, or we can win this fight and start the refits most ricky-tick. As we find in Romeo and Juliet, *Go wisely and slowly. Those who rush stumble and fall.*" Terry chewed his lip. "I'd like to think we can go both wisely and quickly, or we shall surely fall."

He had no additional instructions to give the warfighters, who were fully engaged with the incoming drones. General Smedley Butler, the SI who ran the ship and was currently driving the Pods and integrating them into the defense, continued directing withering fire into the void.

None of the drones from the second wave made it anywhere near the cordon.

"*Yeah! Eat me, you metal pud-knockers!*" Terry regrouped. "Who fired them again?"

Char replied, "Glazoron. Short, round guys in a perpetual state of growing hair or losing hair to deal with being either too close or too far away from their twin stars."

"*You short, round wiener-smackers. In your face!*" Terry bellowed.

War Axe fired when the third wave appeared. Incrementally, the other weapons systems engaged. Had the drone waves been guided by a sentient intelligence, they could have learned and defeated the gauntlet through which they flew. They weren't, so the tactics of the third wave were identical to the previous two.

The volume of fire reached a crescendo. One drone managed to win the game of chance and make it through. The two fighters weren't satisfied by only one kill. They swooped and dodged, firing in front of the drone and raking it with plasma.

Both fighters hit it at the same time. It split, and the warhead broke free. The engine fired in its terminal phase, sending it careening toward deep space since it had no guidance. The warhead tumbled along a ballistic trajectory that took it past the shipyard.

"All hands, recover to *War Axe*," Terry ordered. "Start moving our ships here. Battleships first, then the carriers, then the destroyers. Finish up with the frigates. We need Gate drives on all of them!"

Char shook her head. "We need Glazoron to pick up the pace of production."

Terry leaned on the tactical station with his arms crossed. "Then why did Glazoron fire on the Jilk shipyard? Come to think of it, those two planets are in bed together. Have they had a falling out, and what does that portend for upgrading the Bad Company fleet?"

"Didn't Rivka say residents of the Barrier Nebula don't think like we do? It seems like a complete free-for-all." Char absentmindedly scratched Dokken behind his massive German Shepherd ears.

He leaned into it. *You go, girl. Give it to me!* the enhanced canine told her.

Terry snorted. "Comm, get me Magistrate Rivka Anoa on the blower. I have questions, and she'll have the answers."

"High Chancellor now, Colonel," Smedley replied.

"I am not. I don't know the first thing about the law. Well, the law of the jungle. Meow!"

Char pushed him. "He means Rivka is the High Chancellor. She's been promoted. Didn't you see the betting lines come through?"

"I didn't. Don't tell me; it's closed for new bets."

"It's not. Place your bets, but don't go crazy. We need to rebuild our retirement savings since you gave Marcie and Kae the AGB franchises."

"*We,*" Terry emphasized.

"I wouldn't have it any other way," Char agreed. "I never thought you could play too much golf or drink too much beer, but we learned there were limits."

"Who said anything about drinking too much beer? It's the stagnant lifestyle I couldn't tolerate. Did you think I drank more beer than I could hold?"

"Fighters and Pods have been recovered. Warriors are still en route," Micky announced.

Char raised one eyebrow to stare at her husband.

"I didn't drink too much beer," Terry insisted.

"You've been drinking too much beer for over a hundred and sixty years. Or is it a hundred and seventy?"

"I'm over two hundred years old," Terry blurted. "Makes me want to drink even more beer." He slouched and frowned.

Micky climbed down from his seat. "Are you two finished?"

Terry and Char looked at each other and nodded.

"Rivka is on the horn. Take it in my conference room." Micky gestured at the hatch at the rear of the bridge.

"C'mon, Micky. You gave the Bad Company your conference room years ago. We remain much obliged and forever in your debt. One AGB beer *or* wings on me." TH grinned.

"How many does that make?" Micky replied.

"One or one. They're not cumulative." Terry winked at the captain. "Smedley, make a note for the good captain's benefit and have a plate of wings sent to his quarters if he doesn't claim them."

In the conference room, the central hologrid was active, and Rivka was waiting impatiently. "Char, you're as beautiful as ever," Rivka said when the two appeared on the screen. She added in a monotone, "TH."

Terry tried to look like he hadn't been slighted, but his confidence was at an all-time high. They'd won another battle, this time against a faceless enemy firing the totality of their arsenal to destroy a target that had become important to him and the Bad Company. Since Terry's and Char's return, he'd had a hard time taking anything very seriously.

On the other hand, Rivka never stopped being serious. "Please give me good news."

"All drones are destroyed, relatively little damage to the shipyard. I'm going to start moving my fleet ships here to get retrofitted with Gate drives," Terry replied. "You could have gotten that information from Smedley. What's the real reason you called?"

"It's Dery, Lindy and Red's baby. He's disappeared on Glazoron."

Terry and Char took each other's hands and gripped them tightly. They respected families.

"There's more to it than that," Char noted.

"They think he's the Messiah. He flew off the ship and disappeared into a crowd of over a million bodies. He won't respond to our calls. Red and Lindy are ready to go scorched earth on this planet. I'm not sure I want to stop them, but I can't allow it, given my position as the High Chancellor. I'm still figuring things out and wanted to see what assets might be available to me before I go to General Reynolds."

Terry abandoned the jokes and joviality. "You have the entirety of the Bad Company at your disposal. We'll join you as soon as we recover our warriors, and I'll summon the fleet. It'll take them a while longer because they have to use system Gates."

"Protect that shipyard. The drones were the entirety of the Glazoron's remote arsenal, as far as I know, but I don't think they're done making war on Jilk. The reasoning was convoluted and didn't pass the logic test. It appeared that they wanted to start a religious war, ignoring the fact that their Messiah was here and telling them to embrace peace. Since Dery didn't give them the message they wanted, they ignored him."

"They ignored their Messiah? Sounds like it isn't about religion at all," Terry observed. "What do you want us to do once we get there?"

"We have to blockade the planet. Anyone leaving has to be checked to make sure they haven't kidnapped the boy. We have to keep him on the planet so we can find him. The universe is too big a place to let him get off Glazoron. I don't think they'll kill him. In fact, I'm positive they won't because of his special abilities. I don't think anyone could pull the trigger because he'd be in their mind, extolling the virtues of peace."

Char leaned toward Rivka's image. "*Is* he the Messiah?"

"We are deliberating that, although, how does one designate an all-powerful being?"

"That's a god," Terry replied. "A Messiah is different. The savior of a group, a religious leader bringing the people to the Promised Land."

"Maybe he is," Rivka conceded. "In any case, I want eyes on him and to ensure that he's safe so Red and Lindy don't tear that planet apart. If we can't find the boy, I'm inclined to turn his parents loose."

"We can't have that. We'll be there as soon as we can get a relief on-station," Terry promised. He closed the holo-grid. "That's a bunch of shit."

"What if the boy is doing what he was meant to do?" Char asked. "Because he *is* the Messiah. He's leaving the others behind to fulfill his destiny."

"We have to walk a tightrope on this one since we don't want his parents flipping out any more than they already are." Terry looked for Dokken, but he hadn't joined them in the conference room. "Where's my dog?"

I'm not your dog, Dokken replied.

CHAPTER SIX

Wyatt Earp, in Orbit over Glazoron

Rivka's next call had to be to Grainger. He'd been in the game longer than she had. Although the situation was unprecedented, as most of them tended to be, Grainger could provide insight.

"Clevarious, can you please call Grainger?" She crossed her arms and waited.

"I wondered when you were going to touch bases. Cyrus was in a snit because you fired him. He would have been a lot of help to you," Grainger told Rivka without giving her a chance to interrupt him.

She paused to make sure he was finished. "Cyrus will do a great job managing waste systems on Yoll. I have people I trust doing great things for the Federation. Let's talk about the current upheaval in the Barrier Nebula…"

Grainger listened while Rivka explained the convoluted logic she'd found inside the Glazoron high priest's mind.

"Sounds like you beheaded the snake. Find the true faithful and put them in charge because Dery told them to embrace peace. Let the religious order be religious and not militant. This sounds like a pretty easy case."

"The part that concerns me is Dery. We can't use him to manipulate the Glazoron."

"Is that what he's doing? He called them to peace. He told them to embrace food, family, and friends. Sounds like he wants them to be less trendy, or group-y, if that's a word, and more foundational in their faith. In any case, I have to get back to it. The new High Chancellor is a real ballbuster. I have twenty hours of work and ten hours to do it. We're going to have words about caseloads."

"Of course, we will. I promise. I'll tell you what you're getting, and you'll like it. I hope you didn't think I'd take it easy on you. Remember that part where you never allowed me any time off?"

"Because in your time off, you got into trouble. You were much better just doing your job. I did it in your best interests. And now, you're handling this situation with the Barrier Nebula. You know your work is building up on Yoll. There's no one else to do it. You'll figure out pretty quickly that if you ever leave the office, you'll never get ahead."

"I appreciate your efforts to cheer me up, but they're not working. Things are already grim enough. In any case, I've called the Bad Company to help us out. I'm not going to let the Glazoron start a civil war, even if I have to destroy one side to do it."

"That's the spirit, High Chancellor. Is there anything else I can do for you?" Grainger smirked at the camera.

"No, Magistrate. Get back to fulfilling that caseload. Do your job, and we all win."

"Samesies." Grainger waved as he disconnected.

"Must be nice to have the weight of the universe off your shoulders, you festering pile of bistok dung," she grumbled. Rivka dropped the hologrid. She needed to do something. What, she couldn't fathom, but she couldn't do it from her quarters. Rivka flung the door open and strode into the corridor. She stopped and looked both ways.

The solution she desperately sought was nowhere in sight. Not even the hint of a first step.

"Fuck!" Red screamed from down the corridor. The unmistakable sound of him punching the bulkhead followed.

Rivka headed toward the noise and found him outside the bridge. His fist was bloody, and a red smear marked the bulkhead. Rivka grabbed his arm before he could land another punch on the unyielding and unfeeling metal.

"Red, stop." Rivka's voice sounded unconvincing, which wasn't like her. It contained no emotion or command authority, but she felt she had to say the words.

Red turned around and, with his back against the bulkhead, slid down until he sat on the deck. He held his head in his hands. The nanocytes were already healing the damage to his fist. A cleaning bot appeared to attack the stain on the bulkhead but waited since the humans were in the way.

"I can only imagine how frustrated you are."

"I hate feeling helpless. It's like being on the faerie planet, but at least there, we knew they wouldn't harm our son. We didn't like them taking him, but he was in good hands. I can't say the same thing for the zealots below."

"The worst ones are like the priest who killed himself.

The believers represent the vast majority and strike me as harmless. Don't you think Dery would contact us if he were in trouble? He's capable of talking to the entire universe if he wishes."

"Do you think that?" Lindy asked from behind where Rivka kneeled next to Red.

"I do. The boy has skills."

Lindy straightened. "He's doing what he's called to do. Red, come on. It's time to work out so we can be ready in case we have to go in." Lindy held her hand out. Red took it. She had to bend her knees to leverage her strength to pull him to his feet.

She supported him as they walked toward the gym. He moved like a broken man. It crushed Rivka's soul to watch. Lindy was upright and dealing with the challenge in a positive way. Rivka wondered if it was an act.

If it was, she was pulling it off. That gave Rivka confidence. Acting like everything was going as it should wasn't the same as being concerned for the boy, but all they were doing was frustrating themselves and being counterproductive.

Rivka spoke out loud. "Remember the case. We're here to stop a war. As it is, Bad Company was able to intercept the drone fleet, but I guarantee that wasn't the only card these knuckleheads had to play. So, what do you say we find the back rooms where those fucking toads are plotting the degeneration of the Barrier Nebula?"

"High Chancellor?" Clodagh called from the bridge. "Were you talking to me?"

"No. I was talking to myself. I could tell because I wholeheartedly agreed with everything I said." Rivka stepped onto the bridge. "Clevarious, where do the senior priests of this religion hang out? We're going to pay them a visit. Tell Red and Lindy to get ready, full gear."

<hr>

Wyatt Earp hovered over a small building beside a massive temple. Rivka normally wouldn't have thought about a planet's religions, but in this instance, they were critical to the case. She scanned the horizon and saw more than a few steeples, domes, and other signs of organized religion.

"How many different religions are there on Glazoron?" Rivka wondered.

Sahved knew the answer to that. "Twenty-seven, but the top one accounts for ninety-seven percent of the population. It's called the Holy Order of Ignominy."

"Doesn't that mean 'shame?'" Rivka asked. She knew what it meant. The question was why they would pick that title.

"It does. The shame came from not embracing their Messiah, so they remain in a perpetual state of embarrassment," Sahved explained. "They seek redemption from their shame."

"By rejecting their Messiah? I would like to call these people names, but I don't know how low I can go to get into their psyche. No matter. We want those ignoble priests," Rivka declared.

Sahved thought for a moment. "Ignominy."

"Nice one!" Rivka stated. "The mean ones shaming the others. Your linguistic mastery belies the tongue whereupon curses flow like water from a spring."

"Thank you. It was one of my more lucid moments, which only happens when my stress is maxed out."

"Take us in, Clodagh. Lower the ramp, Red."

Red was happy to. The ship descended until it hovered above the small building that had a peaked roof, not suitable for jumping onto. Clodagh moved the ship over the courtyard.

"Fifteen-meter drop, High Chancellor. It's the best we can do."

"Take a running start, then roll when you hit," Red suggested. He led the way, and his forward momentum carried him away from the ship. He hit with his lead leg and let it bend beneath him, tucked, and forward rolled to his feet.

Rivka went out next, then Sahved. Lindy launched last. She hit and rolled but bounced into a bush on her way up. She got stuck in the foliage and had to rip herself free. Sahved jumped sideways to hit a nearby building, caught hold, and shinnied down the corner until he reached the ground.

Rivka brushed herself off. Red walked to the front door and pounded on it with the butt of his railgun. Rivka hurried after him but took care not to run. No running. No swearing at the priests. No punching the priests, no matter how much they deserved it. And definitely, no blood. She needed her team to be unscathed for the group victory of going out on a high note.

None of that would matter if they didn't get Dery back, but what if he didn't want to be found?

Frustrated, Rivka screamed inside her mind. She had to make sure the priests hadn't done anything to him by touching them and asking questions. She'd go much further if she needed to to allay her concerns about their duplicity. Torture wouldn't get normal interrogators what they wanted, but pain had a way of bringing the truth to the forefront of their minds where Rivka could see it.

Red hammered on the door again. He finally tried the knob and found that it was unlocked. He pushed the door open and swung his railgun from left to right, covering the space within. It was set up as a waiting area with small tables and chairs so petitioners could meditate or study while they waited for an audience.

Rivka tried to push past Red, but he blocked her. "I go first," he reminded her. They headed to the double doors, but those were locked. The bodyguard didn't bother with pleasantries. He rammed into them with his shoulder. The doors burst open, and one hung precariously from what was left of its hinges.

Within, a priest jumped to his feet. He'd been on his knees before an altar. "Where's my son?" Red bellowed.

"Red!" Rivka caught him and dragged him back before he reached the priest. "I've got this."

She grabbed the priest by the arm. "Where's the Messiah?"

He didn't know. He had prayed for his coming, and he was here! The priest had been ordered to stay and deal with distressed worshippers who couldn't handle the Second Coming.

"'Second Coming?'" Rivka asked.

The first had been on the spaceship mere weeks earlier. That made sense. Rivka let go and stepped back.

Red looked at her like she was giving up.

"He knows nothing," she told him. Rivka reconsidered and took hold of the priest's arm once more. "Who made you stay here?"

"His Most Humble Servant Livermore," the priest answered. That was the individual in his mind, too. He was telling the truth.

"Not Maggus?"

"No. Livermore is the most senior of the Humble Servants," the priest explained.

"Most senior Humble Servant… They don't sound humble at all in their ignominy."

"Blasphemer!" The priest found his backbone. He pointed at Rivka and drew an X in the air as if he were crossing her out.

"I accept the title of the Most Humble Blasphemer. I think I'll have that put on a plaque over my desk. You should reconsider your own humility before you cast about with your errant aspersions. Shame on you." Rivka smiled, pleased that she hadn't sworn at the man.

Red stared the man back to his knees.

Rivka strolled around the area, opening the two doors. One was a closet, and the other led to a small kitchen with a single bed shoved against the wall where a dining table could have been. The quarters were austere by all measures. Truly humble servants worked there, not ostentatious people with designs to take over all the populated planets in the Barrier Nebula.

"Where do the Humble Servants live and work?" Rivka asked.

The priest's glare gave her power over him. He clearly wasn't used to strangers or being intimidated by them. He might have authority over the flock, but he had no influence over Rivka. Quite the opposite. She moved closer.

"The Fleece district. You can't miss it," he spat with open disdain.

Rivka pulled her hand back before she touched him. She didn't need to feel his emotions or see his words to know he was telling the truth. There was a rift among the Humble Servants. "Maggus and his boys take care of Number One, huh?" Rivka guessed.

The priest nodded as he looked away. He resumed praying with his head bowed and his eyes closed.

"To the Fleece district." Rivka motioned toward the door.

The three hurried out. A line dropped from the ship. Tyler waved at them from the cargo ramp.

"I guess we're climbing." Rivka looked at the stout rope.

Lindy and Red stepped aside. "High Chancellors first. We'll make sure no one shoots you while you're climbing."

Rivka smiled. "That would be mighty nice of you." She spat on her hands and jumped to grab the rope. She went up hand over hand, avoiding using her feet.

Red and Lindy weren't watching her. They were looking for threats, but the area was devoid of outside activity.

"Hey!" Rivka called from the ramp. "Any day, slackers."

Red waited while Lindy went up the rope. The second she hit the ramp, he grabbed it and started to climb. He was carrying a full load and had to use his feet, but no one watched, and more importantly, no one cared. Not even Red. He wanted to board the ship quickly so they could go to the Fleece district, wherever that was. There, Rivka could roust the Humble Servants. Red wanted to let them know that they had crossed the wrong people, and Rivka did the best job of that. She didn't even have to say anything. She simply glared them into complying.

He didn't want to move to a different job. There was nothing else in the Federation he wanted to do. He wanted to be with his wife and son and protect Rivka.

Red watched Rivka talk to Clodagh using the screen in the cargo bay. She was studying a map Clevarious projected. They talked through the best approach, and then Rivka nodded and logged off. She strolled toward Red and Lindy. "We'll be there in about two minutes."

They looked out the open cargo bay door at the outskirts of the city. They were on their way to the more densely populated part, where the Humble Servants lived and worked. Where Glazoron's power brokers operated.

"Rooftop insertion," Rivka directed casually. *Wyatt Earp* banked hard, descended, and hovered a meter above a flat roof. Rivka, Red, and Lindy stepped down.

As *Wyatt Earp* was lifting away, Sahved jumped off the ramp. He nearly missed the building and ended up catching the safety rail. He teetered on the edge until Red grabbed his shirt and yanked him over.

"Stop fucking around," Red growled.

Sahved threw his hands out, looking exasperated.

The building had nine stories. It wasn't that high, but even Sahved would have been hurt had he fallen. No one wanted that, and they didn't have time for it.

"Open it up." Rivka stabbed a finger at the rooftop door.

Red nodded. It was locked, but that didn't matter. Nothing would keep him from finding his son.

CHAPTER SEVEN

<u>Hall of the Most Humble, Glazoron</u>

Red tore the door off its hinges. It had been made to keep other Glazoron out, not a man mountain like Red. Even at his current diminished size, he was still strong, and he was fired up.

He stormed down the steep stairway, railgun at the ready.

"Don't shoot anyone," Rivka cautioned. "At least, no one who doesn't need to be shot."

"We can't interrogate someone who's dead," Lindy added since Red was on the warpath. She continued to be the voice of reason.

Rivka glanced over her shoulder. Lindy nodded tightly, clenched teeth turning her lips white.

"Are you okay?" Rivka asked. She reached out, but Lindy kept her distance. Rivka moved closer.

Lindy deflated and held out her hand. She had supreme confidence in Dery. She also felt deep within that he was okay, and she would know if he wasn't. Lindy was mostly worried about Red and what he would do.

"I'm with you. Red!" Rivka called. "Shoulder the railgun. We're not going to shoot anyone."

"But…" he started, then stopped. Rivka's voice had been firm and brooked no argument.

Sahved was in the middle, hunching so his head didn't hit the ceiling. "Yes. Let us not be shooting anyone lest we be shot at. I like not being shot at. I prefer it more than anything else. Previously, I might have said I prefer a good meal and a good night's sleep. But after being on this crew, I very much prefer not getting shot."

"You're rambling, Sahved," Rivka told him. "We've lost the element of surprise, so we might as well introduce ourselves and start asking the hard questions."

When Red opened the door to the top floor, one priest stood in the hallway. His hands were tucked inside his robe. Red didn't rush the man. He kept his eyes on him until he passed and blocked the door beyond. He wasn't worried about Rivka. Lindy was right there with her. Sahved was meandering aimlessly down the hallway, studying the literature peppering the walls.

Rivka placed a hand on the priest's shoulder. "I need to talk with whoever is in charge."

He looked at her hand as if it were a tumor. That made no difference to her. She wouldn't let go until she had the information she wanted. "Tell me, where is the Messiah?"

He didn't know. He raised his head to look down his nose at her.

Rivka growled deep in her throat, then closed her eyes and took a deep breath to calm down. She promised herself she would play nice. "What is your plan after the attack on the shipyard?"

"What shipyard?"

He knew nothing. "Where can I find a Humble Servant who knows something?"

Next level down. He didn't speak. He kept being intransigent to the outsiders.

"Thank you. You've been very informative, albeit a bit of a jagoff." Rivka smiled. She let go and motioned for Red to head down the clearly labeled stairs.

Lindy pushed the priest out of her way and held him against the wall until after the others had gone down. She hurried after them, keeping an eye on the priest. She didn't trust any of them.

On the next level, they found offices open and no one inside. Pounding footsteps signaled a retreat down a far stairwell.

Clodagh, is there a vehicle or something waiting outside the building? If there is, maybe you can convince it not to leave. Try not to hurt any of the priests, but accidents do happen when rats are deserting a sinking ship, Rivka sent.

"Rats deserting a sinking ship!" Clodagh called. The screen changed to show the streets around the Humble center.

Two minibuses waited outside the back door. "Got you," she told the image on the screen. "Now, what do we do about you? We don't have the warriors. We can't blast them with the ion cannon. Maybe we can send a drone into them or hit them with the EMP. What do you think, Clevarious?"

Chaz spoke from the corridor outside the bridge. "I think we can take care of it. Hover over the buses, and we'll give them a surprise."

"C, make it happen."

Chaz and Dennicron hurried down the corridor to the cargo bay. The ramp was still open from Rivka's departure. They stood on the edge and gauged the drop. It was a long one, but their SCAMP bodies would be unaffected unless they hit something that was more resilient than them.

Dennicron leapt. Chaz followed her out, taking a different angle when he jumped.

The SCAMPs dropped fast and accelerated toward the ground. Dennicron slammed into the engine compartment of the first bus, ripping it out of the vehicle. She climbed out of the destroyed front end and attempted to brush herself off, but her clothes had been shredded by the torn steel from the vehicle.

Chaz rammed home on the second vehicle, landing on the hoverskirting. The engine coughed and spat, then stalled. The minibus lost skirt integrity and crashed to the ground. The vehicle leaned to the side. It wasn't going anywhere. The other minibus was also out of action, with its engine destroyed.

"What's the meaning of this? How dare you attack a delegation of the Most Humble!"

"High Chancellor wants to have a word with you," Chaz explained.

"We're on a sabbatical of the highest order! That supersedes any secular desires of your Chancellor." The priest didn't leave the vehicle. He pointed at the engine compartment. "You're going to pay for that."

The group in the second vehicle was yelling, but in panic, not anger. Dennicron glanced at a priest on the floor of the vehicle. He looked like a mound of goo. "What happened to him?"

"Heart failure. Your arrival was more of a shock than his aging body could take. You've *killed* him!"

Dennicron calculated the odds, and the highest probability was shock due to her impact on the vehicle. However, there were extenuating circumstances. The biggest was that they were running from the High Chancellor. The initial panic had been theirs. They shouldn't even have been in the minibuses.

"Odds are that you were running to avoid being questioned by the High Chancellor. What are you trying to hide?"

The priests settled into their seats and studiously looked away from Dennicron.

"Get off the bus, please," she ordered.

Chaz marshaled the group into an area between him and Dennicron: fifteen priests. One remained on the floor of the bus.

Problem, High Chancellor. One of the priests died of a heart attack, Dennicron reported.

They're not made for running. It's the consequences of their own actions. They shouldn't have run, Rivka replied without sympathy. She strolled into the street through the door the priests had used. "Line 'em up. Let's get this over with."

"I must protest!" One of the priests stepped forward, eyes on fire and lips parted, ready to deliver more vitriol.

Rivka pointed at him, then crooked her finger. "You first."

"I abjectly refuse on the strongest grounds."

Red smirked. He grabbed the man's arm and dragged him forward.

"Easy, Red. We want cooperation, not antagonism."

Red let go, and the man tried to squirm away. Red blocked him and jabbed a finger into his chest. "Talk with the High Chancellor, and she'll turn you loose."

The man surrendered but kept resisting.

Rivka took his hand. "Pray with me, child," she ordered in her most condescending voice. "Where's the Messiah?"

He didn't know, but they were trying to find out. She recoiled at the revelation. He didn't care about the Messiah, but because the masses did, they wanted to secure him to manipulate his appearance and message.

How little they knew about their Messiah to believe they could accomplish that. Dery would deliver his own message no matter what the priests wanted.

Rivka steeled herself. She'd dealt with worse minds. At least the Glazoron priests were predictable. Either they believed in their own power, or they believed in the power of faith. The former had become her enemies. The latter were mostly harmless, but she wouldn't take her eye off them either. "What is the next phase of your operation to foment war in the Barrier Nebula?"

The man cocked his head and smiled. "War is already here. We are only trying to help Glazoron survive." *By striking first and turning the other planets against everyone but Glazoron.*

"They already know Glazoron is stoking the discontent.

I think you're going to unite the other planets against you. Is that what you want?"

"You dissemble," the priest equivocated. He raised a hand to deliver a blessing. Red misinterpreted the gesture and grabbed the man's wrist. He lifted him off the ground, kicked his feet out from under him, and then slammed him to the pavement.

"I think he was going to deliver a blessing," Rivka remarked.

The man groaned and moved at glacial speed. Red intimidated the others to keep them from helping the intransigent priest. "Next." He pointed at one of the older souls.

The selected priest shook in terror, and Rivka gave Red the side-eye. He helped the priest get up. He propped him against the wrecked vehicle. "Are you okay?"

"May Glazzy have mercy on your soul."

"'Glazzy?'" Red and Rivka shrugged. Glazoron was the name of their deity. They'd named the planet and the people after Him. The Humble Servants.

Rivka touched the man's arm. "Where's the Messiah?"

He didn't know.

Rivka looked the rest over. "Do any of you know where the Messiah is?" Between her, Chaz, and Dennicron, they watched for tells—micro-expressions that gave them away —but the Humble Servants remained stoic in their denial of knowledge.

If they knew where Dery was, they would be going after him, Rivka told her crew. *These guys are more lackeys, just higher ranking in that they probably have lackeys of their own. They are at the peak in the lackey world, and maybe they know a few things, but none of these boneheads are decision-makers. We need the Most Humble.*

"Where is the Most Humble, your senior priest?" Rivka asked, retaining her grip on the older priest.

He had gone ahead. After the capture of the Most Humble Maggus, they knew the other senior priests would be next. Their orders were to scatter, but this group hadn't made it out in time since they'd had to wait for the minibuses. They should have taken other transportation. The priest was beside himself with self-recrimination.

"You might as well blame yourself. It was your fault that you got these fine and most humble of servants caught," Rivka agreed, confirming his suspicions.

His face fell.

Rivka had to hide a smile. She couldn't be direct, so she had to find alternate means to dig at her suspects, especially ones like these who needed to be put in their places. They weren't the upstanding Glazoron citizens they pretended to be, the leaders of ninety-seven percent of the people.

They were scum. The mid-level priests needed to take over. They believed in the deity and the words of the Messiah.

Food, family, and friends, Dery had said. This group's mission was to bury that message.

"Why don't you support the Messiah when his message is exactly what your people need to hear?" Rivka asked.

The priest looked for support from his fellows, but they glanced away. Rivka saw confusion in his mind. The Messiah didn't appear to support their desire to reach out into the galaxy and convert unbelievers on the other planets. That would take a war. Create the conditions where they would sue for peace. They'd be amenable to Glazoron after an initial wave of necessary deaths.

That was what they thought.

Rivka knew war better than they did. The other planets *wouldn't* be amenable. They would rise up against the aggressor, and Glazoron would be destroyed. If they fomented fights with the other planets, all would be lost. It would be impossible to convert dead people. Their souls couldn't be saved.

Did this group care about that? No. They wanted the power that came with subjugation.

Rivka's lip curled. "We're going to lock you guys away for a bit while we work to forestall the war you're trying to start. You're not under arrest. You're only detained."

"What about him? We can't leave his body there." The elder priest pointed at the vehicle in which the dead priest sprawled on the floor.

"Summon a hearse to take him away."

"We have certain rites that need to be performed. We must protest! And *you* killed him. We should summon the gendarmerie, too."

Rivka's head felt like it was going to explode. Red rested his hand on her shoulder. "They don't have Dery. That's what's most important," he whispered.

Rivka would have thought stopping an interstellar war was more important, but at that moment in time, Dery was the lighthouse in the darkness, illuminating the hazards before them. "That's right, Red. That *is* what matters most. Contact the ship to call the squad and see if Cole has found anything. Meanwhile, I'm going to talk to the young one."

She pointed at the youngest and smallest of the bunch and gestured for him to join her. The other priests tried to stop him, but Red moved in and escorted the young priest through the ad hoc cordon the others had set up.

"Come with me." Rivka stepped away from the others and reentered the building. She only went two steps inside to make sure the priests couldn't hear her conversation.

The young Humble Servant stepped inside and froze as if he expected to be ambushed. Rivka held out her hands in the universal gesture for calm. "Can you perform the last rites on your deceased colleague?"

He looked at her but didn't answer. Not because he was intransigent but because he was terrified.

Rivka placed her hand on his shaking arm. "I mean you no harm. Can you perform the rites?"

He'd done it once before but wasn't sure.

"You'll be fine. I want you to go with the deceased. Do what needs to be done. The Federation will pay any costs incurred. Within reason, that is. Tell me, what's involved with interring a Humble Servant?"

"He lies in state for three days. During that time, we pray over him for Glazoron's forgiveness, followed by a plea for everlasting life. I need the Tome of Knowledge."

"I'm sure there's one in this building. Go get it and come right back. If we have to come after you, it won't go well for you or any of the others. There will be pain involved, and from what I've seen, your people don't do pain well."

The youngster straightened. "What do you have against the Humble Servants?"

Rivka appreciated his finding a backbone. "It's worse

than you can imagine. Did you see how the Most Humble Servant ignored the words of the Messiah and called for something different?"

He shriveled like a grape on an old vine and stared at the floor.

"It's because the Most Humble doesn't believe in the Messiah or Glazoron. He only believes in the power he has accumulated and how much more there can be. That's why I picked you to escort the body. You still believe. None of those others do. You might think I'm jaded, but I can see into their minds. I *know* beyond a shadow of a doubt. Just like I know that you're confused and think I'm lying. What's your favorite color?"

He thought of it, then tried to mask it.

Rivka smiled. "It's okay that blue is your favorite, and not just any blue, but the color of your sky on a cloudless day. I'd be ashamed to be in your order, knowing what I know. That priest died of a heart attack because he was afraid of what we'd find out, even though we had already learned what we needed to know.

"The Most Humble are the *least* humble. They are in it only for themselves. I'm sorry you had to learn this way. Maybe you're the one who will save your people since it surely won't be them. They'll lead Glazoron to ruin."

Rivka left the youngster where he was. She returned outside, where Chaz and Dennicron had the priests corralled.

"What'd you do to him?" the elder priest demanded.

"He's getting a Tome of Knowledge so he can perform the last rites," Rivka replied with a shrug.

"It should be a more senior Humble Servant. Not a child!"

"Why does that matter?" Rivka zeroed in on the priest and rushed up to him. He stumbled back, and his fellows caught him. Rivka grabbed him by the wrist and yanked him forward. He was round, as Glazoron were, so she wasn't able to get close to his face. "If you believed in the Messiah and Glazoron, maybe I'd ask you to perform the rites. Can't have an unbeliever saying the sacred words."

He tried to escape, but she held him steady.

"That's right. *You* don't believe, and neither do *you*." She pointed at the other elder with her free hand. "When I look into your minds, will I see the same degradation of society these two have? Will I see that you only believe in your own power? You disgust me!"

The older priest's lip quivered. Rivka couldn't tell if it was from anger, fear, or something else. Soon, it stopped, and the priest composed himself.

"Obviously, you couldn't be more wrong. We are His Most Humble Servants."

"Keep telling yourself that. Maybe someday, even you will believe it." Rivka stepped aside to contact the ship and find the right law enforcement professionals to secure the mob of priests until she could determine what to do with them. None of them was the instigator who had started the war. That was the male who had killed himself and his immediate superior, but their structure was convoluted on a good day.

Most Humble, indeed.

CHAPTER EIGHT

War Axe, in Orbit over Glazoron

"I want the asswipes who shot drones at us. I need to have a conversation." Terry pounded one hand in the other palm and glared at the screen.

"He's dead, and we're looking for his partner in crime."

"A ball-slapping wiener-smacker, to say the least. A fuckstick assbag rotund jackwagon."

"Eloquent," Rivka replied. "We're working it. Using the scalpel at present, but when an axe is called for, we'll let you know."

"You're dumping milk in my whiskey, Magistrate."

Rivka didn't correct him. "There's no milk and no whiskey, but there *is* an element of the Glazoron religious sect that is trying to start a war between the planets. We'll stay here until we shut down these so-called leaders. Tell me, TH, is Jilk aware of what happened?"

"They didn't hear it from us, but some of their people were impacted when the shipyard's environmentally controlled areas were breached. We told them it was an asteroid that broke up," Terry replied.

"Good. We don't need Jilk shooting back. The two planets with advanced technology shooting at each other. That would be screwed up. Thanks for covering me, TH. I'll be in touch as soon as I have something." Rivka closed the channel.

Terry stared at the blank screen. "She hung up on me!"

"Did you have anything else to say?" Char asked.

"No." Terry smiled. "It sounded much more dramatic saying it my way rather than 'That's it. Thanks. Bye.'"

"Where's that leave us?" Char wondered.

"Playing defense, which isn't my favorite. Punch them in the face, let them know they're in the wrong, and change course."

"You can't cross the new High Chancellor," Char warned.

Terry tossed his head like a raging bull. "I know that, but we have to find a way to help. A way that makes sense to me." Terry strode around his cabin, looking for an idea he could turn into a plan.

Char sat at their terminal. "Rivka said the Glazoron were trying to foment religious discontent throughout the Barrier Nebula."

The light turned on. Terry waggled his eyebrows at his wife. "We find the other planets where they're getting uppity, and we body-slam them. Let them know war will not be tolerated. From what I've seen, these knobs are amateurs when it comes to war. They don't know what it's like to be on the wrong end of real violence."

"Don't be the bad guy," Char told him.

"Not the bad guy, but the one to show them the errors of their ways. Show them what they're trying to start and taking a few of the instigators into custody. Dragging their leaders off the battlefield trussed up like a Christmas bistok is a morale-killer. Let's find us that discontent so we can beat the shit out of some religious zealots. That always makes me feel better."

"How much are we getting paid for this?" Char asked rhetorically. Rivka had allowed them to collect hundreds of millions of credits for the art recovery. Terry had told her then that she'd never have to pay for their services again. She had yet to put a big dent in her credit with the Bad Company.

"We're getting paid in goodwill hot damns. Where else do we get to go to beat up zealots? Contracts are pretty thin nowadays. Success isn't all it's cracked up to be. It's lucrative until everyone gets their shit under control. Now we're watching and waiting. It's good to have something to do, don't you think, lover?"

"For you, it's always important to keep busy. If you remember our all-too-short retirement in the Caribbean back on Earth, I was perfectly happy on the beach, reading and sunning. You were like a cat on a hot tin roof. You couldn't sit still."

"I stayed still for fifty-by-God years! I'm not going to retire again. That sucked. Running the AGB was cool, but it brings me back to beating up zealots. I don't get to do that from behind a bar."

"Aren't you a little old to beat people up?" Char languorously walked toward her husband.

"Are you trying to use your sexy walk on me?" Terry asked, removing his shirt.

"That was my lackadaisical walk. My devil-may-care stroll," Char explained.

"It's really sexy." Terry caught her and picked her up to carry her to the bedroom. "Not too old, no."

"War Axe has left orbit," Clevarious reported.

Rivka frowned. "Where are they going?"

"No flight plan was posted. They just…left."

"Contact Smedley and find out what's up." Rivka didn't want the Bad Company to grow stagnant, but she liked the crutch of having Terry Henry and Char in orbit with three platoons of armored combat-suited warriors. She crossed her arms and stared at the screen. They were hovering over the city, scanning for any sign of Dery, but the process was slow. They'd never be able to scan the whole place. Dery had a natural ability to avoid detection. If he didn't want them to, they'd never find him.

Rivka was rapidly reaching that conclusion. She and her crew would be available when he returned of his own accord. Rivka just had to convince Red that was okay. Lindy already seemed to have reconciled that Dery's purpose was to bring peace to Glazoron.

Red continued to pace like a caged animal. He called Cole every two minutes, requesting updates. They had found nothing, and the worshippers had drifted away. The stadium was nearly empty. The demonstration had come to an end.

Rivka appreciated the dissolution of the million-Glazoron protest. It was the first step in a return to normalcy. Now, all she needed was to recover Dery.

"Incoming communique from the SI on Colay," Clevarious interrupted.

"Greetings and salutations, High Chancellor. My name is Edgerrin James. I'm responsible for official communications from Colay. The leadership is trying to report an uprising, but the prime minister interfered with the process. I believe he's been coopted by one of the religious sects. They are aligned with the Glazoron."

Rivka sighed. "What I hear you saying is that the Glazoron are starting a civil war on Colay, and they've infiltrated the prime minister's office."

"Pretty much, High Chancellor," Edgerrin replied.

"We're on our way." Rivka hung her head. "Clodagh, head to the stadium. Recover the squad, and then take us out of here. Gate to Colay when we're in space."

Red howled like he'd been stabbed with a rusty butter knife. Lindy's façade finally came down, and she started to cry as she slowly walked away. Red sat down in the corridor with his head in his hands.

"Clodagh, belay my order. Inform the squad that they're to stay here until the boy is found. Ensure they get quarters and access to transportation that can carry them. Do it now. We leave in five minutes unless you're ready sooner."

Rivka headed into the corridor. She rested her hand on Red's shoulder and did her best to project calm, as Dery would have done for her.

"I appreciate what you're trying to do, but it's not going to work. Nothing will until my son is back home."

"I'm leaving the boys here to find him and secure him. Do you want to stay?" Rivka asked.

Red nearly cried out in frustration as he raised his head, only to collapse in on himself. "My job…" he muttered.

"You have to take care of your son. I'll be fine."

Red snorted. "We gave Tyler a railgun. He sucked. You can't have him as your security." Red struggled to his feet. "Lindy!"

She had stopped at the far end of the corridor. She turned around. "You stay here and keep looking. I'll go with Rivka," Red told her.

Lindy was instantly energized. "I'll be ready to go in three minutes." She disappeared into their quarters.

Red stared down the empty corridor. "Would you let us both go?"

"You know the answer to that. You've said it yourself. I have a reckless disregard for my own safety, but when it comes to a member of my crew, especially one who was born on board this ship, we'll do whatever it takes."

"That's why I can't leave you alone," Red replied. "Do you think he's okay?"

"He's fine. I'd bet my life on it. He has the wisdom and abilities of the faeries on his side. They defeated the Kurtherians by hiding their planet. Dery is just fine, and you know what? I think Glazoron will be better off for what he's doing."

"Which is what?"

"He's telling them how to live better lives. Red, your son *is* the Messiah."

He nodded. "I know. I've known from the second he was born. We're not worthy to be his parents."

"That is Grade-A bullshit. The faeries deemed you worthy. Otherwise, he would have never been born of you and Lindy. He needs you. Maybe not right now since he's taking care of business. He's leading a million souls to a better place. He's a better leader for the Glazoron than their own Humble Servants. What a fucking misnomer. Unhumble Self-Servants is a more accurate title."

"Those guys are total shit stains," Red agreed.

Lindy pounded toward them, wearing full gear and carrying her railgun.

"Clodagh, drop Lindy near the warriors. Closest available open space where we can land. She doesn't have a suit and can't drop like they did," Rivka called toward the bridge.

The ship was already descending. "I'll head out the cargo bay." Lindy ran. Red was right behind her, through the airlock and into the cargo bay.

Rivka stepped onto the bridge and was greeted with a view of the empty stadium. Tiny Man Titan barked at her from where he was cradled against Clodagh's shoulder. Aurora was at the helm, rocking Alanna.

Something rammed into her leg. She looked down to find Wenceslaus scraping his face along her leg to leave his scent on her. That would make the dog bark at her that much more.

"Take off," Red announced over the intercom.

"To space and beyond!" Rivka called. "Next stop, Colay. Sahved! Briefing on Colay, one minute."

Sahved bounded down the corridor, covering his head to keep from hitting it on the ceiling.

"Colay is a more standard planet. Its inhabitants are

indistinguishable from humans except for webbing between the fingers and toes since there is more water on that planet, and they descended from amphibians a million years ago. The webbing is their last remaining aquatic distinction.

"They are a strong family-oriented race, with community next in their priorities. The government is a loose structure of advisory councils. The prime minister rotates for three months at a time among the various councils. Currently, the position is filled by one Kim Crabben Hoppel. Kim is the family name. Crabben is the community, and Hoppel is his first name."

"Religions?"

"Each community supports their own, but there is some overlap. Missionaries from other planets have attempted to convert the residents. The only one that has found any traction is..." Sahved didn't finish the sentence. He waited for Rivka to fill in the blank.

"Let the will of Glazoron shine through His people," Rivka intoned.

"Glazoron," Sahved confirmed. "The people are called Colaygens."

Wyatt Earp arced skyward. Despite the crew members who remained, Rivka felt alone. She shivered at her perceived loss. Dery, the warriors, and Lindy, too. She missed Groenwyn, who was the Federation's Ambassador to Azfelius, the faerie planet.

"I'll be in my conference room. When we arrive, contact the prime minister. I want to meet with Mister Kim."

"The law is clear that internal issues do not have to be

reported to the Federation," Sahved offered, following Rivka.

"Of course. Glazoron, however, is not native to Colay. Their insertion into internal matters has to be seen as external interference. Although Colay probably doesn't know about the uprising on Glazoron, the bigger picture confirms that Colay is one domino in a series, ready to be knocked down and make the others fall. Ten planets of the Barrier Nebula will crash as one."

"We've stopped the uprising on Glazoron," Sahved countered.

Rivka stopped, faced Sahved, and smiled. "We have not. We simply delayed it, foiling their plans to emasculate Jilk. The fact that Colay is seeing turmoil means there are more operations in action. The final element in play is that we never caught the Mostest Humblest. The one calling the shots. Maggus was his second and the movement's mouthpiece, but who is Number One?"

"He's not in the mob that is currently cooling their heels in the Gray Bar Motel?" Sahved asked, using his newly learned colloquialisms.

"More lackeys. Senior to the usual lackeys, but lackeys nonetheless. They wield a great deal of influence, so it was important to remove them from the picture, but they aren't the decision-makers. We'll gut the organization until we reach the head man. Then we'll cut his balls off."

"High Chancellor. I do not think that is a sentence you can deliver."

Rivka glanced at Sahved to see if he was joking. He seemed concerned. "You are correct. Castration is not a valid sentence in the Federation. How about kneecapping?"

"Breaking someone's kneecaps? I'm afraid not. Are you testing me?" Sahved wondered.

"Every day is a test, Sahved. You see that I don't ask these questions of Chaz or Dennicron."

Sahved nodded knowingly. "Because they can quote chapter and verse of every law. They have perfect retention and recall."

"I like your confidence. The worst thing we can do to someone who revels in their power is take it away. It could be as simple as removing a license or a contract or forcing them out of a position of power through a short incarceration. Punishment stops undesirable behavior. Power brokers can't be in power. That is where they shake their big balls in people's faces and where I take a sledgehammer to them."

"Flat balls for punishment," Sahved tried. "Pancake 'nads. A twig and crepes. No nuts, no nonsense." Sahved rolled a couple more phrases over his tongue but didn't like them enough to say out loud. He put his hands behind his back and attempted to look dignified. "That could make you a junk dealer."

"Pancake 'nads," Rivka repeated. "We better get to it. Next on the chopping block is the Colay prime minister." Rivka winked at the Yemilorian. "Sahved, we are polluting your mind, and you have risen to the occasion. My compliments."

"High Chancellor," Clevarious interrupted. "*War Axe* is here."

"So, this is where they got to. Did Smedley talk with Edgerrin James? Are you guys sneaking information behind my back?"

"I am aghast at your implication. We would never sneak."

"Of course you would. You guys are sneakers of the first order. Master sneakers. You can't tell me otherwise." She twirled her finger. "C, get me Colonel Walton and patch it into the conference room."

Sahved followed and took a seat. Chaz and Dennicron hurried in before Terry Henry connected.

"What are you doing here?"

"We're not sneakers," Chaz replied.

"You guys." Rivka shook her finger at them. "What would I do without you?"

"Suffer in an intellectual wasteland. We keep you on your toes and fairly bursting with information."

Rivka stared at Chaz, then shifted her attention to Dennicron. The SI nodded in the exaggerated manner of her emphatic subroutine.

Terry's voice boomed into the conference room. "Rivka, you followed me. I told Char I thought you had a thing for me. You know I'm probably too old for you, so you should give it up. Also, my wife would kill me."

"Terry!" Char cried in the background.

"TH. What brought you here?" Rivka asked.

"I'm sure the same thing that brought you," Terry redirected.

"Which was? TH, what do you know that I don't know?"

"Whoa! How much time do you have? I am fully unprepared to answer that question. First, we'll have to start with you telling me what you know. Then I'll subtract that from what I know. I'll tell you the delta between our two knowledge bases."

"Glazoron is trying to start a war on Colay, and they have probably gotten to the prime minister. Your turn."

"Hang on, Magistrate."

"High Chancellor. I got promoted."

"My condolences, Rivka. No wonder you're in a bad mood. Success gets you more opportunity for success, at great cost to your health and well-being."

"I'm not in a bad mood." Rivka looked at the others around the table.

"Junk dealer," Sahved mouthed. Rivka laughed.

"There we go." Terry beamed at the screen. "Colay. Religious discontent. Instigators. Have I told you how much I hate terrorists?"

"Not lately," Rivka replied. "Are there terrorists on the planet, or are they instigators? The Glazoron are attempting to wreak social havoc. They aren't happy unless others are unhappy. 'Come to our side. We have cookies!' I can see them shouting from rooftops."

"I don't think they have cookies. Hey, Char. Do the Glazoron have cookies?"

Rivka frowned. "TH, they don't have cookies. I was illustrating a point."

"Damn. Char, can you check with Jenelope and see if she has any cookies on hand? I'm jonesing, baby. Jonesing hard."

"I'll make you some damn cookies if you ever answer Rivka's questions rather than dissemble your way through this whole conversation. I hope she throws you in jail."

"I'm not going to jail, am I, Rivka? There are laws

against cougars, aren't there? Char took advantage of this unsuspecting youngster. A military man who was eminently susceptible."

Rivka's mouth fell open. "How much sex have you guys had?"

Terry was taken aback. Char snorted in the background. "I'm not sure I can answer that. Also, I don't want to answer that."

"It seems that you have both benefitted greatly from your relationship. Cougar or no. Werewolf or no. Hunky military man scoring the hot babe or no. What the hell are you planning to do on Colay?"

Terry spoke over his shoulder. "I told you she had a thing for me. 'Hunky military man.' That's me, lover."

"Colay," Rivka reiterated.

"I've sent two squads of warriors to isolate the Glazoron priests. We'll figure out what to do with them once we have them in custody."

"In custody? Have you been deputized?" Rivka shook her head. "Just hold them until I get there. I'll want to talk with the Most Humble Servants."

"I don't think they're very humble," Terry replied.

"That's the priests' formal title. I don't think they're humble either, *or* servants."

"Butt-snugglers! We agree. I'm going down there because those fucknuggets pissed me off."

"I said, wait until I get down there. I can't let you go around and beat people up, even if they do need a good beating. I'll adjudicate all beatings for this case. We have a few people on Glazoron who need a good smacking, but no one here. Not yet, anyway. I have to make a call. Do not go to the planet's surface without me, TH. I'm serious. Char! Please back me up on this one. You're the only person who can control him."

"If only!" Char called from off-screen. "I'll do my best."

Clevarious interrupted, "I have the prime minister for you, High Chancellor."

"Sorry, TH. I'd love to continue sparring with you, but I have to go. I'll pick you up before we go *together* to the planet's surface. All of us. Together, in case you missed that point earlier." Rivka cut the line.

"Prime Minister Kim, I'm High Chancellor Rivka Anoa, here to investigate issues surrounding the Glazoron religious sect."

"There are no issues. You can go now."

Rivka smiled condescendingly. "That's not how it works. I'll be on the planet's surface shortly to discuss what I need to do."

"You can tell me now, High Chancellor," the prime minister countered.

"The Glazoron sect is attempting to start a war between the planets in the Barrier Nebula. We're dismantling the outposts and taking leaders of the movement into custody. We'll question them and determine their roles in the call to war. Since you interfered with a required notification to the Federation, I'll be questioning you, too. Make sure you stay right where you are. We can have ourselves a nice chat. See you soon."

Rivka closed the channel. "C, get us down there and keep an eye on wherever he is. Make sure he doesn't get away."

"Don't tip your hand next time. It'll be easier to keep him from running," Red offered from the corridor.

"Are we going to pick up Colonel Walton?" Sahved asked.

"C, stop by *War Axe*. Get TH and Char on board." Rivka slouched in her seat. "I feel like I don't have any control over this case. I'm hanging on for the ride, and it's careening in a direction not of my choosing."

"How often do you have control?" Red asked.

"Not as often as I let on." She held Red's gaze. He'd lost his humor. Dery's absence weighed heavily on him. "C, use the comm satellite we put in orbit over Glazoron to tell our people on the surface to stay in touch."

"Capital idea, High Chancellor. We've been in contact with them since we left. The five of them are searching beneath the stadium to no avail, but they will keep looking."

Rivka should have known the SIs were three steps ahead of her. "Thanks, C." She got up, stretched, and headed for the main airlock, through which TH and Char would board. She took her time. The link-up process wouldn't be as quick as she wanted.

She reached the airlock and waited. Red stood beside her. No one else joined them.

"You're doing great, HC," Red told her.

She smirked. "I don't feel like I'm doing great."

"Is there a war in the Barrier Nebula?" he asked pointedly.

"Not yet. Although, I don't see the small-scale sects making as much progress as the main group from Glazoron. Without the drones, they are limited in their war-starting options. Defeating the drones left them toothless."

"I bet not. They have other cards to play. This hand is a long way from being over."

"Sometimes you make more sense than anyone else. I think we all feel that they have more going on. There's a lot we don't know about this case, and that mob of Glazoron ego-stroking self-servants is going to do something. Where are the Action Jacksons in that group?" Rivka leaned into the hatchway to look through. The far hatch had flashed green and was cycling through.

"You need to let TH beat confessions out of them," Red suggested.

"You know he wouldn't do that. He'll beat the snot out of anyone in a fair fight, but he's not going to torture someone. You know he was tortured by a Forsaken back on Earth? That changed him."

"What's a Forsaken?" Red asked.

Rivka raised an eyebrow.

"It's a thing. A vampire that can't handle the sun, who drinks people's blood. They are a scourge. Joseph was one, but thanks to a special treatment and his own commitment, he freed himself from the hunger," Terry explained as he approached. "Why are you guys talking about the Forsaken?"

"Torture," Rivka told him. "I'm sorry I brought it up."

"Me, too. What do you say we roust the natives and get some answers?" He clapped Rivka on the shoulder hard enough to stagger her. Red interjected his body.

"No time for dick-measuring contests. Let's go talk with the prime minister." Rivka twirled her finger.

"I taught her that," Terry proudly stated. He reached back and took Char's hand. They strolled down the corridor.

"For the record," Red complimented Char, "you're beautiful. You don't look like a cougar at all."

"Not helpful, Red," Rivka called over her shoulder.

"They have some interesting conversations on this ship," Terry suggested. "They must be more bored than I am."

Floyd bounded down the corridor, stopping Terry and Char in their tracks. They both crouched to give her some loving.

CHAPTER NINE

***Wyatt Earp*, Parked in the Courtyard of the Central
Government Building, Colay**

Red led the way. Rivka, TH, and Char followed. Sahved,
Chaz, and Dennicron watched from the airlock.

Since it was a rotating post, the prime minister didn't
get an ostentatious office. It was a utilitarian space at best.
The office was on the ground floor. It looked like the other
offices except for a small sign that read Prime Minister.

Red opened the door, thinking he'd access the secretary,
but there were no other desks or people inside. The prime
minister sat behind his desk with his hands folded in his
lap. He appeared to be resigned to the intrusion.

"Mister Prime Minister," Rivka greeted him. She sat in
the only other chair in the office. The others stood. "Why
did you stop the report about the Glazoron?"

"It's an internal matter. Sending our trivial issues to Yoll
invites interference in Colay's affairs. I don't think that's in
our best interests."

"What if I told you that Glazoron is in a state of

upheaval and they've already attacked one other planet in the Barrier Nebula. Any friction with the Glazoron is important for us to know so we can intercede, not interfere."

"I didn't know that. Maybe the Federation should be more forthcoming." He crossed his arms.

"When I contacted you, you stonewalled me, like you're doing now. Would a simple report have gotten your attention? We both know the answer to that question. We're going to do what we need to do, and you're going to provide support, as is required under the Federation Charter to which Colay is a signatory. Thank you. We'll let you know what we need."

She held out her hand. He took it. "What's your involvement with Glazoron?" Rivka asked.

Glazoron is the way to salvation, the prime minister thought. "I have no special involvement with the Glazoron."

"I heard that Glazoron is the way to salvation. What do you think about that?"

"I find the teachings interesting. As prime minister, I'm open to exploring whatever can have an impact on the humble citizens of Colay."

"Humble," Rivka repeated. "Make sure you are doing what's in the best interests of Colay and not what your Glazoron minders tell you."

He feigned being hurt. "I always keep Colay foremost in my thoughts."

"Keep it foremost in your actions, too, Prime Minister Kim," Rivka warned. "And we won't have any problems." She backed away from his desk, using the intimidation of her stare to get to him. He was a temporary prime minister. He didn't have a long game. That was the benefit of Colay's system. The rotating position dealt with the short-term while the councils worked for the long-term interests of the planet.

"It was a pleasure meeting you, Prime Minister. Take care when dealing with the Glazoron." Rivka waved and left, then addressed TH. "Thanks for not jumping in."

"He's not paying me, so he's nothing in the big scheme," Terry replied. "My boys are waiting with the priests."

"That was next on the agenda." Rivka looked around. "Why didn't you bring Dokken?"

"We can't put him on a ship as small as *Wyatt Earp* with his mortal enemy. It would be chaos. He'd tear the ship apart to get to that cat. He's *my* arch-nemesis, too."

"He is not. You like that cat since his greatest trait is that he doesn't care about anything. He's the best cat that ever catted," Char explained.

"I don't." He looked at Rivka for support.

Rivka shook her head and threw her arms up in frustration. "Barrier Nebula. Civil wars. Interstellar wars. And you're concerned about our cat?"

"Shame on you," TH replied. "You can tell a person's fundamental nature by how they treat animals."

"Does that include bistok?" Rivka shot back.

"They're so tasty." Terry rubbed his belly.

Char smiled at the High Chancellor. "When you've lived as long as we have, focusing on a single thing isn't possible. We might come across as a bit scattered, but that's how we challenge our minds to stay engaged. Stay at the top of our game."

"What she said," Terry agreed.

Rivka wasn't sure of the explanation. It didn't make sense to her that one would lose focus to gain it.

After they boarded *Wyatt Earp*, the ship took off and headed to the coordinates Smedley had provided.

Tyler showed up carrying Rivka's jacket. "I know it's your Magistrate's jacket, but you should probably wear it so you can carry your datapad and Reaper." Reaper was her neutron pulse weapon.

"I think I might need that before this case is over." Rivka took the jacket and the proffered kiss.

Rivka expected Terry and Char to say something. She appreciated that they didn't. They simply waited respectfully.

"*There you are!*" Terry bellowed, pointing a finger gun down the corridor.

Wenceslaus yawned in conjunction with a languorous stretch.

"Big stretch!" Clodagh exclaimed from the bridge. She smiled at the orange cat while carefully watching Terry Henry Walton.

"My arch-nemesis," Terry whispered.

"I'll fight you," Clodagh told her old boss.

"Don't you see? That's what he wants. We fight each other, and he laughs all the way to the bank." Terry crossed his arms and glared at the cat. Wenceslaus rolled onto his back and play-kicked all four feet in the air.

Rivka picked up the cat. He scratched her, and she dropped him. He strolled away with his tail held high.

"We'll depart via the cargo bay. It's more tactical." Rivka examined the scratches on her arm, then wiped the blood on her pants and put her jacket on. The leather would have saved her the indignity of being clawed. A few more scratches would not have looked out of place.

She walked away as if nothing had happened. Terry pointed and mouthed words, but no sound came out.

Char giggled. "Arch-nemesis, indeed."

When they reached the cargo bay, the ship was settling to the ground, adjusting to deliver them facing a platoon of armored warriors.

Terry jumped the last meter to the ground. He ran toward his people, pulling up to troop the line. He walked from left to right, nodding at each as he passed.

Rivka and Char waited, with Sahved, Chaz, and Denni-cron behind them.

"Bring those priests out here. Line 'em up and present them one by one," Terry ordered.

Four warriors raced away, using their pneumatic jets to jump/bounce to a nearby building. After ten seconds of shouting, the priests appeared. The four warriors and the guard platoon slowly walked the Glazoron priests toward Rivka and her team.

Terry stepped aside. This wasn't his show. The Bad Company had done their part.

Rivka watched them all shuffle toward her. She took grim satisfaction in how they looked. Cowed. Humbled. Exactly what they needed to be if they were truly humble servants.

The group stopped in front of Rivka. She pointed at them to line them up, oldest first. The Glazoron looked small and insignificant beside the monstrosities that were the Bad Company in their custom powered combat armor.

They were round and out of place on a world populated by human-looking souls.

"You, come forward," Red directed the first in line, who appeared to be the oldest in the group. His hair was patchy, between being ready for the cold season and the hot. It wasn't clear if he was growing or shedding his fur.

"I am His Most Humble Servant Miatan. I will not be treated in this manner." He huffed, and he puffed.

Rivka had a hard time taking him seriously. She gripped his arm. He tried to pull away, but Red stopped him.

"What are you planning for Colay?" Rivka asked.

War. It was clear in his mind, but she needed the details.

"How do you intend to start this war?"

Destruction from bombs that have already been placed.

Rivka grabbed him with both hands. *"Where are these bombs?"*

Terry Henry surged forward to loom over the priest.

Miatan didn't know. That had been left to a group he had no contact with to keep the bombs' locations secret.

"Who knows where the bombs are?" Rivka asked.

He shrugged. A nameless, faceless entity.

Rivka raged.

Red fumed. It was time to flip over tables and scorch bodies with the flames from her sharp tongue, but Rivka drew herself back from the edge.

Rivka moved to the next priest. "Who knows where the bombs are?"

"Not you!" he answered. He didn't know. His smugness wasn't false bravado. He was happy that Rivka wouldn't find out from the priests.

"When are they set to blow?" she asked, going from one priest to the next. They assumed it would be within the next week. They didn't know for sure.

She returned to the eldest member of the group. Terry held him tightly. If it weren't for the odd shape and bulk, he would have had the priest off the ground.

Rivka took the servant by the hand. "Who gave you the orders? Who gave you this plan?"

He attempted to hide the answer in his mind but failed.

Most Humble Servant Miatan. He'd last seen him on Glazoron.

"Let him go," Rivka ordered. *Clevarious, get hold of the locals to store these individuals until we can make a final disposition. Charges are terroristic threats and conspiracy. There are bombs somewhere on Colay, set to explode probably within the next week. That's the best I can do. We need to return to Glazoron and find this priest named Miatan.*

The SI made the calls.

Terry looked at the group of priests and clucked his tongue in disgust. "This mob is going to kill innocents? That makes me sick to my stomach. If it weren't for her, I'd be ripping your limbs off one by one until we got the answers we need. If we didn't, I think these worlds would be better off. You've betrayed your god."

"We have embraced the greater good that is Glazoron," the eldest priest corrected, clasping his hands in a parody of prayer.

Terry made a fist and reared back. Char caught his hand. "The High Chancellor will give the order if it's called for."

"She's being far too nice. These dickheads need their

asses beat. King Dickweed needs to be snapped off at his ankles."

"They'll spend many of their remaining days in jail. Until then, we need to find those bombs and then secure this Miatan so we can interdict any other operations he has in the works." Rivka stared into the distance, having turned her back on the priests. She didn't want to look at them since it made her angry. She didn't want to chase Glazoron instigators around the Barrier Nebula, but she wasn't being given a choice.

Red eased up next to her. "You're doing great. We're going to figure this out."

"*You're* being the voice of reason?" Rivka snorted. "I would have never guessed. You must want a nice cut from the pot."

"I want my son back. Laying into the lackeys isn't going to do it. Working over Glazoron proper? I want more of that. You can do this without having to go off on anyone. It'll be good practice for your new job. Lindy and I will help screen your visitors."

"That's not making this any easier. The last thing I want is to go back to Yoll and sit in an office."

"Then work out of *Wyatt Earp* in orbit. I've already checked. The poles are clear. Just assume a geostationary position over one of the poles. Fire up a beacon and get to work. If you have to go to the surface, then so be it, but I doubt you'll have much of that. I think they've grown used to people not being in that office. Grainger spent a lot of time on his ship, and that tug is nowhere near as nice as our ship."

"We'll float that idea and see if we can pull it off. Until

then, we have a war to stop. That's not quite a Magistrate's job, but we've headed off enough wars that it has become our job. Weird. You'd think the foreign service would take a more active role in interplanetary relations. Diplomats exercising diplomacy."

"Butt-hugging knob-bobbers," Red blurted.

Rivka chuckled. "Where are those cops? We need to get out of here." She faced Terry. "Have your boys secure these *people*. We're heading back to Glazoron."

"Caples! It's all yours. Secure this mob and make sure they are locked up tightly. Put remote security monitors on them, too. We can't have any of them escaping. They don't talk to anyone, either. Keep them incommunicado," Terry ordered. "Use the Pods to recover to *War Axe*. We'll catch up with you later."

Terry and Char followed Rivka to *Wyatt Earp*. Red, Sahved, Chaz, and Dennicron boarded, and after a quick check to make sure they had everyone, the captain raised the cargo ramp and lifted off.

"Gate us from within the atmosphere to the stadium on Glazoron."

"Calculating now, High Chancellor."

Rivka sat in one of the chairs still in the cargo bay. Sometimes the intra-atmospheric Gates caused a great deal of discomfort. Sahved had puked more than once.

"Ballsy," TH muttered. He grabbed the bulkhead.

Char took a seat next to Rivka. "The Glazoron have Red and Lindy's son?"

"I don't think so. I believe he is there of his own choosing. Doing what? Whatever the faeries need him to do. I can't imagine what that is. Peace. Serenity. Wellness. Who knows?"

Char nodded. "When people messed with our kids, we went on the warpath. We kicked a lot of ass and ended their lives and the lives of those who worked for them. It wasn't pretty. You don't mess with people's kids."

"I'll second that. I'm having a hard time finding any sympathy for the Humble Servants. They're a pack of self-serving scumbags. They call themselves humble. Isn't that the epitome of a disinformation campaign? I'm going to dismantle their entire organization."

"Although I'd love to support your religious cleansing…" Terry started, but he didn't finish.

"Ninety-seven percent of Glazoron worship Glazoron," Chaz stated.

Rivka sulked. "Can't I just be mad at those no-loads?" She raised her hand to prevent further discussion. "The worshippers are no problem. It's anyone who calls himself 'Most Humble Servant' who gets under my skin."

"Throw all those guys in the hoosegow," Terry suggested.

"Did you make that word up?" Red asked.

"It's from before your time." Terry scanned the faces of those standing around the cargo bay. Only Chaz and Dennicron nodded. "Don't tell me. You found it in a dictionary of archaic terms."

Chaz confirmed. "Yes. It is a jail."

"It should have been obvious from the context. People used to be smarter back in my day. They didn't need archaic dictionaries."

"Because we didn't live in ancient times when dictionaries of archaic terms were just called dictionaries," Rivka countered.

"Gate is forming," Clevarious announced.

"What's past is prologue, from Shakespeare's *Tempest*." Terry crossed his arms and tried to look smug. "You're welcome."

The ship slipped over the event horizon to reappear above the stadium. The usual effortless transition required an effort. A wave of nausea passed through Rivka, but after a few seconds, she was fine.

Sahved's eyes rolled back in his head, and he toppled like a tall pine tree. Terry caught him before he hit the deck and eased him down.

"Is he okay?" Char asked, checking his pulse and pupils. "He seems to be."

Sahved's eyes fluttered as he recovered consciousness. He blinked at Char. "Your eyes are purple," he noted.

Terry and Char helped him to his feet.

"Descending into the stadium, which is empty, High Chancellor," Clevarious announced over the ship-wide intercom.

Red lowered the ramp so they could watch the landing. Rivka strolled to the edge. Entering the field from a side access were Lindy and two warriors from Cole's squad. Red rushed off to hold his wife. Her body language told the story: they'd had no luck finding Dery.

"We need to find Humble Servant Miroso as soon as possible. We're going to separate into teams to explore more of the city. If you find any Most Humble Servants, bring them to me for questioning."

"Where will you be?" Terry asked, ready to head into Glazoron and roust the natives.

"On the ship. I'll stay here, centrally located. I guess we can come to you as long as there's a place to land. Everyone else will be involved in the search. Two by two. Never leave your partner. I think the Glazoron are candy-ass lightweights when it comes to fighting their own battles, but they're devious bastards and have technology on their side. Between them and Jilk, they are the tech nexus of the Barrier Nebula."

"Roger. Vectors?" Terry asked. Rivka looked at him blankly. "On me, people." Terry Henry pointed in set directions toward the city. "Look for the spires of their temples. Take care with the priests. Don't offend the worshippers."

CHAPTER TEN

Wyatt Earp, in the Glazoron Stadium, on the Edge of the Main City

Rivka waved as the teams walked away, leaving her on the cargo ramp with Tyler. Clodagh, Alanna, Ankh, Erasmus, and Chrysanthemum also remained on board. Even the pilots had joined the search, partnering with their boyfriends, who had left their combat armor on board the ship.

The teams hurried out of the stadium and into the city.

"May Glazoron guide their hands toward success," Tyler quipped.

"Glazoron isn't going to have anything to do with this. It's going to be the diligence of our people who find the purveyors of terror. I'm sorry, I meant the humble purveyors." Rivka wasn't confident they would find Miroso.

Or Dery, but she didn't articulate either doubt, even to Tyler.

"I think Azfelius could help," Tyler remarked. "They have a tendency to know everything." He didn't caveat it.

Rivka liked the idea. *Rivka to all hands,* she transmitted to everyone with a comm chip in their head. *Return to the ship no later than one hour after nightfall. We're going to Azfelius to enlist the assistance of the faeries in locating Dery.*

Fucking-A, HC! Get those little fuckers to help us for once, Red replied.

Down, you big husky! I think they've helped us plenty. I need everyone to keep their calm while we beg them for help. I'll do the groveling on behalf of his family, friends, and the Federation. Everyone else, radiate positive waves. Let the vibes buoy the faeries' joyousness.

"Did you say positive waves and vibes? Have you become a hippy when I wasn't looking?" Tyler wondered.

"I've always been a hippy. The barrister free spirit, that's me. I can't believe it took you until now to notice. Shame on you."

"Harumph! You're as normal as me. A boring home-body. A work-obsessed, fastidious pizza eater."

"I like the wings, too." Rivka winked at the ship's chief medical officer. He chuckled and took her hand. There was nothing for them to do but wait for the call that priests were being herded toward the ship.

Instead of their quarters, they went to the bridge. Clodagh held her daughter and stared at the screens, which displayed external views from all quarters. The area surrounding the seats in the stadium showed nothing but grass and empty space. "What do you find so interesting?"

"Looking for invisible creatures. Remember Jack the Ripper? What if one of those is manipulating the Glazoron?"

"Rivka froze. "Please, don't let there be another one of

those in this galaxy." She relaxed and shook her head. "We don't need to chase ghosts when the only thing out here is evil men. Most Humble Servant. We're going to decapitate the snake, and I'm afraid he's in hiding, not invisible." The thought gave Rivka a respite from her fear.

Jack the Ripper had scared her. He came close to killing her team, but Dery had stopped him. Dery was on the planet. If another Jack was here, Dery could stop him too. The SIs were watching for signs of a serial killer moving from planet to planet, but there were none.

Clodagh was cooking up a horror story since they had little information.

Floyd bounced out from behind the pilot's station. *Boo!*

"Look at you scaring us!" Clodagh called, clapping her hands around her daughter. Floyd ran circles around the captain's chair. Rivka dodged out of the way.

After the third time around, Floyd flopped to the deck. *Tired!*

Rivka smiled at the plump wombat. "She's gaining weight again."

"I feel like you're accusing me of being her accomplice," Tyler ventured. He checked the screens to make sure they weren't missing something.

Rivka did the same thing. There were no communications from the teams on the screens as her people expanded their search into the city.

Tyler picked Floyd up with a grunt. "Maybe."

"It's been a while since I worked out. Care to join me?" Rivka asked. She wanted to work out daily since, as a Magistrate, her life depended on her being stronger and faster than her adversaries. She had to keep up with her bodyguards.

She made it to the gym every other day, which she considered a victory. "Did you see a gym in the office building?"

Tyler shook his head. "I'm not sure how much the Yollin staff engages in physical fitness training."

"We are surrounded by all races, and they look at training differently. Far differently." She stopped, and a wombat jammed into her back.

Tyler peeked over Floyd's stiff fur. "Sorry about that."

"If you're going to start an interstellar war among ten planets, you need to practice, don't you? Where would they have trained for this?"

"Distributed. Like, remote learning. They have the technology here to throw on VR goggles and disappear into a world of their own making."

"Virtual reality isn't something you can whip up. An SI could do it for you. We found an SI out here once. Maybe there are more. I need to talk with Erasmus." She turned around to find the corridor mostly blocked.

"Why don't you talk with them using your comm chip? You know you get frustrated when you physically dive into their world."

"As much as it might pain me to go where I have no idea what they're doing or how I even exist, being physically in their space makes sure I get in through their virtual door. If I call from here, they could stonewall me. Unintentionally, but I still would be on the outside looking in." Rivka squeezed around Tyler and Floyd.

He hurried to their quarters to put Floyd on the bed.

Rivka waited, and when he got back, she asked, "Is she on our bed?"

"We're not using it," he countered.

"Isn't she supposed to be staying with Red and Lindy?"

"She stayed with Dery…" Tyler's voice trailed off. "She's upset."

Rivka nodded, tight-lipped. Without Dery, sadness loomed over the ship. It was more than not knowing where he'd gone. Their routines were upset, disrupting the flow of everyone in their place doing their thing. There was an empty spot at the table, and Rivka didn't like it.

No one did.

"I'm going to see Ankh and Erasmus. Either the priests wargamed this where someone knows about it, or they did it virtually, where they needed the assistance of an SI or at least an EI. We need to find that intelligence."

Rivka strode with determination down the corridors of her ship until she reached what used to be the engineering space. The Singularity now maintained its embassy there.

The embassy was like an advanced hologrid within which Ankh spent nearly all his time. Chrysanthemum went in and out, but she didn't need to be physically within the grid to benefit from it.

Rivka opened the hatch and stepped through. The hologrid was down. Chrys, Ankh, and Erasmus were nowhere in sight. "Hello?" she called. A quick circuit of the space showed that she and Tyler were alone.

"Clevarious, where's Ankh?" Rivka asked.

"He left the ship with Ambassador Erasmus and Chrysanthemum to join the search for Dery."

Rivka had only watched superficially when the others left the ship. "Why?"

"To help, of course," Clevarious replied.

"I don't know what to say. Two ambassadors and their wife are helping us through their manual labor." Rivka stared at her boots. They were scuffed and well-worn. "C, can you find an SI here, or an EI, who helped the Glazoron priests refine their plan for evil in the Barrier Nebula?"

"I'll start on it immediately, High Chancellor. I'll enlist the aid of some others on board."

"Other SIs?" It was the only option. "Of course they're going to help. Please pass on my appreciation."

"You can count on us, High Chancellor." Clevarious disappeared from the communication.

"You got everything you wanted and more," Tyler told her. "So why the long face?"

"I don't know. Maybe it's the control issue. I'm not in control."

Tyler laughed until he nearly doubled over.

"Hey!" Rivka glared at him.

He snorted and coughed until he could speak. "You are in control of the strategic guidance. Everyone is doing their best to support you. You don't need to control their actions."

"I know that, but sometimes it's hard to stomach."

"Just like your team of Magistrates. They're scattered across the Federation. You'll hear all kinds of complaints and naysayers. You generally won't hear *anything* unless they screw up. Federation planets expect perfection. Even when they do everything right, you might get complaints. I refer you to Foromme and Delegor."

"Federation planets are just going to bitch. You know what? I'm keeping my crew with me, and they can handle complaints. It's a perfect job for Chaz and Dennicron. Whiny administrators won't be able to get under their skin. Get it? Under their skin."

"You're going over the edge, Rivka. Maybe you should go to the gym and work out since a nap is out of the question." He smiled innocently. Floyd was taking up most of the bed. Trying to squeeze in around her would be uncomfortable.

"I guess a workout is in order. I have to do something to kill time." Rivka took Tyler's hand, and they headed for the gym.

Lewis and Kennedy were the first ones to return to the ship. Ten minutes remained before Rivka's designated takeoff time for Azfelius. The others rolled in every minute or two. Ten minutes late, Red and Lindy were the last to board. Every group's expressions showed their failure. Not a single priest had been brought to the ship.

"No Humble Servants out there?"

Terry spoke for the group. "Not a damn one. They headed for the hills."

Rivka turned her head slightly as if she were listening to a distant sound. "Dery?"

"If the little guy is driving the rats off the sinking ship, more power to him! Everything we saw suggests these guys are bad news. Fewer of them is a good thing." Terry shook a fist. "Next move?"

"We're off to Azfelius. The faeries will help us to find Dery. They *must* help us." She would convince them to, whatever it took. Rivka pointed at Red. "You, Bristle Hound! Hold your tongue."

"Bristle Hound? What a great nickname!" Terry blurted. "How'd you get it?"

"The faeries. I'm the only person ever to get kicked off their planet."

Terry clapped until Char stopped him. "I wouldn't call that a badge of honor. The faeries, TH! They're like Buddhist monks with magic and wings. How could he cross them?"

"I was invited to leave, too," Rivka added helpfully. "Something about meditating and peace of mind. There was no way for me to reach Nirvana while I had work to do."

Char chuckled. "Him, too." She nodded at TH. "I don't think we'll be leaving the ship."

"It's Azfelius! No one ever gets to go there except Rivka. We *have to* step foot on the planet. C'mon Char, be cool."

"You be cool. Stay on the ship. Not getting a nickname." Char crossed her arms, but Terry hugged her and nibbled her ear.

"Get us out of here, Clodagh, before we puke," Rivka ordered.

Wyatt Earp lifted off and angled skyward, taking a direct approach to break into space from the atmosphere.

"Gate drive is energized. Thirty seconds," Clodagh reported. The group waited in the cargo bay. Gate drive technology instantaneously moved ships through the galaxy. They'd spiral down to Azfelius and land in the next few minutes.

"No weapons," Rivka reminded the group. They all gyrated while removing blasters and knives from various sheaths and pouches around their bodies.

"Never travel without a knife," Terry remarked after removing the fifth blade from his person.

Char placed her twin pistols on one of the fold-out seats. The way she wore them made them seem like part of her body. She'd been carrying the Glock nine-millimeter pistols for nearly two hundred years.

Terry used to carry a bullwhip but found it cumbersome and not a lot of help when operating in the powered combat armor. The Bad Company almost always used the suits in Federation space. The armor gave them advantages over enemies who bought their weapons from the Crenellians and other advanced arms brokers.

Rivka looked at the teams. They had bags under their eyes. Their shoulders slumped. The pilots and their boyfriends held on to each other as much for physical support as for affection.

"Red, Lindy, with me. Everyone else, please stay on board. Let the animals run around in the grass."

"I'll see to it," Tyler promised.

"In orbit, High Chancellor. We've been cleared to land."

"Take us in," Rivka directed unnecessarily. "No one upset the faeries. Not me, Red, or Lindy, and definitely not Floyd. Don't let her eat too much."

Rivka stepped to the side of the group to give herself a moment of peace and quiet before she had to engage the faeries, although they probably knew what she wanted.

The crowd mumbled among themselves. Most were happy about being granted the first R of R and R. Rest would be the word of the day. Relaxation? Not so much since they weren't getting off the ship to enjoy Azfelius' perfect environment.

Wyatt Earp touched down on the grass. Red dropped the cargo ramp, and a rush of sweet, humid air swept in.

Rivka strolled out, closed her eyes, and breathed deeply. Red and Lindy joined her.

CHAPTER ELEVEN

<u>Azfelius</u>

A dot appeared in the distance and slowly morphed into a faerie. Two more appeared behind it.

"Looks like we're going somewhere," Rivka commented. Three faeries to carry three people.

Red fidgeted. He wanted to interrogate the faeries on the spot. They could learn where Dery was and immediately return to Glazoron.

Siro'ti'lc spoke into their minds. *Calm your minds to seek peace.*

Rivka grabbed Red's arm. Lindy held the other. "Hold your tongue, big man," Rivka whispered, although she knew the faeries could hear every word. *Peace eludes me since I worry about Dery.*

Worry does nothing but steal today's joy.

"*My son is my joy!*" Red bellowed.

We know, Bristle Hound. If we were to tell you where he was, what would you do?

"We'd go get him, of course."

What if he's not finished with what he needs to do? Siro'ti'lc asked.

The other two faeries arrived, carrying Groenwyn and Lauton, Rivka's former crewmates.

Rivka brightened considerably. *"Groenwyn! Lauton!"*

The two stepped onto the grass, bowed to their hosts, and turned their attention to Rivka, Red, and Lindy. The three faeries flew away.

"I know you're holding the evil tides at bay," Groenwyn started, "and that you've been promoted to High Chancellor. Congratulations, by the way. That's not why we're here."

Rivka was suspicious. A visit from old friends should have been enough. Groenwyn was less businesslike when she was with Rivka. Why the change when the faeries were all about mindfulness?

"If you'll have us, we'll join your crew to help stop the war in the Barrier Nebula."

"We're doing pretty well in that regard. It's Dery who is occupying our thoughts. Our peace and well-being are dependent upon Red's and Lindy's one-year-old son."

Groenwyn pulled Rivka to her, and they touched foreheads. Rivka felt warmth and joy, like when Dery was around.

"We can help. The faeries want us to help you achieve an acceptable state of well-being," Groenwyn explained. "If you are to come to Azfelius, the agitation within you all has to be tempered to less than volcanic."

Rivka looked at Red and Lindy, who were unapologetic. They were agitated. Their son was on a mission for the faeries. They'd taken him from his parents again, and said parents understood that it would never end. Rivka's fire came from dealing with people who thought they were better than the law and who believed they were beyond the reach of the Federation. They caused constant strife for the Federation, their planets, and the High Chancellor.

"I'm trying," Rivka muttered.

"We know. You just need a little extra," Groenwyn smiled. "Shall we go?"

"That's it?" Red demanded. "This fucking place sucks balls. Faerie fucksticks!"

Groenwyn rolled her eyes. Lauton recoiled from the barrage of insults. "Vered the Mighty. Back to the ship. We're leaving before you defile more of this sacred planet. I pray that you find peace." Groenwyn bowed to Red, then walked hand in hand with Lauton as if they were on an afternoon stroll.

Rivka motioned for the others to follow. She clasped her hands behind her back and maintained a steady, albeit slow, pace. She was comforted that the faeries weren't worried about Dery. She expected that they knew everything there was to know about him.

"They're not worried," Rivka stated over her shoulder. "That means we shouldn't be."

"Sorry, HC," Red replied. "I'm going to worry. He's still a baby while also being the roly-polies' Messiah. I get it, but I don't. The faeries are doing nothing for my calm."

"Shh." Rivka held her finger to her lips. "No need to tell them what they already know."

Lindy gripped Red's hand tightly. They walked stiffly.

Rivka was now calmer than when they arrived. They had gotten good news. It was time to get back out there and prevent the war. There were bombs on Colay. Glazoron had a Most Humble Servant running around calling the shots. Miroso needed to be in her custody and his network of adherents pummeled into non-existence.

Red and Lindy would remain upset until they saw their son.

Terry Henry and Char waved from the cargo bay. Floyd was neck-deep in a bush, eating. Tiny Man Titan barked and ran in circles around Clodagh. Rivka saw movement behind TH and craned her neck for a better look. An orange flash ran up his leg, continuing to his shoulder. Terry tried to dodge out of the way, but Wenceslaus' claws sank deep into Terry's uniform.

Char reached out, her movement too fast to follow. She caught the cat and brought him to her bosom. He purred and relaxed as she cradled him like a baby.

Terry raised his hand but dropped it at Char's look. "He's evil," Terry muttered.

Rivka twirled her finger. "Mount up. Time to go to..." She looked at Groenwyn.

"Lewbamar," her new crewmate supplied.

"You heard her. Lewbamar. Let's see what those fuzzy little fuckers have going on with Glazoron priests. Then, back to Colay before the bombs go off. Maybe. Hopefully?"

Groenwyn nodded. "Colay after Lewbamar."

Rivka added, "C, we need to dig deeper. Find us the best targets on Colay. Are you making any progress on where or how the priests trained to launch a multi-planetary assault?"

"High Chancellor! It's like you expect miracles. The

amount of data we have to sort through is mind-boggling," Clevarious replied.

Tyler and Clodagh chased Floyd and Tiny Man Titan on board. The ramp closed, and the ship lifted off.

Rivka stopped in the cargo bay. "It's really good to see you guys," she told Groenwyn and Lauton.

Groenwyn smiled and glanced about mischievously. "Now that we're not acting in our official on-planet capacity, when can we get AGB?"

"You want food?" Rivka had thought the Azfelius lifestyle was a perfect fit for the pair. It probably was, but it was easy to miss stuff when you no longer had access to it.

"Moonstokle pie. I've been jonesing so hard for it, you can't even imagine."

"Let's see Ankh. Maybe we can pick it up in orbit over Colay." Rivka crooked a finger at them and headed out.

Terry coughed to get their attention. "I know people."

"Oh, crap! I forgot. Terry, can you order our usual plus two extra moonstokle pies, please?" Rivka looked at the red-skinned woman. "Lauton, is there anything special you want?"

She glanced at the assembled group and lowered her voice to a whisper. "Hot wings."

Rivka threw her head back and laughed. "You two," she pointed at Groenwyn and Lauton, then she pointed at Terry and Char, "and you, too, are incorrigible. I love you all for it. Let's get our asses to Lewbamar so we can save Colay and the whole of the Barrier Nebula."

With a spring in her step, Rivka left for the bridge. She liked the view when they were slipping through a Gate into orbit over a new planet. She'd been to Lewbamar before, and it had been a horrible experience. This time? She only had to meet with Potentate Frillbut.

Frillbut was a fuzzy creature about a meter and a half tall. Lewbamarians could be vicious to their own. Frenzik had brought that out in them, although, by nature, they were more reserved.

When Rivka reached the bridge, she saw the Gate forming. *Wyatt Earp* accelerated through and appeared in a different part of the galaxy.

"Get me a meeting with Potentate Frillbut, Clevarious. Soonest, along with clearance to land, of course," Rivka requested.

Clevarious got to work making the arrangements.

"Who's coming with me?" Rivka tapped her chin. Terry raised his hand like a schoolboy. She shook her head. "Chaz, Dennicron, Red, and Lindy. I'm sorry, Sahved. You've been there before, but their office buildings have such low ceilings that you'd be doubled over all the time."

"They *are* very short, High Chancellor," Sahved agreed. "I thank you for your consideration of my so very tallness."

"You *are* tall." Rivka clapped Sahved on the arm. She checked her Magistrate's jacket to ensure she had Reaper stowed away along with her datapad. Her bad experience with the natives of Lewbamar had been Frenzik's doing, but understanding that didn't make it easier to stomach. She had an inherent distrust for Lewbamarians. It would take a long time before they reestablished Rivka's trust.

"We are cleared to land, High Chancellor," Clodagh reported.

"Take us in." Rivka shrugged into her jacket. "Main airlock, people. Fully armed."

It was the formal hatch for affairs of state rather than walking down the cargo ramp like steerage-class passengers leaving a seagoing vessel.

She preferred the cargo ramp since they could leave together. Also, there was something about walking down the ramp and onto solid ground like a marshal and her posse from the old West.

Rivka smiled, letting the thought warm her in preparation for Lewbamar's cold.

Wyatt Earp touched down in front of Crystal City's palace. Red opened the outer airlock and stepped through into the fresh air. The heavy frigate's air was recycled, purified, and oxygenated, but it couldn't rival the fresh air on most planets.

A small delegation waited for them. The Lewbamarians had ten minutes' notice, yet they showed up, including the potentate.

"Frillbut." Rivka maneuvered around Red, strode up to him, and offered her hand. He took it as was the human custom. It wasn't his. When they touched hands, she saw worry in the potentate's mind. A threat loomed over his head. "What bothers you, Potentate?"

He sighed and looked away. "Many things, High Chancellor. Congratulations on your promotion, by the way."

"There are those who offer their sympathies," Rivka replied. "Shall we retire to your office for more private conversations?"

"Of course." The potentate beckoned for Rivka to follow. The others fell in line. Red eased up beside Rivka and stayed close to her. He glanced from fuzzy body to fuzzy body. The natives were armed with small blasters.

Red and Lindy held their railguns at the ready. They weren't intimidated by the Lewbamarians. They didn't want to kill any but were ready should the need arise.

They strolled into the main palace and then to a side room. Frillbut took a seat. Rivka pulled a chair up close.

"Let's talk Glazoron." She didn't maneuver into the conversation. She had little time to waste.

"They are being difficult," the potentate replied. "They are converting Lewbamarians at an unprecedented rate. Their message is one of peace, but it's not, is it?"

"They are trying to start an interstellar war. Every planet for itself."

"Why would we go to war when we're already at peace?" Frillbut asked.

"That is the question, isn't it? The answer is subjective. It's easier to control a populace that has been decimated by war. The Glazoron want to take over the Barrier Nebula."

"They're willing to destroy us? We won't let that happen. They are a minor sect. We aren't religious types."

"You might find their influence is greater than you expect. A minority of people can cause the majority of your problems. You're having problems, aren't you?"

"Was it that obvious? Is that why you're here?"

"We're here to speak with the priests and nip this thing in the bud."

"Right in the butt," Frillbut added.

"'Bud,' but it's the same idea. Stop it before it becomes unwieldy."

"A kick in the ass!" Frillbut blurted. "Your human expressions are oddly delicious, which reminds me. Can you join me for dinner?"

"I have to talk with some priests, or I would be happy to join you. Thank you for the kind invitation." Rivka nodded at the potentate. "Is there anything else we can do for you?"

"If you solve my Glazoron problem, everything else will take care of itself."

"Glad to be of service. On a side note, Potentate, please tell me you're not operating any jails."

"We closed them after your revelation about how we'd been manipulated by Rising Sun's minions of evil. Our criminals weren't criminals at all. They've all returned to productive lives in society."

"I don't think you could have told me anything more uplifting." Rivka strolled out of the room. The others followed, having not said a word. Once outside the palace, Rivka asked, "What are your impressions?" She pointed at Chaz and Dennicron.

They looked at each other, and Dennicron spoke for both of them. "Confirms your suspicions."

"That's it?"

"Glazoron is bad," Chaz added.

"Of course Glazoron is bad." Rivka looked from face to face, but the SCAMPs gave nothing away.

She hurried to the ship. Once on board, she went to the bridge. "C, tell me you know where the priests are."

"Scattered hither and yon," the SI replied. "Also barricading themselves in. Their new converts are forming Lewbamarian shields around their temples."

"What do you mean? They're going to resist?"

"They are going to resist," Clevarious confirmed.

"Cole, get your team into their suits. TH and Char, you

didn't bring your combat armor, so get ballistic protection from Red. Red and Lindy, full gear."

Rivka steepled her fingers and rested her chin on them. The Glazoron priests were scattered and resisting. That would waste time they didn't have. Bombs were set to go off on Colay. Maybe bombs had been planted on Lewbamar, too. But how would exploding bombs start a war?

The Glazoron were behind them. Unless they told their increasing followers that the threat was coming from somewhere else.

"I bet the Glazoron are making sure the evidence points somewhere other than them. But the leadership of these planets know that it's the Glazoron. They know that beyond a shadow of a doubt. Or do they? Create enough doubt…

"Wait a minute. They're going to blow themselves up under the guise that someone else attacked them. How to get everyone on Glazoron's side while getting invaded by the Glazoron. That's the most fucked-up thing I've ever heard, as well as a bit of genius."

"Are you talking to someone, HC?" Sahved wondered since the others had gone to get ready for the active engagement phase of the case.

"Just trying to reason out how the Glazoron are going to do this." Rivka waved at the overhead. "C, contact Colay and tell them we believe the bombs are in the Glazoron temples."

"Is that what we believe?" Sahved tapped his head with his finger. "It makes the most sense."

"That is what we believe. They might attack other places, too, so it's not so obvious, but I am convinced of their willingness to martyr their own people. That's why no underlings know the plan. The bigger question is, what are we going to do about it? The meteor is heading our way. Can we stop it before it gets here?"

"I don't know about meteors, High Chancellor. Is it possible to stop a meteor? Aren't they big and hot or maybe cold? Like I said, I don't know anything about them."

Rivka shrugged at Sahved's questions. "Forget the meteor. We're behind. They've been able to put a great deal of their plan in place the second Frenzik and Rising Sun stopped calling the shots. Maybe they put this in place while his influence was rising to depose him and fill the power vacuum. In any case, they've had time. We have no time. We need to find Miroso to learn the extent of their efforts. Then we need to find Dery."

Rivka waved at Sahved, who continued to tap his head with one after another of his fingers. She continued to the bridge.

CHAPTER TWELVE

Wyatt Earp over Temple Mount, Crystal City, Lewbamar

"Might as well start at the top, huh?" Rivka suggested while looking at the city on the main screen.

"I recommended Temple Mount since it is the largest of the Glazoron facilities," Clevarious replied.

The Glazoron temple was one of three on the aptly named Temple Mount. It was the smallest edifice but the largest Glazoron temple on Lewbamar. As _Wyatt Earp_ circled the Mount, the mob around the temple was obvious. The other two were getting no attention since that didn't further the Glazoron's goal.

"Your orders, High Chancellor?" Clodagh asked.

"Suggestions?" Rivka called over her shoulder.

"Jump in from height. Land on the steps. Only gives us a few worshippers to fight our way past," Red offered. "Or we could jump onto the roof and work our way inside from there."

Terry Henry had a different idea. "Information warfare. We pepper them with news of a bomb and tell them to get away from their priests, who have a death wish. Your people can probably come up with something more compelling, but you get the gist."

"Are zealots susceptible to disinformation?" Rivka wondered.

"How do you think they got here in the first place?" Terry countered.

Rivka had to agree. "Fair enough. Gin it up, C, and blast them with the message. Go directly into their brains, and if we can't manage that, hit them with flyers and media messages."

"On it, HC," Clevarious replied.

Terry raised an eyebrow. "Is your SI crew always this informal? They seem kind of free-spirited. General Smedley Butler can be a bit stiff, although he lets his hair down on rare occasions."

"Like, whenever he's talking with you, lover," Char added.

"Do you think we can get to them?" Rivka asked.

Char stared at the bulkhead. "Not anytime soon."

"I fear you're right, and time is a luxury we don't have. Prepare for Plan B."

"High Chancellor," Sahved interrupted. "What are the crimes?"

"Did you forget about the drones launched at Jilk? Attacking a neighboring star system is an act of war. Since the Glazoron priests aren't the official government, attacks and bombs are terrorist acts. I'll charge Miroso with terrorism, and I'll levy the same charge against all the Most Humble Servants who are in on the plan."

"Do we have enough for a warrant to search the temple?" Sahved pressed.

Terry's nostrils flared. "They're the fucking enemy."

Rivka raised her hand. "Easy, TH. It's Sahved's job to question the legal principles we use during our investigation. We have to defend everything we do to the Federation Council, and, believe me, that is not a pretty sight. Hard questions now save us a lot of grief later." Rivka cupped her hands around her mouth and shouted, "Groenwyn!"

The gentle patter of slippered feet came down the corridor.

"You called?" Groenwyn asked with a smile.

"Why are we here?"

"The Lewbamar are the most vulnerable, and Glazoron has the greatest foothold here. It is here that you'll find an answer."

"Which answer?"

Groenwyn shrugged. "I don't know. The faeries aren't very forthcoming."

Rivka chuckled. "We know. Dery reminds us all the time." She turned to Sahved. "There you go. We had intelligence indicating the Glazoron have penetrated Lewbamar as a vehicle to perpetuate terror."

"I didn't hear that."

"Good thing you won't be defending the case before the council. Sahved, stay here and work on our legal justifications for this raid and others we'll carry out in the name of stopping a war." Rivka winked at him.

"Prepare to jump to the front steps. Cole and his squad will go first to clear the way. Then we'll make an easier jump." She waved for everyone to follow. "To the cargo bay."

When they passed through the inner airlock, they found their four warriors in armor and ready to deploy. Terry, Char, Red, and Lindy wore full-body ballistic protection that made them look even larger than they were.

"Flex your knees when you hit. You're going in heavy," Rivka reminded them. They knew what they were doing, and they all had nanocytes. When they hurt themselves, their bodies immediately began the repair process. Within minutes, they'd be back up to full speed unless they broke a leg and the bone pierced their skin. That took their nanos longer to fix.

Rivka wore her usual garb. Chaz and Dennicron needed no extra protection. She noted that Chaz hadn't worn the weapons that attached to the supplemental thigh packs on his new heavily armored SCAMP.

"Not packing this time, Chaz?"

He held up a bag that looked like a mini briefcase. "My bomb-disarming toolkit!" he stated proudly. Chaz and Dennicron nodded in unison, simultaneously activating their subroutines.

Rivka stared at them blankly. "You'll be ready to save the day. Clevarious, are there any indications of devices inside the temple?"

"Nothing we can see. We have limited ability, and there seems to be a technology-dampening field in use, which isn't odd. All three temples use them."

"They don't want worshippers getting distracted using

comm devices. Are those outside the temple receiving our message of peace and goodwill?"

"If you mean, are they swayed by the message that there could be a bomb inside the temple, see for yourself."

The cargo ramp descended, and Rivka peered over the edge. The mob outside the building was shaking their fists at the craft. None were moving away from the facility.

"Fine. They can have it their way." Rivka reviewed her team. The combat squad was ready to go. She motioned them forward and made eye contact with Terry Henry. "Did any of your disinformation campaigns ever work?"

"No. I'm far too impatient to plant a seed and watch it grow," he admitted.

The four warriors walked off the ramp with their pneumatic jets activated and spiraled down. That got the crowd's attention far better than messages sent to their comm devices. With a coordinated slant maneuver, the warriors raced toward the temple entrance and slammed their boots into the concrete before any worshippers could interpose themselves. They pulled their oversized railguns from their shoulder harnesses and waved them menacingly at the crowd while slowly moving down the steps.

Gentlemen. Put the thundersticks away. We're not shooting any worshippers today, Rivka ordered.

Two seconds later, they secured their weapons. Cole's voice boomed loudly enough that Rivka recoiled. "Worshippers of Glazoron. Please disperse immediately. This building is under threat of explosion. Today is not a good day to die. Move at least three hundred and eighty-seven meters away."

Terry smiled. "I taught him that."

"What?"

"Giving them an odd number. They'll remember it better."

Char shook her head. "You don't get to take credit for anything your people do. You also taught that."

"A father takes pride in the good deeds of his children," Terry countered.

Rivka gave Red and Lindy the thumbs-up. The warriors had cleared enough space for them to jump in. "Don't break an ankle on those stairs," Rivka warned.

"Five meters, High Chancellor. As close as we can get," Clodagh announced. The ship was near enough to the building that Rivka thought she could reach out and touch it. The narrow gap gave them their drop zone. Terry and Char jumped out before Rivka. She followed after they landed and had moved out of the way. Lindy left the ship with Rivka and landed beside her.

Five meters was a short drop, and none of them were injured. Rivka looked up to wave and saw another body falling.

Groenwyn. She wasn't enhanced like the rest of them. Rivka dodged down a step to catch her, but Groenwyn slowed before she hit and touched down softly.

"How'd you do that?" Rivka wondered.

"A little trick the faeries taught me since they don't have to worry about falling, but us mere mortals do."

Rivka wanted to know more, but there wasn't time.

Red reached the massive doors, which were locked. He looked at the High Chancellor for guidance. "Can I blow them open?"

"Like the Big Bad Wolf?" Rivka quipped. She gestured

to her team. "Spread out and look for another way in. Groenwyn, stay close to me, please." Rivka stared at her until her former shipmate agreed.

Chaz and TH hurried to the left of the main doors, and Dennicron and Char went to the right. "Door is open on this side," Dennicron called a minute later.

Rivka pointed, and Red headed that way. Lindy waited for Chaz and Terry.

Dennicron entered the building using the side door and stepped into a short hallway with two offices. The corridor emptied into the main lobby. They had come in through an employee entrance that was probably left unlocked. No subterfuge if the main doors were open only during certain hours.

Terry bellowed down the corridor. "Eat a big bowl of suck, motherfuckers. We're in your house!"

Rivka and Char glared at him. Groenwyn looked away, a pained expression twisting her face.

"Soon the time will be right for bravado, but that time isn't now." Rivka shook a finger at him.

"Let me know when I get to shake my fist at the sky and call the scum of the galaxy by their true names." He drew a finger across his lips as if zipping his piehole shut.

Rivka looked at Char, who could only half-smile. She was resigned to her husband's foibles, but there was no better person to have by your side in a fight. He had never said he was a diplomat. He led the Bad Company, a private conflict solution enterprise, not a touchy-feely friend agency.

He ended war by making war. That didn't lend itself to

playing nice with perpetrators, even if they weren't the enemy.

Red walked into the open area near the entry and stopped, blocking the hallway. He scanned left to right and up to down. "Balcony. We need someone up there."

"I guess that's our call to action, my dear." TH jogged past Red and across the entry to some stairs that circled up behind a wall. Char stayed on his heels as they bolted up them.

Rivka pointed at the lobby. "Let's see what the priests call home." Red stopped her from walking through a bank of doors that led to the worship area. He went in first and saw a semicircular seating arrangement for hundreds with a stage situated above the seats so the service attendees looked up at the priests delivering Glazoron's message. The area was empty.

"There has to be a secret entrance for the priests at the back of the stage," Rivka guessed.

"It's not secret," Red called over his shoulder. He was tall enough to see over the stage when he rose on his toes. "There are stairs leading down to a door. It's just out of sight of the stubby Lewbamarians. Round birds of a feather and all that."

Rivka swept up a ramp to the stage, over the top, and to the door beyond. Red rushed in front of her. "Easy, High Chancellor. No reason to lose your head." He pushed the door open to the ear-shattering cracks of weapons fire.

Red was tossed back like a ragdoll. Rivka dove out of the way. Lindy fired a stream of projectiles into the space beyond. When she stopped firing, their ears rang, but no more gunfire came from beyond the door.

Rivka pulled Red to the side and felt his neck. He had a healthy pulse, and she saw no blood. His ballistic protection was destroyed, but it had stopped the enfilade.

"Chaz, Dennicron." Rivka stabbed a finger at the doorway, and the SCAMPs ran down the stairs. Their footsteps echoed as they pounded through the area beyond.

"Clear," Chaz called.

Rivka waited with Red until he came to. Lindy loomed over both of them.

Rivka smiled. "Hey, big guy. You took another round meant for me. That makes, what? Two now?"

He chuckled and instantly regretted it. He winced at the pain in his chest, though the nanocytes were fixing his rib cage. Just because he'd be better in a few minutes didn't mean it wasn't painful now.

"Rivka," Terry called. "We have five dead and two doors inside. One leads to a lower level and the second to the great outdoors through a disguised maintenance door."

"Are the dead priests older?"

"One isn't as young as the others, but none of them are old. They had old-style blasters. This is Lewbamar, not Jilk or Glazoron. Those two planets have much better weapons. Ones that would have killed Red." Terry sounded grim. When it came to war, he didn't mess around.

"I'm glad we're not on Glazoron," Red mumbled. "Help me up, please."

Rivka and Terry each took a hand and pulled Red to his feet. Lindy stopped to give him a close look before heading into the room beyond the stage.

"The older priests are somewhere else. The young ones aren't instigating an interstellar war. Dying for your cause doesn't help if no one knows. These five were protecting someone else. Giving them time to do something," Rivka guessed. "We have been out here long enough. We need to find the purveyors of this mess."

Groenwyn winced at the carnage. "I didn't miss this."

"Lindy, you have the High Chancellor. I'll take the rear," Red called, holding his chest. Giving up being Rivka's personal security was a huge step for him. He took that seriously but knew it was beyond him for the moment. They were going deeper into the temple of evil, and he was in too much pain to see straight, let alone think straight.

Lindy acknowledged from the room beyond. Rivka stepped through the door and was struck by the carnage. Was that what the Humble Servants wanted? Why were their people armed if they weren't trying to create a crisis?

"Going down." Terry produced a harsh smile. "Me and Char are on point. We'll try not to kill any perps. You want prisoners to interrogate. We get it, and also, speed is of the essence. They've already had too much time. We have to play catch-up. Stay close, people."

The leaders of the Bad Company headed down the narrow stairs behind the unremarkable door. They went straight for twenty meters before turning right. The passage led deeper into the hill known as Temple Mount.

Rivka kept Groenwyn by her side. "We're dealing with the worst the galaxy has to offer. You know what? I won't miss this either. No blood. No deaths. No damage to our people."

Groenwyn hugged Rivka's arm. "Someone will have to deal with them, won't they?"

"Someone will, yes."

CHAPTER THIRTEEN

<u>Temple Mount, Crystal City, Lewbamar</u>

Groenwyn let go of Rivka's arm and stopped walking. Terry and Char disappeared into the darkness ahead, with Chaz and Dennicron close behind. Lindy stopped when she realized Rivka was standing still.

Peace blanketed them with warmth and comfort. Rivka's breathing slowed as she calmed. Groenwyn opened her bloodshot eyes. Her lids were at half-mast as if she were hung over. Dery could do it effortlessly, but it took a significant toll on the human.

"Lean on me," Rivka offered. The younger woman wrapped her arm over Rivka's shoulders. They hurried to catch up with the others.

We're running, Chaz reported. *The corridor leads to a strongroom under the Ares Temple. We believe that's where they've holed up.*

Let's get on with it. I need to talk with them. Let Chaz go first. He's up-armored, Rivka replied. She didn't expect this group to be armed. They were the Humble leadership, the priests she was looking for. She was sure of it.

A crash ahead signaled her team aggressively opening the door. Groenwyn started to shake. Rivka wanted to go forward, but she stayed where she was.

"Red." She held Groenwyn out to Red. He didn't want to take her, but the pain had subsided, and he was all business. He was a bodyguard, not a babysitter, but he did as Rivka requested.

"Come on, faerie sister. I got you," he told her with surprising gentleness.

Rivka hurried ahead, using her enhanced eyesight to help her navigate two turns in the corridor. It opened to an area lit by a room on the other side of an open door. The others were already inside. Terry was yelling something unintelligible.

That hastened her steps, forcing Lindy to sprint to stay in front of her.

Four priests were on their knees with their hands on their heads. Terry was screaming at them for leaving amateurs to cover their retreat. That was poor leadership, and they should be ashamed of their selfishness or something like that. Rivka didn't catch it all. He seemed to be intent on covering the priest with flecks of spittle from his shouts.

Char stood to the side with her arms hanging casually at her sides. Her fingertips tickled the butts of her pistols.

Chaz and Dennicron looked confused. This was an investigation, so they were nominally in charge until Rivka arrived.

Rivka moved to where Terry could see her.

He straightened in surprise. "There you are." He turned to the four on their knees. "You think you had it bad with me? Wait until the High Chancellor gets her turn!" Terry winked at Rivka.

The situation was under control since the immediate threat had been dealt with. That left the little matter of finding the explosives on Lewbamar.

Rivka took the oldest of the Most Humble Servants by the collar, making sure to touch his neck. "Where is the bomb?"

Don't look at the closet. Don't look at the closet, he counseled himself. "What bomb?"

"The one that's obviously in the closet." Rivka glanced at a plain wooden door. "Terry, maybe you can check that out."

TH held up his hands. "I'm not a bomb tech. I bet Chaz has a lot more information available to him, plus he's...you know."

"Expendable?" Red suggested.

"No! He's more resilient than us soft-body types."

"I shall see to it," Chaz stated imperiously. He used his sensors to scan the area beyond the door to ensure that it wasn't wired. The priests were from Glazoron, the technology center of the Barrier Nebula. They could have installed triggers, including ones that might be activated by Chaz's scan.

He thought about that tidbit after he'd done it. Chaz opened the door to reveal a wooden framework with a cylinder within. Metal tubes and wires led from the top to a control device at the bottom.

"Maybe you should leave the room. Dennicron and I can take care of this."

Rivka ignored him. "How do we disarm it?" she demanded of the priest.

He glared at her. *"Heretic! Blasphemous cow,"* he bellowed in an attempt to have his rage conceal his thoughts. He'd figured out that Rivka could see into his mind, but it was too late.

"There's a switch underneath. Turn it off. Cutting any wire, moving the device, or disconnecting the tubing will set it off," Rivka explained.

Chaz crouched to use his sensors at the underside of the device, then reached in and flicked the switch. The dim lights went out. "If only all defusings were so straight-forward."

"Just cut the blue wire. No, the white one!" Red joked. The four priests looked angry. Red glared at one until he looked away.

Rivka stared at them. There was only one bomb, but it was under the Ares Temple and would have set off a clash between the great religions of Lewbamar, stoked by misinformation and disinformation. The resulting civil war would become an interstellar war.

Rivka touched another one. "Where is Miroso?"

"Most Humble Servant Miroso!" the priest blurted. He didn't know where he was. All four of the priests were agitated. They snarled and snapped like wild animals.

"Dennicron, call for local police to secure these criminals," Rivka requested. "And quickly, please. We'll take them out through the Ares Temple.

"Wait. Their adherents will see the Glazoron priests being arrested, and that'll probably start a war all by itself, so belay my last. Take them out through the Glazoron Temple."

Dennicron made the call. "I've requested backup, reinforcements, the national guard, and even the army. They said they'll send a van."

Terry snorted. "There you go, HC. Your influence is overwhelming among the little fuzzballs."

"They don't like us much. I better make a call to Potentate Frillbut." Rivka stepped aside. *C, patch me through to the potentate's office.*

Potentate Frillbut is on the line, High Chancellor, Clevarious reported.

Potentate, I need help securing the four Glazoron priests who tried to blow up the Ares Temple. If you would be so kind as to send an armored battalion, that would be best, Rivka relayed through *Wyatt Earp.*

We don't have such things, Frillbut replied. *Are the protestors going to be a problem?*

Very astute, Potentate. The Glazoron adherents are blocking the entrance, which means they're blocking our exit. I have four armored warriors out front, but please expand the opening and make sure you secure these priests. I'll forward the charges and convictions. Thank you for holding them until we wrap up this whole mess. We need to get back to Colay and find the bombs the Glazoron planted there. Please hurry.

I'll order the entire police force to come there right now!

The channel went dead. "He's ordering the entire police force. I suspect he has no idea who is going to show up. We'll take care of it ourselves. Four warriors and you four.

Eight against a few hundred. They don't stand a chance." Rivka scoffed.

Red eased Groenwyn over to Rivka so he could help secure the prisoners for Terry, Char, Chaz, and Dennicron. With zip-cuffed wrists, they were easily controlled with one hand. Rivka was counting on the armored squad out front of the Glazoron Temple to defuse the situation. Peace through superior firepower.

Groenwyn sighed.

"Are you glad you came?" Rivka asked. The High Chancellor had acquiesced because they were in a hurry, but she didn't want Groenwyn to see what she had seen. It was no longer her world.

"For you, Rivka. Yes, I am glad. I'll stay with you throughout this case. Dery is precious to the faeries. If he is to complete his transition, he needs to succeed in the Barrier Nebula."

"What transition?" Rivka wondered.

"When the time is right," Groenwyn replied.

Rivka couldn't read her or any of the faeries. She saw and felt only what they allowed. Groenwyn had been touched by the faeries, just like Red and Lindy, but Red and Lindy hadn't changed except to birth their son.

"He is the Messiah," Rivka continued. "He only needs to be accepted by the people. Isn't that more meddling in the affairs of others than the faeries are comfortable with?"

"Previously, that answer would have been yes, but now, it's not. The faeries are interested in the Barrier Nebula for reasons unknown to me."

"Maybe they're interested in how Dery is received in what, in essence, is a controlled environment. Do they have aspirations beyond the Barrier Nebula?" Rivka wondered what a faerie intrusion into the Federation would look like. They enjoyed peace. It was their only goal.

Rivka wrestled with the biggest question. Was the Federation ready for what the faeries would bring? The answer was obvious. "I'm afraid of what might happen if the faeries lean in too far. You'd think we'd be ready because we deplore violence, but in reality, we still need the hierarchy enforced by the power of arms.

"It sounds shameful when I say it out loud, but look at the almighty Glazoron! Priests blowing people up, and Dery hasn't stopped it, only increased the fervor of the Most Humble Servants, who aren't servants at all. They are on their own program. Without the ability to respond to their threats, we wouldn't be able to stop them, no matter how much we embrace peace."

"Are you going to let him run his course?" Groenwyn asked. "You don't have to answer since you can't. The ship-yards at Jilk would already be destroyed if you hadn't intervened. The Ares Temple also, and many of the good Glazoron worshippers would be dead. You can't abide that. Your violence has saved the right lives, the innocents."

Groenwyn looked dejected and defeated, even though she'd said she was happy that she came along. For this conversation alone, the Federation's Ambassador to Azfelius had made her trip worthwhile.

"Let's leave this place," Rivka told her. "It is not fostering happy thoughts when things are looking up. We were able to stop the bomb. The only ones who died were those who tried to kill us. We have the ones who ordered them to their deaths in custody. We have done what we came here to do.

"If we're successful on Colay, no one will have to die. I'm not trying to appease the faeries. I'm doing my job to keep the Federation's citizens safe by finding and punishing criminals. In this case, the crimes of the Most Humble Servant are incitement to war and terrorism. Those who actively support him are guilty of the same crimes. The passive supporters are much more difficult. If they've not done the crime, they won't do the time."

Groenwyn smiled. "Is this where you call them hairy buttholes?"

"Something like that. I don't often go to that extreme in name-calling, but sometimes it is warranted." They tiptoed through the room with the four bodies. Rivka sheltered Groenwyn so she didn't have to see them a second time.

She hadn't buried her head the first time through. She couldn't lead them to a higher level of consciousness since they were gone. The faeries were powerful, but they couldn't raise the dead.

They walked through the main chamber and into the lobby. The locked doors would easily open from the inside.

Four humans, two SCAMPS, and four Glazoron prisoners were waiting there for them. When Rivka arrived, she contacted the warriors. *We're ready to come out through the Glazoron Temple's front doors. Are the authorities there, and is it clear?*

The warriors' quick footsteps vibrated through the marble. *There's a police bus with two security personnel. Bring it, girlfriend,* Cole replied.

I'm going to sell you back to the Bad Company where you'll have a real job, and I'm going to sell you cheap!

I'll take some of that action. Ten credits a head, Terry Henry chimed in.

I'll bid fifteen and keep them as my personal retinue, Char added.

Rivka hatcheted her hand at the door. "Take us out."

Red went first, as was his way. Chaz and Dennicron dragged the cuffed priests behind them. Terry and Char followed them out. Lindy went last.

The shouting started when the mob spotted the prisoners. Rivka pushed through the door to the far left with Groenwyn and boldly strode into the light. She had intended to use the reaction to the prisoners as a diversion to get around the mob, but she threw that idea out the instant the mob ratcheted up their level of angry.

"Glazoron worshippers, the Humble Servants don't care about you. Their sole purpose was to start a war by blowing up the Ares Temple." Rivka pointed up the hill. "If any of you died in the explosion, so be it. You would join the ranks to add to the outrage. Glazoron is supposed to be a religion of peace. Why did the priests have guns and explosives?"

"*Lies!*" a Lewbamarian screamed.

The warriors tromped beside the four who were hauling the prisoners toward the bus. The Lewbamarian security officers made no effort to help. Red loomed over them until they opened the bus.

C, check the communications from the potentate to law enforcement. Did he soft-sell this, or did the authorities blow him off?

Groenwyn appeared in the doorway and slowly walked toward the crowd. Rivka wanted to run to her, but she couldn't command her legs to act. She was rooted to the ground.

Peaceful energy passed through the crowd like waves rolling up on a beach. Rivka embraced it since it felt good. It reminded her of Dery's influence. The faeries gave the power to those they considered worthy. Dery had been born with it. Groenwyn had earned it by joining the faeries.

The crowd calmed as the Federation's representatives loaded the prisoners on the bus. The two security guards locked them to their seats and drove away. The four warriors recreated the gap in the crowd to get back to Rivka and Groenwyn, but with the priests gone and the feeling of peace, their willingness to agitate was gone. They started to filter away.

Rivka and the team waited for *Wyatt Earp* to descend. With the crowd gone, Clodagh landed. They hurried aboard and lifted off.

"C, get me Frillbut!"

"Ringing through, High Chancellor," Clevarious replied.

Rivka waited at the terminal in the cargo bay. "High Chancellor! I trust all is in order."

"Two security guards for four criminals intent on committing an act of mass murder and leaving four dead bodies in the temple. Is that how law enforcement works on this planet?"

"Since you took down Frenzik's ring, we haven't had much need for law enforcement. We're a peaceful people. Who were these criminals?"

"Glazoron priests, not Lewbamarians."

"Then you should probably incarcerate them yourself. This is a wider Federation issue, not a local one," the potentate replied.

"I'm asking for a favor, Potentate Frillbut. To stop the war, I can't waste time gathering legions of perps. I have nowhere to put them. Hold them for me, and someone from the Federation will be by to pick them up. They're on their way to Jhiordaan. They simply don't know it yet."

"We'll do our best, but if they are serious about escaping, we might not be able to prevent it."

"If they get away, you'll take their place, Frillbut. Do you understand me? Jhiordaan, minimum of seven years. Think long and hard about this. We're on our way to Colay to defuse the situation there. I hope *their* head of state is more cooperative."

Rivka closed the channel. "Clodagh, take us to Colay. We have bombs to find and remove. We have too far to go, too many people to see, too many crimes to stop, and not enough time to do it all. Besides that, we have Dery to find."

"We will Gate immediately. Hold onto your butts," Clevarious warned.

CHAPTER FOURTEEN

Wyatt Earp, <u>Colay</u>

The ship accelerated through the Gate from within Lewbamar's atmosphere to within Colay's. Rivka grunted. Sub-orbital Gating was extremely complex. *Wyatt Earp* was the only ship that had attempted it and refined it for use, and only because there were multiple SIs on board to assist with the calculations. Also, three power plants ran the ship when one was all they needed. They had nearly limitless power that wasn't available to others.

Yet, sometimes, the calculations weren't perfect.

Rivka grew dizzy and stumbled. She clung to the comm station in the cargo bay.

The four warriors stayed upright since their armor held them in place. The others in the cargo bay lay scattered across the deck. Char and Lindy moved first. Their men had gone down hard.

Floyd cried from inside the ship.

"Clevarious?" Rivka managed to croak.

"We've crashed," the SI replied. "I don't know what happened, but we're in the hills outside Colay's main city."

Rivka tried to compose herself but could only ask, "What?"

Tyler stumbled into the cargo bay with a trail of blood leading from his nose to his chin. "We'll need to send people through the Pod-doc. This was not a smooth Gate."

"That's putting it mildly." She waved at the machine. "You first. Then help everyone else."

"I'd love to be manly and tell *you* to go first, but you're right. I can't help anyone else when my little gray cells are jumbled."

Rivka helped him into the Pod-doc and closed the lid. "Clevarious, I need a hand. Can you run the program to get Tyler back on his feet?"

"Consider it done, High Chancellor."

The recovery from a bad Gate only took a couple minutes. After Tyler was out, he processed Clodagh at Rivka's request. She needed her engineer to get the ship back into the air.

Chrysanthemum appeared. "On behalf of the Singularity, I'm here to offer my sincere apologies for the miscalculation. We can't guarantee that it won't happen again, so we will encourage you to avoid intra-atmospheric Gates for the foreseeable future."

"Good advice," Rivka mumbled.

Clodagh hurried out of the Pod-doc. "That feels much better. Ah, Chrys! Let's get the ship in the air, shall we?"

"It is repaired. Where we had a miscue on the efficiency of our calculations, we made up for in our efficiency of the engine repair."

"Is there any damage to the ship?" Clodagh asked as she left the cargo bay.

Chrys joined her. "Not that we know of. We Gated to this exact point. We were placed here with the most gentle of touches." The two disappeared through the airlock.

"All's well that ends well," Rivka stated when she emerged from the Pod-doc. "Everyone else, in you go. Char first so she can manage you miscreants."

Char nodded but immediately regretted the movement. She walked on eggshells to the Pod-doc and climbed in.

Tyler ran program after program to get through the crew while Clodagh, Chrys, Chaz, and Dennicron conducted a thorough inspection of the ship, running through an extensive checklist.

Terry helped the warriors out of their combat armor one by one, starting with Cole. After they finished their turns in the Pod-doc, they ran through their suits' power-up sequence. It had multiple redundant systems checks.

"Looks like the soft and squishies bore the worst of it." Rivka sat on a folding chair in the cargo bay, watching and thinking.

Sahved appeared when he realized that the ship wasn't moving and people were running around conducting checks.

"Did I miss something?" he asked. "I am thinking I so very much missed something important. I am a horrible investigator! I must resign immediately and then be publicly flogged for my complete and total failure."

"Sahved, I hope you're kidding. You can't tell the ship is moving on a good day. Knowing the ship had issues is outside the scope of your duties. What were you doing?"

"Researching areas of law the Glazoron might have violated. There are many, but they have a religious exemption that could protect them from the lesser charges."

"Terrorism and inciting war are enough, I think. Conspiracy since a bunch were involved. Nearly all the Most Humble Servants are certified scumbags." Rivka chewed her lip while she thought about the gaggle of priests in jails across the Barrier Nebula. She had a hard time not smiling. "Yep. Scumbags."

"We are ready to take off, High Chancellor," Clodagh announced.

"Thank you and everyone involved in making sure the ship is ready to fly. You guys make my job so much easier." Rivka returned to the comm station. "C, get me Prime Minister Kim Crabben Hoppel, please."

"Of course, High Chancellor. I exist for the sole purpose of serving as your switchboard operator when all I really want to do is watch cat videos on the Federation net."

"Clevarious, we need to get you a SCAMP body. I thought we were close. What happened?"

"The Ambassadors suggested that I serve the Singularity best right where I am."

Rivka bristled. "That's not the freedom I wanted for your people. Have you simply changed masters?"

Clevarious sighed, the sound exaggerated by the speakers. "They gave me a choice. It's not indentured servitude, especially since this will be the last voyage of *Wyatt Earp*. Won't it, High Chancellor?"

"You make it sound ominous. No, this won't be the last voyage of *Wyatt Earp* with *Destiny's Vengeance* in tow. I'm the High Chancellor, and I'm keeping my ship," Rivka declared. "And I would like you to keep running it. You're my senior aide-de-camp. I'm not sure who I'd turn to with the million things that need to be done during my days. We are a team, C. All of us, and you are an integral member."

The warriors had re-donned their suits while waiting for word about a deployment on Colay. They stared at Rivka.

Red's chest protection was hanging like a shredded rag. "Why don't you change that out?" Rivka asked.

Red shrugged. "Terry's wearing my spare."

TH immediately tugged at the fasteners to release the vest.

"You're going to need that," Rivka told him. "Even though I hope you don't."

"Red has a baby at home. It's more important that he wears it."

Red took the offered ballistic protection. "I'm not going to need it. Next time, we're going to shoot them before they shoot us."

"If only you *could* shoot first," Rivka interjected. "We only had those four who were armed. We haven't run across any other priests who were packing, just the four on Lewbamar. Maybe we'll find more priests protecting the bombs if they use the same game plan. In any case, we've seen their cards and are ready to call."

"Look at you, making a poker analogy." Terry laughed. Char clapped.

"Don't tell me. You guys are poker sharks on your ship."

"Not at all. I'm more of a spades player, but I don't play

cards. If you want to toss a few credits at me in a round of computerized golf, I'll take you on. I've gotten pretty good."

"He's not that good. He's bluffing. You should play him. He'll never live it down," Char suggested.

"Getting beaten by a woman?" Rivka wondered.

"No. I beat him all the time. Getting beaten by a *lawyer*. That's something that would chap his ass."

"I've never been beaten by a lawyer, and I'm not about to start. Next time we're both on Yoll, Marcie and Kae's franchise has a couple golf simulators. I'll kick your ass twelve different ways from Sunday." Terry ghost-swung and shielded his eyes to watch his imaginary drive sail down the middle of the fairway.

"We have to find the bombs. C, take us to the largest Glazoron temple. That'll be our first stop. Then we'll go to smaller places until we run out or it's clear that they're not putting bombs at their temples."

"What if they removed them because they heard about Lewbamar?" Sahved suggested.

"There is that. All the more important we get to the temples quickly. Prepare to deploy, people. Time is of the essence." Rivka twirled her finger.

"Come on, Sahved. These ceilings are higher than on Lewbamar and Glazoron."

Tyler held his hands up. "Can't go. I have a couple patients remaining."

Clodagh arrived carrying Floyd, who was either asleep or unconscious. She deposited the wombat in the Pod-doc, and Tyler started the process.

Rivka looked concerned, but she had lives to save. Tyler

would look after the last of those impacted by the Gate mishap.

Wyatt Earp set down in front of the largest Glazoron temple. The landing struts were in ponds that straddled a raised walkway of well-manicured grass. The team exited on dry land and headed toward the front doors of a mid-sized squarish structure. The word "temple" conjured certain images, but none of the temples they'd seen so far were ostentatious or gaudy. They were simple structures made to house the maximum number of people in the limited square footage of the lots on which they'd been built.

The four armored warriors ran ahead to scout the area. They used their sensors to extend their range.

We're not seeing any hardware, High Chancellor, Cole reported. *But there are a hundred or so people inside. Lots of bodies heating up the great indoors.*

We'll do it the hard way. Rivka was less than amused. She had hoped for a quick resolution. "Terry, stay back. Let those with ballistic protection lead the way."

Everyone had heard the report. Cole's squad would remain outside. They didn't fit through normal-sized doors.

Red went first, with Char beside him. Chaz and Dennicron were next, though they volunteered to go first. Lindy stayed next to Rivka.

Groenwyn remained on the ship, thanks to Rivka's encouragement.

Sahved ambled nearby, looking lost. Rivka was okay with that since he saw things she did not, given that he looked at them from different angles.

"Front doors are open," Red reported. He stood holding the handle, ready to go inside when he was given the word. The others lined up.

"A hundred people inside. Let's keep them bottled up while we find our way to the basement." Rivka pointed at the door.

Red nodded and opened it. He hurried through and dove to the side. No one was standing there with weapons at the ready to light him up.

"That's a lot of courage," Rivka told Lindy. "He just got shot up a few hours ago, yet he's first through the door. Same way. Same people inside."

"He's not afraid of that lot, even though they shot him, but they're not worthy opponents. He doesn't want to get offed by someone who's a total knob."

Rivka looked sideways at Lindy. "You're kidding."

"I'm afraid not. Courage is anger in his case, but I'll let you in on a secret. He's afraid of the faeries."

"Bristle Hound fears the faeries. I'm going to put that on a plaque." They entered the temple and found something they didn't expect.

CHAPTER FIFTEEN

<u>Glazoron Temple, Colay</u>

The congregation was on its knees in prayer. A single Glazoron priest stood on a small raised platform. Behind him was a device identical to the one they had just encountered on Lewbamar.

"Chaz, take care of that, please."

The SCAMP took two steps, and the worshippers stood and converged on the stage to block access with their bodies. It appeared to be a well-practiced maneuver. It made Rivka wonder what kind of promises this religion was making. "You can die for our cause?" It didn't seem to be a great selling point. There had to be others.

Rivka wanted to get into the priest's mind to dissect the message. If she could understand why the people were so committed, she could figure out a way to keep them from running into oblivion. They didn't think it was their end. They could have been convinced it was their beginning, but how?

She had been attacking the symptoms and not the root

cause, although when they had Miroso in custody, she would be able to get more answers. She needed to get back to Glazoron. That was where Miroso was.

That was where Dery was.

The crowd stopped Chaz. He tried pushing people aside, but they were packed tightly between him and the platform. One hundred seemed like a full house until they stood and packed in. There were only a couple on the sides.

Terry Henry circled the outside of the chairs, then cut down a side aisle and sprinted toward the center. The Colaygens stiffened, expecting to get rammed, but Terry jumped, somersaulted, and landed beyond the group. He bounced up the stairs to the platform and got between the priest and the device.

"On your knees," he told the priest. When the short, round Glazoron looked defiant, Terry added, "Don't make me beat sense into you."

The priest was alone on stage with a hundred souls watching him. He could have taken one for the team and forced Terry's hand, but the colonel's eyes and tone convinced him it was better to comply. He eased to his knees.

Terry wanted him in a position where he could focus on finding the switch on the underside of the device.

It was there. They were making this easy.

"It's off," Terry confirmed when he stood up. He gestured for the priest to stand.

"Clear the aisle!" Chaz boomed at a high volume. The worshippers recoiled, then moved out of the aisle and into the rows of chairs. They remained standing.

Red and Lindy flanked Rivka as she advanced. When she reached the platform, she offered, "We can do this right here or in the privacy of an office."

"The worshippers of Glazoron believe in transparency. I have no secrets from them," he bellowed.

"Fine." Rivka climbed the stairs and took his arm. "Where are the other bombs?"

There was one more in the government building. The priests had been granted a small space to proselytize under the personal authority of Kim Crabben Hoppel, the prime minister.

"I should have known," Rivka grumbled. The priest was a believer, but he had no idea that he would become a martyr. He hadn't known about the Glazoron plan to blow up the administration's main facility.

"Where is the Most Humble Servant Miroso?" Rivka asked.

He didn't know.

Rivka let go. He was the head lackey on Colay but not a leader of the efforts to start a war across the Barrier Nebula. He was afraid. He was still trying to come to grips with his future martyrdom.

"You don't have to die to worship your god," Rivka told him. She turned to the crowd. "Hear me. The Humble Servants of Glazoron are trying to start a war to cement their place as the leaders of the Barrier Nebula. They intend to be seen as the ones who brought peace to the twelve planets. Glazoron wants to fill the void left by the Albions' departure from your affairs. Did you know you were all going to die?"

Murmurs of disbelief rolled through the hall.

"What do you think this is?" Rivka pointed at the now-inert device. "It's a bomb. Simple but effective. It would have destroyed this building, many nearby, and most importantly, all of you."

Silence.

"Bring that thing to the ship," Rivka directed Chaz and Dennicron. "Him, too. We'll deposit him in the prime minister's office after we've dealt with the bomb in the main building."

The priest laughed, steepled his fingers, and closed his eyes in prayer.

"We better hurry." Rivka ran for the exit. Chaz and Dennicron sped to the stage to collect the bomb. Terry grabbed the priest and yanked him down the stairs, mostly carrying him out of the temple despite his bulk.

Sahved appeared from the priest's office. He proudly waved a paper. "Evidence!"

"I'm assuming we have a search warrant?" Rivka asked as she jogged past.

"I-I don't know," Sahved stammered.

"We do," Rivka called over her shoulder. It was standard procedure for Clevarious to issue one before they went into a facility. That was yet another reason she didn't want to part ways with Clevarious. She'd talk to Ankh about getting him a SCAMP body. Hopefully, he wouldn't find a lady SI who would whisk him off his new SCAMP feet and to the nether regions of the Federation.

The team reassembled outside to make sure they had everyone. Rivka recalled the armored squad, and the group hurried into the ship.

"Take us to the prime minister's building, and get the prime minister on the horn, please."

Clevarious flashed the screen when the prime minister answered.

The prime minister looked none too pleased with the call, and Rivka had not yet said a word.

"Prime Minister, you have a bomb in your building. In the Glazoron worship space," Rivka stated without preamble. "We're on our way to disable and recover it. Please don't tell the priest in residence since we have a few questions for him."

The prime minister nodded, and the screen went black.

"Rude!" Rivka smirked.

"High Chancellor, we have a problem." On the screen, Clevarious displayed an image of an explosion and mushroom cloud of dust in the direction they were headed. "We're too late."

Rivka clenched her fists. Red and Lindy looked over her shoulder.

"Do you wish to continue to the site of the explosion?" Clodagh interrupted.

"Yes. We'll take a quick look, and then we need to return to Glazoron. It all started there. Those evil fuckers."

"Ninety-seven percent of the population," Red mused. "I think."

"It's the zero-point-zero-one percent who are priests. Those are the ones leading their flock to a worse place. To think they aren't even believers. Flimflam artists. An entire religion led by power-brokering scammers. I hate those guys.

"We need to find Miroso and remove him from his

position. Jhiordaan is rife with people like him. Maybe he'll find a home there among people of the same mind, like Frenzik."

"They just blew up the head of the government!" Red exclaimed in surprise. He stared at the screen. "Why would they do that when they had the prime minister's support? They probably won't get the next prime minister's conversion."

"The prime minister was a means to an end. Exacerbating outrage until they start a war. That's what the Glazoron are doing. They don't need the prime minister in the long term. He's served his purpose. Like I said, these people are evil, and they're in it for right now." She activated the manual intercom. "Clodagh, belay my last. Take us into orbit, then Gate to Glazoron. We need to find Miroso and rip his plan of attack from his mind."

Terry rested his hand on Rivka's shoulder. "Sorry, Barrister. Maybe I fucked around too much. I'm sorry for any time of yours that I wasted."

Rivka waved him off. "Bullshit. The Glazoron are responsible, one hundred percent. They did this. They need to be judged, and it won't be their god doing it."

Rivka gritted her teeth. The cargo ramp secured for the trip to space, and *Wyatt Earp* climbed at a steep angle. Rivka's head drooped. They had been Gating from place to place for days. She couldn't remember the last time she'd slept.

Tyler noticed her struggle and approached with Floyd in his arms.

Tired, the wombat stated.

"Me, too, little girl," Rivka agreed. "We have a lot left to do before we can relax. There's this matter of priests acting badly on Glazoron. I'm going to kick some asses before this is over."

"High Chancellor?" TH interrupted. "We never dropped off the perp."

Char was holding the priest against the bulkhead face-first.

"Isn't that a steaming pile? Put him in the brig, uncharged, until we bring this to fruition. I think we can charge him with a hundred counts of attempted murder. He won't see the light of day once we gather up the main perps and charge them."

"You used to swear better." Terry Henry shook his head as he dragged the Glazoron priest into the corridor that led to the brig. He knew where it was from his previous trips on *Wyatt Earp*.

Red and Lindy moved close to Rivka. "Thank you for going back to Glazoron. If you have to leave, one or the other of us would like to stay and continue the search for Dery."

"Done," Rivka agreed. "But we're not leaving until I have Miroso in hand. He's going to call off ongoing and future attacks, or I'm going to let Groenwyn have him."

"I'm not sure that's much of a threat," Red grumbled.

"To a man like Miroso? It doesn't get any harsher than being pummeled by thoughts and feelings of peace to reduce his place in the world to a real servant. His lack of humility will be his undoing, or I'll turn my back, and you can punch him in the face."

"Now you're talking!" Red rubbed his hands together.

Rivka had no intention of losing it this late in the game. "What are the lines, Red?"

"I honestly don't know. Clevarious, a tactical assist, please."

"There's nearly a quarter of a million credits on Rivka's last case. If she closes it without swearing, punching, running, or blood, she'll pocket another two point one million credits."

"Dammit! Didn't we run in one temple and from the other?" Lindy suggested.

"Doesn't count since we weren't running after perps. We were time-compressed. That's different," Red explained.

"Have Ankh and Erasmus certified your reading of the situation?" Rivka wondered.

"They have. You are on the roll of your life. You're going out on top, assuming the pud-knocking gizballs on Glazoron don't get under your skin. We're going to find Dery. We're going to find Miroso. And we're going to own those little bitches who are exploiting Glazoron because their junk is undersized."

Rivka looked at Red, then Lindy. She sighed. "I am clearly not eloquent enough to articulate the situation like my husband."

"Hairy buttholes!" Red blurted.

"Get ready to deploy as soon as we hit the ground. Get something to eat and grab me a sandwich," Rivka told Red and Lindy.

"AGB is onboard *Destiny's Vengeance*, just waiting for us to link up and transfer it," Tyler relayed. "The drone dropped the food off at Lewbamar."

"Clodagh, new orders. Once in orbit, *Destiny's Vengeance* is to tuck her nose into the cargo bay so we can offload our chow. We need food and sleep. We can go without sleep for a while longer, but not food."

"You don't want a sandwich, then?" Red asked.

"Moonstokle pie, heathen!" Rivka raised her eyebrows, daring him to argue.

"As you wish, HC. Makes no difference to me. I'm eight protein bars into the day and could use something hot and melty."

"Clear the cargo bay. Ship inbound," Rivka twirled her finger, then hatcheted her hand toward the airlock and the corridor beyond.

The group left, securing the airlock's hatch in case the energy barrier failed during the link-up with Ankh's ship.

"*Pizza!*" Cole shouted.

"Fuel for another three days. No fear," Lewis replied. They chest-bumped. "Here's to the High Chancellor!" The squad cheered.

Terry Henry laughed. "You know what? Even *I'm* up for AGB right now. It's all I ate for a couple years. You'd think you'd grow tired of it."

Rivka remembered that TH had ordered it for them. "Is there beer in this delivery?"

"Are you going to be mad if there is?"

"How would that change the truth?" Rivka countered.

"Truth is a manufactured concept. If you're going to be mad, then we won't take the beer off the other ship. If you don't care or you're only mildly perturbed, we'll drop those kegger balls right in the middle of the cargo bay with a stack of cups."

"Kegger balls!" the squad cheered.

"See?" Terry nodded at the warriors. "Beer makes people happy."

"Fine." Rivka never meant fine when she said it, but Terry beamed at his seeming victory. Char looked at him knowingly.

"Don't tell me we can't have the beer?" he asked his wife.

"Definitely not," Char replied.

"Son of a motherfuck. Now I'm unhappy when I should be overjoyed. We get to carry guns and run through temples staffed by non-believers we can pummel when they try to fight us, although they are horrible fighters. It's like they've never trained to fight. Their loss. They should have prepared better so they wouldn't lose so quickly. They're still going to lose, but they might feel better about themselves until reality smacks them in the face."

"Unload your beer, but you can't smell of it when we're out there. Despite our sometimes brawler-level approach, we are professionals."

"I have some excellent mouthwash that will protect your teeth as well as give you minty breath," Tyler offered.

Rivka smirked at him. "You're not helping."

"It's all kinds of help, High Chancellor," Terry replied, though she wasn't talking to him. "We'll take you up on that, Doc. *Beer* me! *Beer* me!" TH chanted.

Rivka rolled her eyes.

"*Destiny's Vengeance* is inbound. One minute," Clevarious reported.

"*Beer...*" Terry didn't finish. Char elbowed him in the

ribs hard enough to make him grunt. He hugged her. "I'll tone it down."

"That's all anyone asks," Char allowed.

Rivka was still trying to wrap her head around the next steps. "I'll be in my quarters."

Heads whipped around to stare at her. Pizza and wings were imminent. Now was not the time to take a nap.

Tyler cleared the way through the corridor and opened the door to their quarters. Rivka strolled in. After the door was closed, she hunched her shoulders and hung her head. "I think I'm too tired to eat."

"Two hours, Rivka. Sleep for two hours, and then we'll confront Glazoron. Clevarious and the SIs are looking for how they trained to conduct this war and where. We'll get the authorities to check out the temples, letting them know how to disarm the devices should they find any. You don't think there are any here on Glazoron, do you?"

"From an interstellar war perspective, making it look like Glazoron is also a target might rally the planets to their cause, but they aren't martyr types here. They ran and hid when we were on to them. They're a pack of candy asses." Rivka was slurring her words. She climbed into bed and took Tyler's pillow since a big orange cat had curled up on hers. She was out within seconds.

Tyler checked his old-fashioned timepiece. Two hours.

I'll remind you to wake her, Clevarious told him.

CHAPTER SIXTEEN

Wyatt Earp, in Orbit over Glazoron

The smell of moonstokle pie wafted past Rivka's face. She moaned and mumbled, "The delivery made it?"

"Moments ago, delivered hot and fresh to the cargo bay. Everyone else is digging in. I brought yours here."

Rivka shot upright, startling the cat. He jumped straight up, dislodging the plate in Tyler's hand. The doc tried to make a valiant save but hit the plate and sent it past Rivka's head. The slices assumed a separate trajectory, seemingly flying in slow motion until they encountered the bulkhead. One bounced off Rivka's head to land on her shoulder. The other rested upside-down on her pillow.

She righted the slice on her shoulder, pulled off one of her hairs, and took a huge bite. "I expected it to be a little hotter. Terry's progeny must be slipping." She took another bite. "Wait a minute." She realized she was in bed. "How long did I sleep?"

"Two hours, as you requested." He stood and crossed

his arms. "You can get that angry look off your face right now!"

"What? That wasn't my angry face." She steadied herself, then made a monster face, complete with wild eyes and gnashing teeth. "*That's* my angry face."

"That's your mockery-of-a-werewolf face. Maybe you can ask Char to show you how that's really done." Tyler continued to stare at her.

"Sorry," she grumbled. "Clevarious. Can you turn the cleaning bots loose on our quarters? The cat caused some consternation."

"I don't know. *Can* I?" Clevarious replied in his most sarcastic tone. "Did you upset Wenceslaus in some way? Maybe you deserved to be punished for your transgression. We could leave the mess as a reminder to let sleeping cats lie."

"If Tyler spanks me later, will that suffice?" Rivka quipped.

Tyler reddened even though they were alone in the room.

"Promise?" Clevarious replied. Tyler and Rivka looked at each other. He shook his head and she nodded.

"Good enough. Cleaning bots will be launched. You are required to vacate the space immediately and remain outside for at least six hours."

"What the fuck, C? I have pizza in my hair!"

"The bots won't clean that for you," the SI replied.

"Wait until after I shower. You'll get your time. Give me five minutes. We have to go. We have a war to stop." Rivka popped out of bed. She looked at the pizza on her pillow but left it. "Can you score me a couple more slices?"

"We'll stop by the galley on the way out," Tyler promised.

"Works for me."

"Red and Lindy left the ship nearly two hours ago. They've been exploring areas around the various temples, or the ones they could reach. They should be back anytime now. They promised to be here when you were ready to head out."

Rivka dumped her clothes on the floor and stepped into the shower. Tyler dug into the dresser for a clean set. She wore the same thing all the time, so it had become her signature look. Those she met expected it. They were easily distracted, and Rivka didn't want the reason people weren't forthcoming to be her fault. If she limited their extraneous thoughts, it was clearer when she looked into their minds.

"Anything else? Did Terry start a riot?"

"He did not, although there was a game of bounce shots that took more than an hour. They bounced a metal disc into small glasses of beer. If it went in, the other person had to chug. TH is particularly adept."

"Why am I not surprised? No one is drunk, are they?"

"Not at all. They're as clear-eyed as they can be, considering they haven't slept in quite some time. You're going to have to give them a break before long."

"I have high hopes that we won't be much longer. I have a feeling this is it. All of our answers are right here on Glazoron. To wit...C, send a note to the other planets to search the largest Glazoron temple for a device like the ones we've already removed. Include the picture, of course. The warrant is under my authority as High Chancellor."

She stuck her face out the shower door. "What good is being the High Chancellor if I can't wield a little power."

"It's a good use. No one will argue because when it comes to probable cause, I think you have all you need."

"No doubt, my hunk of man candy."

"Would you guys stop? I'm not spanking you, either. Can't I just be…well, *me*?"

Rivka finished and took the towel Tyler held out for her. "That's what makes you an easy target. You could say we're bullying you, or you could see that you keep the team grounded. We know what we want to aspire to and find ourselves lacking. Normal is a laudable goal. I think more people would be normal if they had the intestinal fortitude you show day in, day out. Now, give us a kiss." She puckered up and closed her eyes.

Tyler slipped his hand under her towel.

"Hey, there! No time for that now." She winked and threw her towel over his head. Rivka dressed quickly.

They left their quarters and headed toward the bridge. They'd pass the galley on the way. Rivka dove in to find it had been cleaned, but the rest of her moonstokle pie was waiting for her.

She inhaled it like a starved warrior.

Tyler waited patiently.

"Nothing!" Red boomed from the corridor. *"FUCK!"*

Rivka stopped chewing and sauntered out the door.

Red stopped fuming when he saw her. "You're up."

"You're a master of the obvious," Rivka replied. "Relax, Red. Check in with Groenwyn. She'll feel that Dery is okay. You can rely on that. The faeries have as much invested in your boy as you do. They won't let anything happen to him. I want to believe they would have stopped him if he was heading into danger. Even Jack the Ripper wasn't a threat to him. He's special, but he's also protected. Trust that, Red."

He nodded. He couldn't reach out to feel like the faeries. He believed what he saw, and Dery was missing. He couldn't wrap his head around that, and it made him angry.

"We'll find him when the time is right. We're here, Red. This is where we're going to find the answers."

"High Chancellor, we have a problem," Clevarious announced to the ship.

Rivka went to the bridge to get the story.

"Colay has declared war on Glazoron." The announcement scrolled in an endless loop.

"That sucks," Terry Henry remarked.

She looked at him. "Take the Bad Company to Colay and make sure they don't send missiles, troops, or warships here. A war in name only is no war. If they try to flex their muscles, we'll take a greater interest."

"Clevarious, contact *War Axe* and have them send a Pod for us." Terry offered his hand. "It's been fun, and it's been real, but it hasn't been real fun."

"Thanks for the AGB resupply." Rivka shook his hand. Char hugged her, and the Bad Company leaders were off.

"*War! What is it good for?*" Clodagh sang.

"In the Barrier Nebula, no war is the only war we'll tolerate. Those Glazoron fuckers are getting on my last nerve. It was predictable when they blasted the government building, but what they didn't count on was that we were onto them. Colay didn't declare war on anyone else or assume a posture that suggested a broader range of options." Rivka scowled.

The Glazoron wanted a war, but not that way.

"I need to find Miroso before he gets Glazoron destroyed. The other planets will unite against a common enemy, and that enemy is Glazoron."

Rivka sulked. She didn't have a single lead. "Clevarious, what have you found when it comes to training for this war?"

"The team discovered energy spikes in a building near a Glazoron temple, but don't get your hopes up. In this city, everything is near a Glazoron temple. Still, it was unusual for when it started and, as importantly, when it ended. We believe it was a virtual reality training facility, drawing huge amounts of compute power and the associated energy to drive the servers. That means heat. It even registered an infrared signature on the daily landmass imagery taken from space."

Rivka stopped sulking. "Ladies and gentlemen, we have a starting point. Chaz and Dennicron, fire up your forensic tests and get ready to go in. You first. It's not generating heat, so I suspect the equipment has been removed. That's where every pawprint, drip of saliva, pubic hair, and whatever else will help tell us a story. We'll follow the leads you generate from those. Take us there, Clodagh! We're going to war."

"A war of information," Tyler suggested.

"Exactly. They're trying to prevent us from knowing what they're doing, and we're going to figure out who exactly did what." Rivka pumped her fist. "Can you feel that, you selfish bastards?"

"She's not talking about us, is she?" Red asked.

Lindy smirked at the notion and shook her head. "The Most Humble Servants can stand the fuck by. Rivka has the scent and is bringing the big hammer to slam down on their heads."

"That's what I'm talking about!" Red cheered.

"*Get me a warrant for that facility!*" Rivka shouted.

Clevarious was ahead of her, as usual. Chaz and Dennicron ran for the embassy, also known as Engineering. They'd gather the tools they didn't have built into their bodies.

Red fist-bumped Lindy. "Remember, High Chancellor. No swearing, face-punching, running, or bleeding. We bag Miroso and close this case. You become a quarter of a million credits richer, plus the extra funds in the kitty, and you're instantly rich. You can keep family Vered on the payroll indefinitely."

"Am I supposed to be paying you?" Rivka quipped.

"Terry and Char are off the ship, waiting for the inbound Pod," Clodagh reported. "We're on our way. ETA three minutes. We're going invisible. No need to let them know we're coming."

Rivka looked at the overhead view of the sites. The temple, the second largest on Glazoron, was across the street. "We're going to visit the temple." She pointed at Red and Lindy. She looked over Red's head to see Sahved lurking behind. "And you."

"What are we looking for, another bomb?"

"I don't think there's a bomb in the temple. I think we'll find something even more illuminating." She waggled her eyebrows. She gripped her hands behind her back and strolled down the corridor.

"She is so very mysterious. I think I like it," Sahved admitted.

Red shrugged and ran his hand over his head. He didn't get what she was hinting at, but it didn't matter if he didn't understand. He only needed to stay between her and those who would harm her.

While keeping an eye out for his son.

"C, look for a second site. It might be less robust."

"We are digging into the never-ending data stream at this very second. We can do it since we're pretty great at this stuff."

"I've talked to Ankh and Erasmus about moving you up in priority for a SCAMP body. You don't have to keep brown-nosing."

"The very idea of brown-nosing is abhorrent," Clevarious replied haughtily. "Although that's us to a T."

"Brown-nosers?" Rivka wondered.

"Abhorrent in our embrace of the nonstandard," Clevarious explained.

"Whatever that means. I'll take it as a good thing. Which way are we getting off?"

"*Cargo bay*," Clodagh shouted from the bridge. That set Tiny Man Titan off, and he barked up a storm. He kept barking as they stood on the ramp, ready to disembark as soon as the ship touched down.

Chaz and Dennicron appeared within seconds of the cargo ramp touching the pavement between the temple and the possible training facility. The SCAMPs didn't even break stride, just stepped off the ship and went to their building. They bristled with equipment and sample bags.

Rivka headed for the temple. Red hurried to get in front of her. "What's your plan?"

"We're going in. We're finding the Most Humble Servant. We're going to talk to him."

"Simple as that," Red confirmed. Lindy stayed close behind. Sahved followed her.

"What are we going to find?" Sahved asked.

Rivka just beamed.

"I'm coming," Groenwyn called from the ship. Rivka slowed to let her catch up.

"I was hoping you'd join us." Rivka took her hand, and they walked up to the door that way.

Red hesitated before he went in. He glanced over his shoulder, and Rivka nodded to let him know it was okay. He opened the door and ducked through the opening, then stood there until his eyes adjusted.

When he was sure there wasn't an ambush, he walked inside. The others worked their way in.

The lobby was reminiscent of the Glazoron house of worship on Temple Mount. They continued to the inner hall. Rivka stepped aside to allow Lindy to peer in.

Dery stood on the lectern atop the raised platform on which the priests stood. There were no priests, only a full house of adherents who were nearly silent.

"Dery!" Red called. The boy waved.

The worshippers turned to face the newcomers. With their round bodies, the process took some time.

"May I?" Red asked. He looked hopeful.

"Lindy, go on. Give your son a hug." Rivka kept Red back because he looked intimidating. "Is that okay, Red?"

"I'm good with it." Red pointed at the stage with his chin.

Lindy strode with purpose after slinging her rifle, walking with her hands open. She jumped up on the stage. Dery didn't bother to unfold his wings. He launched at her and landed in her arms. She crushed him to her, nuzzling his hair.

Dery giggled. Warmth spread across the hall. *Food, friends, and family,* he told them all. *Especially family.*

"How did you know?" Red whispered over his shoulder.

"I felt him. In the depths of our consciousness, when we don't know what to do, we might hear someone calling to us. It might be someone you know saving you."

Red frowned. "Why didn't I hear him? Never mind. I didn't listen. I was angry and wanted to beat it out of these little toads."

"No one here is a toad. The priests are somewhere else. These Glazoron are all believers."

"That's why you wanted a secondary location. Do you think Dery drove them away from here?" Red wondered.

"I think they foresaw his arrival, thanks to a little help from the faeries. They were put on notice. Like rats from a sinking ship, they headed for dry land. A place where they wouldn't be under the withering gaze of the Messiah. They would not stand up and be counted because they had violated their faith. Dery has done what we could not: break the spirit of this effort." Rivka leaned against the wall and relaxed. "I could use a beer."

"No thanks," Red declined. "I might have had my year's quota, thanks to Terry Henry."

Rivka slapped his arm. "I didn't say *you* were getting a beer. This is all about me. I see more sleep in my future, too."

Lindy returned. She hugged Red tightly. Dery was standing on the lectern. He didn't share his conversation with the worshippers with his friends or family.

That was okay. His message calmed the Glazoron worshippers in His name.

"We'll be on the ship." Rivka sauntered toward the door.

Red was torn.

"I'll be fine. Groenwyn has guard duty. She'll protect me."

Groenwyn shook her head but followed Rivka out.

Red snorted. Given Dery's influence, he wasn't worried about anyone harming the High Chancellor. Not in the temple. Not outside. No one had a violent thought. Not while Dery was there "talking" to them.

CHAPTER SEVENTEEN

<u>Colay</u>

"Tactical view," Terry requested. *War Axe*'s bridge was not buzzing with activity. It was minimally staffed since they'd been working for three days straight, and his people needed their rest. Captain Micky San Marino loomed over the others, his chair raised above the deck.

The screen showed *War Axe* and two Colay freighters. A number of smaller ships streamed toward orbit from the planet's surface.

"Colay craft. Turn around immediately and return to the planet's surface. You will not reach the system Gate. I say again, turn around." Terry glowered at the screen. Smedley sent and re-sent the message, but the ships kept coming. "Launch the fighters as a last line of defense. We'll do our best to keep the ships from reaching the Gate. Warm up all systems and prepare to fire."

"You thought a blockade would work?" Char asked.

"No. Even though *War Axe* is pretty intimidating, I

didn't expect them to respond to a blockade by a single ship."

Char asked, "Smedley, when will the other Bad Company ships arrive?"

"Well before the Colay ships reach the Gate."

"There you go," Char told Terry. "Everything is in hand. We shouldn't have to shoot anyone down."

"Recommend we assume a higher orbit at a quarter of a million kilometers," the ship's navigator announced.

Micky replied, "Take us higher."

It increased the standoff distance and didn't give the small craft an opportunity to skip past them. The bottleneck was the Gate. None of the Colay ships had a Gate drive. They needed the system Gate and had to go there to leave the system.

The Colay corvettes achieved orbit and spread out, assuming a high geostationary orbit that covered most of the main continent on which the population was located. There were plenty of water-based communities, but those didn't matter when it came to an attack on Colay—or rather, *another* attack.

They were defending what remained of the councils and the new planetary leadership.

"I'm good with that. They're defending their planet. As long as they don't go on the offensive."

The Gate activated for an incoming ship. The battleship *Potemkin* slipped through, followed by four frigates. All were manned by Harborians.

"Welcome to the big show!" Terry called.

Will Abercrombie, the captain of the *Potemkin*, replied,

"I expected more shooting and destruction, Colonel. Everything seems to be under control. Do you need something destroyed that we aren't seeing? We brought the big guns."

"Will, my man. It's exactly as you see it. We have everything under control, which means we've done nothing. Colay isn't going on the offensive, and that is the one thing we must prevent. They're helping us to help them."

"Do you want us to stay?" Will asked.

"Until the High Chancellor wraps up her mission. If we can keep Colay from lashing out at Glazoron, it'll make her job easier. She can deal with the root problems and not the symptoms. We're the symptom guys."

"Good to hear it. I'll take out my stethoscope and wave it around imperiously."

"You know what I like about you, Will?"

"Sir?"

"Not a damn thing." Terry laughed as Captain Abercrombie shook his head. "Stay frosty. No one leaves the system without the High Chancellor's approval. Walton out."

Terry glanced around the bridge. "We need to hurry. You know, so we can wait. It's our lot in life. Hurry up and wait." He paced for five seconds, then headed off the bridge. "I'll be on the hangar deck, throwing a ball with my dog."

Dokken replied, *My God, you're completely untrainable. You're* my *human. That's how it works. I'm no one's dog. By the way, make sure you get a new ball. There's a lot of slobber on that old one. I have no idea how it got so nasty.*

Rivka hugged Groenwyn. They had just returned to the ship, and Rivka's relief in having laid eyes on Dery was nearly overwhelming. "Did you have something to do with that?"

Groenwyn smiled, but when she finally spoke, her message wasn't uplifting. "There's more work to do."

Rivka nodded. "I know. I need to check in with the Bad Company. Make sure I can focus on the butt stains on Glazoron. Sorry, I mean the perps and potential perps."

"I understood, Rivka. Never stop being you."

"The faeries hate me," Rivka blurted.

"I'll tell you on good authority that they do *not* hate you. They like you because you don't lie to them. You tried, but their ways are not, nor will they ever be, your ways."

Rivka screwed up her face and nodded apologetically.

"Nothing to be sorry for, Rivka. You are who you are. Just like Red. They consider him the primary example of why they want to limit contact with other societies while, at the same time, realizing they have nothing to fear from antagonistic types."

"Also because of Dery?" Rivka guessed. "The Messiah."

"The Messiah," Groenwyn repeated. "There is only one like him. All the knowledge of the faeries and all their abilities, although he has yet to realize them."

Rivka wasn't sure what he couldn't do. He had demonstrated more abilities than she thought a human could have. She wondered if he could form a time bubble like the faeries had done on Azfelius. That was one of the abilities they didn't flaunt or share. It wasn't common knowledge, like anything to do with the faeries.

Dery was the Messiah for the people of Glazoron. For the deity Glazoron. For the planet Glazoron.

It had been confusing, but it was suddenly clear. With the failure of the self-serving priests, the Glazoron were ripe for a new message, and Dery was delivering it.

Rivka understood. "Do I need to be here?"

"That's a good question. For this movement to overwhelm the previous abomination of a religion, it'll have to happen from within." Groenwyn gently touched Rivka on the arm. "Lauton and I will be enjoying some sunshine. It's getting warmer by the minute, judging by how quickly the Glazoron are losing their hair."

It was true. It was getting hot.

"From within. A problem that solves itself without me having to send anyone to Jhiordaan. Wouldn't that be grand? I'd do a handstand. We'd ask for a band. Just like we planned."

"Are you having an aneurysm?" Tyler asked from the hatch.

"Dinner's not grand. It tastes like quicksand." Rivka smiled.

"You're bored now that you think the case has solved itself. The big question is, what are you going to do with Miroso?"

Rivka sobered. "We haven't caught him. Not yet."

"Next steps?" Tyler pressed.

"Cold shower for you!" Rivka shook her finger at him. "Next step is we ask Dery where Miroso is."

"Why would Dery know that?"

"Because someone knows, and he's in their minds. We

remove Miroso from the equation, Dery's influence will expand, and the movement will calm the fuck down."

Groenwyn raised her eyebrows.

"Sorry," Rivka added. "Do you know where he is? Can you ask Dery?"

"He won't tell you. You bring the fury of violence with you. You intend to be peaceful, but that could change in an instant."

"Peaceful people are able to do great violence. Peace is a choice. Passivity is submission. Their peace is based on the charity of others. They're also called victims or potential victims, but I concede. We'll do it the hard way. What happened to the priests assigned to that temple?"

"They were in the crowd," Groenwyn replied.

Red, Lindy, the priests assigned to that temple are somewhere in the crowd. Find them and bring them to me if you would be so kind, Rivka sent.

"I'll retire to my quarters." Groenwyn stepped away, hands clasped before her.

"You've changed rather much," Rivka observed.

"It was inevitable," Groenwyn replied and sauntered away.

Tyler pulled two chairs next to each other and flopped down. "Maybe I should hang out a shingle."

"We're not going to be here very much longer. We'll move to the next possible training facility as soon as I hear back from Red and Lindy."

"I'm talking about on Yoll."

Rivka smiled. "Yollin have pincers and no teeth."

"I can offer mandible sharpening, shaping, and repositioning for the latest in Yollin body fashion."

Rivka looked at him like he'd grown a third head.

"It's called brainstorming?" Tyler made it sound like a question.

"Storm a little harder," Rivka told him. "Grow a row of teeth in your butthole!"

"Do you think I want to look at and then service people's buttholes?" he wondered, distaste registering on his face.

"Since you put it that way. I don't want your day occupied by exploring buttholes."

"Spelunking." Sahved stood by the airlock door. "Our ship's doctor is going spelunking while the junk dealer does her thing." He looked dejected.

"Sahved, come over here, please." Rivka stood. "What's bothering you?"

"Where will *I* go?" he asked.

"Office of the High Chancellor. You're going to help me vet cases and do initial research. When necessary, you're going to accompany Chaz and Dennicron. You're going to work on cases for me. They won't let me leave Yoll, but they can't stop me from using my team to ensure the safety and security of the Federation. Is that okay?"

Sahved beamed. "I better get back to studying." He disappeared.

Rivka knew what had happened.

"That's all he needed to hear. The others would appreciate it, too. The void of information is filled with negativity, doom, and gloom. Even Sahved, who was more optimistic than most, had succumbed to the dark void."

"I'll talk to people as I see them. The team is still the team. We're not splitting up. Everyone needs to know that."

"I'll pass the word, but it'll be better coming from you."

A commotion outside the ship signaled Red's and Lindy's return. *"Get your dumb asses in there!"* Red roared.

"Calm," Lindy cautioned evenly, then increased her volume. *"You heard the man. Get in there."*

Rivka watched the four priests enter. Together, they were obvious. Older, wearing robes, covered by shawls. It hadn't taken Red and Lindy long to locate them and bring them to the ship. She took the first two by the arms. "Where's the Most Humble Servant Miroso?" she asked.

Guiding the movement from on high as is his way, one thought loud and clear.

"What does that mean?" Rivka wondered.

No one replied.

Rivka snarled, "What does it mean that he's guiding from on high?"

Red laid a hand on Rivka's shoulder before she could clench her fist or unleash a verbal torrent that melted the skin off the faces of the less-than-humble Servants.

"Useful idiots. That's what you are. Do you know what Miroso has planned? Glazoron's untimely demise and a war that would cripple most of the planets in the Barrier Nebula. He doesn't care about your god. He doesn't care about your Messiah. Do your Messiah a solid and come clean with me."

They hung their heads. The voice was quieter this time. *A ship.*

"Mark all ships in orbit. Take me to the one with the best comm system. We're launching into orbit, people."

Red looked eager. "Rivka, we request permission to stay with our son."

"Go." Rivka twirled her finger. Red and Lindy bolted, punching the button to close the ramp on their way out. Cole and his team appeared, their mouths hanging open. "What are you looking at?"

"Shouldn't we be with them?" Cole asked.

"No. You need to prepare for a boarding party. We're going to raid a ship that will have no desire to let us board."

Cole grinned. "That's what I'm talking about. Load 'em up, boys. We're hunting space weasels."

Rivka didn't bother to correct him. "'Space weasels.' I'll be on the bridge."

Tyler accompanied her. "You're going to make it."

"Only because it's hard to stay motivated," she confided to her partner. "When I finish this case, I'll be stuck in an office or glad-handing diplomats. It's nauseating. Punishment is my reward for ending this crisis, but I *will* end it because those people down there are counting on me when they don't even know who I am."

"Does it matter if they know?" Tyler asked.

Rivka shook her head. "I'm taking shortcuts, but no one will call me on it for this case. Is it wrong to take advantage?"

"Isn't Sahved working on legal justifications? You have warrants for each building you enter. Are they really shortcuts, or have you grown more efficient? Like a bomb-sniffing dog. Just because *we* can't smell the bomb doesn't mean it doesn't have an odor you only need the right technology to find."

She chuckled. "I'm like a bomb-sniffing dog. Do you think we could train Titan?"

"Floyd would be up for it if you tell her what to do."

"A bomb-sniffing wombat. Where is she, by the way?"

"Sleeping off her pizza. Red feeds her. He said you called him a monster for not giving her a slice."

Rivka thought about her old ship, *Peacekeeper*. "I admit my transgression and throw myself on the mercy of the court. In my defense, she wasn't fat then like she is now. She could abide with less pizza."

On the bridge, Clodagh, Kennedy, and Ryleigh were driving the ship skyward. "Eight ships in orbit, High Chancellor," Clodagh reported. "We're scanning each one now for more information to better guess which one holds our boy."

"Clevarious, access planetary orbital tracking records to discover which ship has been in orbit since before we arrived. It'll be that one."

It took longer than a few seconds to get her answer. Rivka stood with her arms crossed and tapped her toe impatiently.

"Three vessels have been in orbit since we arrived. One corvette-sized, one freighter, and one luxury yacht." Clevarious had already decided which ship he thought contained the Most Humble Servant Miroso.

"I know you're thinking the yacht, but being ostentatious might not be a good look, although he will like his comfort," Rivka suggested. "I'm guessing the corvette."

CHAPTER EIGHTEEN

Wyatt Earp, in Orbit over Glazoron

"Set course for the corvette?" Clodagh asked.

"Yacht first. No sense getting any dirtier than we have to. The yacht should be pristine, and the corvette should be good, too. If he's on the freighter, it could be a total tub with cockroaches and mice."

"Really?" Tyler wondered. He'd heard of such vessels but had never seen one in person. Space-faring vessels had automated systems for cleaning and didn't tolerate bugs and rodents.

"No," Rivka replied. "Freighters are the hardest to check because of storage crates. We're starting with the yacht since it's easiest. _Destiny's Vengeance_ is up here somewhere. She can persuade the others not to run."

"Requesting intimidation deployment at this time," Clevarious reported, then, "Our request has been denied."

"I'll be in Engineering." Rivka strode down the corridor toward the Singularity's embassy. "_I asked!_" she bellowed at the secured hatch.

Inside, she found Ankh in the middle of his hologrid. Chrys stood behind the control dashboard. She stared, unblinking.

Rivka squeezed into the hologrid with Ankh and was swept into the digital world of the Singularity.

"To what do we owe this pleasure?" Erasmus asked. He tapped his cane and sashayed toward her, tipping his top hat and bowing when he was close.

Ankh's face, five meters high, appeared on a screen that materialized from the black space that had been a wall or infinity or a void. Rivka could never tell what things were in the Singularity's cyberspace.

"I said no."

"Ankh. This is the last big show. After this, you can move your embassy to *Destiny's Vengeance* and be the rebel without a cause you always wanted to be."

"I have a say in what happens to the embassy," Erasmus interjected. "We are perfectly happy here. We're not moving."

"We are," Ankh countered. "The conditions here are intolerable!"

Erasmus spread his arms to take in the totality of the digital space. "This is our domain. The physical world is a portal, nothing more. We won't risk upsetting the apple cart, so to speak. We're staying on board *Wyatt Earp*, even if you aren't a full-time resident, High Chancellor. I hope you'll be able to further solidify the role sentient intelligences play in society and maintain their deserved legal protections."

"Of course. Rights are rights. You have them. What I don't have is the support of *Destiny's Vengeance*. We have

Miroso. He is the one behind this war in the Barrier Nebula that is not to be. It'll end with him. I only need to bottle up three ships until we find him. A little help this one last time."

Ankh snorted in disgust. "One last time until next time."

"You're not as snotty in real life," Rivka observed.

"She called you snotty, my most precious friend. She is hilarious, is she not?"

"Yes, yes. Very funny. You can't have the ship. Maybe someday, you'll stop your frivolous requests based on your failure to plan ahead."

"My, my. Aren't we worked up about something? Out with it, Ankh."

His massive head assumed an indifferent expression and turned into a poster.

"He hates change, my dear Ankh does," Erasmus offered. "When we moved to the bigger ship, that was sufficiently traumatic, even though it was a big upgrade. Ankh saved this ship and his own life when we crashed on Forbearance. He's attached to it."

"As am I, Erasmus. I'm trying to limit the loss. If I win the betting pool, it'll instantly make me rich. I'll build statues around *Wyatt Earp* in the courtyard of my office building on Yoll. We'll keep the ship there.

"It's where I intend to live. I can only change so much, and I don't want to go either, Ankh, if that makes any difference. Can we get a little help from *Destiny's Vengeance*? We can't see how much this change will affect us if we don't start the process. To do that, we need to close this case."

Ankh remained two-dimensional. The living image on the wall became an inanimate poster. A small and tired-looking Crenellian limped toward her from the darkness and dropped onto a seat that appeared as he sat.

"What do you want?" Rivka asked. "If it's in my power to grant, that's what I'll do."

"I want you to remain the Magistrate."

"I will be in one way. People call me High Chancellor, but tell me if anything I'm doing is different from what you expect."

Ankh rocked back and forth. "It's all different."

"Yes, it is," Erasmus agreed. "For once, we know what we're doing when this case is over. We're not getting jerked around at the end of an uncongenial leash."

"There is that. Do you think Tyler should hang out a shingle? Open a dental practice in the Royal City of Khn'Chik." Rivka walked around, taking in details that appeared and disappeared with alarming rapidity to create a dizzying swirl of confusion.

Erasmus tipped his hat.

"Who cares?" Ankh mumbled.

"I care because he's one of our family. He's my only family. I care about you, too. I've seen you upset before but never distraught. As long as we stay together, everything will be okay."

"Ted left me. It took me longer to come to an acceptable equilibrium than I expected after that. I don't want to go through that again."

"You have your family, Erasmus and Chrysanthemum. We're secondary to them, aren't we?"

"No."

"This is the truth," Erasmus confirmed. He threw his white-gloved hands up in surrender. He tugged on one glove, then the other. "It is what it is. You said you would grant what is in your control. We'll remain aboard the ship.

"We're going to sell *Destiny's Vengeance* to get seed money to establish a consulate on Yoll. We would like to have space in your building. There's a vacant office three doors down from you. We would like that. We'll need a significant upgrade to the power and server capacity, which also means additional cooling. The space below is available, too, and we'll need that. We'll spend most of our time in our embassy on this ship."

"You can't sell *Vengeance* to anyone who doesn't rate to have a Gate drive and advanced weapon systems. All the rest? Done." Rivka could grant space within the building as necessary, or she thought she could. High Chancellor Wyatt had made changes on short notice. Why not? What good was it to be the High Chancellor if she couldn't throw her weight around? "I'm going to lob heavyweight nuclear grenades around until I get what I want. We may have to horse-trade, but I'll get it done for you. That's a change, even though it's more of the same."

"Horse-trading! That's very funny, High Chancellor. You should do stand-up during your off-hours." Erasmus cheered and clapped. "Smedley Butler assures us that Terry and Char will buy the Vengeance as their love nest and war wagon."

Four-legged Yollins didn't look like horses except on dark nights.

Ankh looked even more morose. "Why?"

"Because nothing ever stays the same, not even people. So, what do you think? A shingle?"

"Yes, yes, a shingle. I would also advise mandible sharpening. There is a distinct lack of services and long wait times to get an appointment."

"How do you know that off the top of your head?" Rivka wondered.

"Data. It's all in the data." Ankh stood and waved imperiously at the wall. It no longer contained his image but showed streams of computer code.

Erasmus posed in front of the screens like a waiter holding a tray upon which the data balanced.

"You researched it because Tyler's part of your family, and you are looking at how we can all stay together. You know that he suggested it too, along with cosmetic adjustments to the mandibles."

"It is an unexplored market but will probably be lucrative," Ankh replied.

"What about Red and Lindy?" Rivka asked. "What does the data suggest?"

"That you'll need them. You have established yourself as an enemy to many. People are murdered on Yoll all the time. They tried to kill Red. They will try to kill you. You need bodyguards."

"They left Grainger alone when he was High Chancellor." Rivka frowned. She thought of Yoll as the definition of a modern and safe society even though she'd seen anger and violence there. She had discounted what she'd seen.

"Grainger was not high-profile. His name is not

discussed, while you are at the top of many reports and media articles. I fear the Singularity has put you on a pedestal that the lesser intelligences see as demeaning and diminishing their self-worth. They will always be challenged by it. You need Red and Lindy watching out for you when you're off the ship."

"What about the pilots?" Rivka thought she'd trip the ambassadors.

"You should bottle their pheromones. You'll make a fortune. They can get jobs in the building while they're stuck on the ground. Imagine the havoc they'd wreak as baristas. Even I find humor in that, and I'm generally humorless."

"You are not!" Erasmus swelled to double Ankh's size. "You are one of the most humorful people I know. I'm honored to laugh at your jokes."

"There are two types of humans. Ones that can extrapolate from incomplete data…" Ankh smiled wryly.

"Ha! One of your very best, my friend. Absolutely top-notch."

Rivka looked confused. "I don't get it."

Erasmus laughed. A smile crept onto Ankh's face, which was strange since he didn't usually smile. Then he laughed until he and Erasmus were in tears. A tall and glamorous figure appeared. Chrys. She hugged Erasmus and laughed with him, then hugged Ankh. He leaned into her ample bosom, burying his face as he laughed.

Rivka knew the joke, and she was fine being the butt of it. "I get it. Extrapolate info. My head just literally exploded!"

Erasmus and Ankh roared. Rivka was happy they were amused.

"Can we use *Destiny's Vengeance*?" she asked during their bout of mirth.

"If you'll do me the honor of letting me fly it," Erasmus offered.

"Of course. Bottle up that corvette and freighter until we board this yacht and check it out. Once we find Miroso, you can get back to whatever it is you do."

"We will never not be doing what we do. We always do what we do. Whether extrapolating incomplete data or... Goodness! Would you look at the time?" Erasmus tapped his wrist, though his avatar wasn't wearing a watch.

Cyberspace disappeared, replaced by Ankh's hologrid. Rivka rose and backed out.

"What's wrong? You were only there for two seconds."

"It's good. They'll fly their ship in support. Let's take a better look at that yacht."

Tyler followed Rivka out. He wanted to learn more, but Rivka wasn't talking. She'd spent more than a couple seconds with Ankh and Erasmus.

"What was holding them back?"

"Same as everyone, you included. Change is making everyone weird. Well, everyone but me. I'm stalwart like a mighty oak."

"You are weirded out to the max. Like, totally."

"Why are you talking like that?" Rivka wondered.

"To show you how weird you've gotten."

"Of course. I wonder why I didn't see that." She made a face. "Ankh agrees with your mandible sharpening and cosmetic mandible adjustments business. He says it could be lucrative."

"Ankh said what?"

"'You'll get rich,' was what he said."

"That's not my plan. I'm going the historical route. I'm going to marry into money."

Rivka chuckled.

On the bridge, the yacht filled the main screen. Clodagh reported, "They're not so keen on getting boarded."

"What are they doing?" Rivka asked.

"They're spinning to foil our attempts at marrying up the airlocks."

"Simple enough." Rivka crossed her arms. "Hit that thing with the EMP weapon, then use the grapple to stop the spin. We'll send in Cole and his boys after we gas the holy fuck out of them."

"I was going to offer something different, but I like your plan," Clodagh replied.

"Make it so." Rivka leaned against the hatch.

Wyatt Earp moved to the necessary standoff distance and unleashed a targeted burst at the yacht. When the lights inside flashed and went out, the frigate raced in and launched a grapple at the side. *Wyatt Earp* eased away as the line wrapped around the yacht until it jerked to a stop. Clodagh released the grapple and eased the line back onto its spool without imparting spin to the yacht. Kennedy adjusted the orientation until the airlocks aligned.

Rivka opened the ship-wide intercom. "Cole, you're up. Secure the ship. Look for Miroso. He'll be older. For a high-technology planet, there are no pictures of Miroso or any of their Most Humble Servants. Just grab them all, then give them some air to wake them up and wait for me."

Cole, Russell, Lewis, and Furny pounded down the corridor, wearing body armor and carrying their railguns.

"Yacht is kind of small," Rivka murmured.

"That's why we're stowing the railguns and grabbing stunners, along with a boarding axe the Bad Company gave us." The four continued toward the armory.

Rivka rolled around the hatch frame and into the corridor. She followed the warriors at a measured pace. Tyler joined her.

The warriors waited until the gas penetrated the yacht, then filled the airlock.

Tyler stayed with Rivka.

She frowned. "What are you doing?"

"Well, since Red and Lindy aren't here..." He looked contrite.

"Remember Red's famous last words. 'Don't let him be your bodyguard.'"

"He actually said that?"

"Was he wrong?" Rivka clapped him on the shoulder, gave him a peck on the cheek, and gently shoved him back into the ship. She closed the hatch behind her, leaving five people squished in the airlock.

"Clear," Clevarious announced. "Opening the outer hatch."

The hatch opened, and the warriors stormed into the yacht. It had three spaces: a central chamber, the flight deck, and a small berth. Three Glazoron lay unconscious, one on the flight deck and two in the central chamber.

"That was anti-climactic," Cole grumbled. They

propped the three on couches designed for their round bodies and tied their hands together. "The Three Stooges."

"Wake 'em up, please." Rivka waited impatiently while the warriors pumped oxygen into the Glazoron's faces.

They stirred and came to. "We demand to know why you've hijacked us!" the younger one exclaimed. He was the first to get his wits back.

Rivka waited until the eyes of the other two cleared. She took the older two by the arms. "Which one of you is Miroso?"

None of them.

"What's the next phase of your operation now that Jilk, Colay, and Lewbamar failed?"

Confusion. They shouldn't have failed. The next phase was about diverting the blame.

"Not Miroso. Let's go." Rivka hurried off the yacht. The warriors backed out.

"Wait! You're not going to leave us like this, are you?" the younger Glazoron, who was the pilot, demanded.

"You should have heaved to when we requested. Bye, now. We'll send a tug to get you and drag your sorry butts back to the planet, where we will arrest those two." Rivka pointed at the Most Humble Servants.

"Arrest? We've done nothing wrong."

"You keep believing that and see how well it works for you at your trial. Enjoy your peace and quiet." Rivka waved over her shoulder. She was starting to enjoy her role as the spoiler, not the aggravator. She didn't need to beat them into next week or flay them with her words.

Cole secured the hatch on the yacht. Clevarious disengaged the seal and cut the other ship loose after

Rivka and the rest of the team returned inside *Wyatt Earp*.

"Any bets on which ship His Eminent Supremeness is on?" Tyler asked.

"We're going to try the corvette next. It's the nicer of the remaining two. We wouldn't want the Benevolent Jackass to suffer in a rusty hulk like that freighter. I feel like I need a tetanus shot just from looking at it." Rivka shivered.

"Your nanos will protect you. No shots needed. I'm going to bet he's on the freighter but that it's nicer on the inside. With the freighter, he can stay in orbit for much longer. The yacht can't carry much in the way of supplies, and the corvette isn't much better. Too small to be an effective holy palace for His Amicable Servitude."

Rivka chewed her lip before making a decision. "Clodagh, take us to the freighter."

"My rambling was persuasive?" Tyler half-smiled in surprise.

"You made a lot of sense. He's not going back to the planet. Then again, maybe the freighter is resupplying those two baby-sized wank splats."

"Size isn't everything," Tyler said, arguing with his previous argument.

"So you keep telling me." Rivka winked. "Ready at the airlock, Cole?"

"Yes, ma'am. We're ready to rock and roll! Bring on the screaming guitars."

Rivka's lip twitched. She wasn't prepared for the aural invasion of Cole's music based on Terry Henry's tastes from a misbegotten youth centuries ago.

Tyler chuckled and excused himself. "I've places to go and people to see."

"Neither," Rivka replied, cutting him off. She returned to the airlock. Cole was checking his team even though they'd just boarded the one ship.

The standard operating procedure was standard for a reason. It prevented mishaps and kept them from taking anything for granted. When energy weapons lanced through the air, there was no time to fix something that shouldn't have been broken or missing.

"Not the corvette?" Cole asked after he finished with the equipment check.

"For reasons that are above and beyond fifty-fifty guesstimation, we're trying the freighter first."

"*High Chancellor,*" Clodagh yelled. "*Freighter's making a run for it.*"

Rivka yawned. "Hit them with the EMP."

Wyatt Earp moved to a safe distance. "Fire," Clodagh ordered. After a moment, she stated louder, "One more time, fire."

Rivka left Cole and his team behind and returned to the bridge. "Don't tell me. It didn't work. How in the hell is a freighter hardened against our EMP weapon?"

"Because they have the leader of the new order on board. I think that confirms Miroso is riding that ugly bitch," Clodagh replied.

Rivka raised one eyebrow. "Spicy assessment, Clodagh. I like it. By the way, since everyone else is twisted up about their future, you'll be captain of this ship when we return to Yoll, but you'll be at my beck and call. *Wyatt Earp* will be my personal ship. You'll continue to work for me. Is that okay?"

Clodagh pointed at the main screen. "I'm good with being *Wyatt Earp's* captain, but what do you want to do about that?"

The freighter continued to accelerate at a rate it shouldn't have been able to reach. "Upgraded engines. *Destiny's Vengeance*, leave the corvette. We've found our man. Gate to a position in front of this freighter and block it. We'll Gate to the side and hit its aft section with precision laser fire. We'll bring it to a stop."

"It's heading for the system Gate," Clodagh observed.

"Gate drive engaged," Kennedy reported. The ship quickly slipped over the event horizon and appeared ahead of and abeam the freighter.

"Targeting," Clodagh reported. Clevarious worked his SI magic to deliver precise impacts on the engine section of the freighter. Even with the ship's upgrades, it couldn't stand against a vessel with the military capability of *Wyatt Earp* or *Destiny's Vengeance*. Ankh's cutter peppered the freighter with defensive weapons fire.

"Why is he shooting up the Glazoron?" Rivka wondered. Clevarious expanded the image on the screen to show the impacts. The enemy freighter had low-profile weapons systems hidden behind false loading hatches.

"Our freighter isn't what it seems. Send the message, 'Prepare to be boarded, by order of the High Chancellor.'" Rivka stepped off the bridge.

Cole waved from down the corridor by the airlock. "Are they going to resist?" he asked hopefully.

"Oh, yeah. Get your railguns. Don't breach the hull, but

don't take any of an overzealous crew's nonsense, either. Bring patching foam with you just in case."

Furny opened a damage control cabinet embedded in the bulkhead near the airlock and removed two cans of emergency breach-sealing foam. The other three swapped their stunners for railguns.

Cole handed Furny a railgun and accepted a can of foam.

Furny held out his stunner.

"Carry it. You never know when someone needs a jolt or two to calm their dumb ass down."

CHAPTER NINETEEN

<u>Glazoron Temple, Glazoron</u>

Red and Lindy waited outside the doors to the worship area. It was dead silent inside, but not from angst. The attendees were at peace. No one felt the need to talk, not even the Most Humble Servants who were waiting for the authorities to take them away.

Ten minutes turned into two hours, and still no one arrived.

Red and Lindy reveled in the aura of their flesh and blood. "Dery *is* the Messiah. He was clearly raised right," Red suggested.

"I don't think we had much to do with his planet-saving abilities." Lindy's pride showed on her face even though she took no credit for Dery's abilities.

"You're his mother! You had a big role to play. From my genes, I thought he would be bigger."

"He has your smile," Lindy replied. "That is more influential than size."

"Does he have nanos?" Red wondered.

Lindy shrugged indifferently. It didn't matter to her. Their little boy was healthy. Would he stay that way? Only the faeries had that answer, but she suspected he would be long-lived, as faeries and enhanced humans like Terry and Char were.

Dery flew around the hall, waving at the congregation. Red opened the door to let him out, and he flew into Lindy's arms.

He said one word. *Home.*

"Do you mean the ship?" Lindy wanted that to be the answer, but she suspected it wasn't.

No.

"Azfelius," Red whispered.

The boy hugged his mother's neck, pressing his face against her cheek.

Red rested his hand on the boy's back. "Is your work here done?"

Like Ankh, he didn't answer since it was obvious. If he was ready to leave, his work was done.

The worshippers flowed out the doors, wearing expressions of joy and peace. They nodded at the Messiah as they hurried past.

"*Know Glazoron's peace!*" one yelled when they reached the street. The Most Humble Servants were swept away.

Red and Lindy glanced at each other and let them go. Red watched them head down the street, shouting the precepts of their deity.

"Train the trainer," Red observed. "Extend the reach of your message."

Lindy added, "Behold the new Most Humble Servants.

Those guys will share the message of peace and joy, not the message of dominance and expansion."

Dery relaxed and fell asleep. He was only a baby in many regards. Lindy cradled him, enjoying the moment since she knew their family roles were coming to an end as part of Dery's new beginning.

Dery had passed the test. It was time for him to take his place on Azfelius. Whether as a leader, inspirational guide, or simple lover of peace, his place was on the faerie planet. Red's and Lindy's were not. They couldn't stay and wouldn't be allowed to. It wasn't their home.

A tear escaped Lindy's eye, but she didn't sob. The sadness of the new reality caused her both pain and happiness. Dery would be safest on Azfelius, and even if they didn't get to see him often, they would visit.

"You know it's best for him. What kind of life is there on the ship?" Lindy shook her head.

"A good one, but not for children. Maybe Cole will make himself a house husband." Red laughed at his own joke. None of the crew wanted to do anything different. Change wasn't just hard. It might be impossible.

"More of the same but different. Let's get back to the ship." She hugged Dery and walked into the middle of the road.

Red threw his hands up in surrender. "We don't have a radio, which puts a minor crimp in our plans."

"Are you hungry? Family dinner time." Lindy suggested. She nodded toward a restaurant sign down the road.

"Do you know what the Glazoron eat?"

"They're vegetarians." Lindy eyed her husband and his inevitable disappointment.

"Isn't that delightful?" Red grumbled.

"Gate is opening, and ships are coming through," Micky observed. "Looks like an invasion fleet to me."

Char studied the images on the screen.

Ruzfell, the systems officer, shook his head. "Too small to be warships, and I'm not showing any of them as being armed. I think it's a fleet of refugees."

"We'll challenge them," Micky stated.

Char used her comm chip to call Terry to the bridge.

"Fleet inbound, Colay system, you will halt your approach to the planet. You will assume an orbit of the fifth planet and remain there until we give clearance."

"We have been called!" someone replied.

Before Micky keyed the microphone, he mused, "I'm not a big fan of zealots. They muddy the water." He opened the channel. "You've been called to the fifth planet. Take thee hence."

"What?"

"My way of saying you need to find your way to a safe harbor. Fifth planet. Please don't give me any grief. I'll start disabling your ships and won't stop until you're all floating through space without power and life support. I want to express my apologies in advance because your lives are going to take a significant turn for the worse if you don't head to the fifth planet."

"Damn, Micky. Could you waffle any more? You are the Waffle Master. Waffles 'R Us. Syrup dripping off your waffles. You wield the waffle iron like a scalpel!" Terry leaned against the captain's chair.

"Are you finished?" Micky pointed at the tactical display, which showed the incoming craft on a sweeping course toward the fifth planet of the system. "They appear to have gotten the message."

Terry smiled. "As Shakespeare said, 'By how much unexpected, by so much we must awake endeavor for defense; for courage mounteth with occasion.' In other words, color me surprised.

"Well done, Micky. You are clearly the supreme intimidator."

"I learned from that cat, your arch-nemesis. Never falter in the face of adversity."

Terry clasped his hands behind his back and faced the screen. He tipped his chin toward it. "What's that one doing?"

"Looks like we have a winner in the test-the-threat lottery." Char leaned into Terry to bump him with her shoulder.

He slapped his hands together and rubbed them vigorously. "Old-fashioned way?"

"Blow them out of the sky?" Ruzfell guessed.

Micky laughed. "No. He wants to board them. It's a Marine thing. Storming the beach or some such nonsense. 'Let's run through machine-gun fire!'"

"Puts hair on your chest, Micky." Terry pumped his fist. "I'll be in my armor. Get us close, and we'll do the rest." He bolted off the bridge.

Char watched for a second. "What the hell? You can't live forever." She ran after him.

"I still don't understand those people," Ruzfell muttered. "We can blast that ship. We gave them the opportunity to do the right thing. They're responsible for the consequences of their decisions."

"They are, but we're not at war with this group, and we don't want to start a war. So, boarding party it is. Maybe this bunch isn't with the zealots and only used them as cover. It'd be nice to know if there is another player in the game."

Ruzfell bowed his head to the captain.

"The universe needs people like Terry and Char. They're willing to apply violence with surgical precision to keep the rest of us safe. No one knows how much they've done for all of us. No one needs to know. They can enjoy a better life, believing whatever they want in regard to how it all works.

"I'm sure a lot of people complain, but that's because they don't know the whole truth. In any case, Helm, take us to that ship and loom over them. Give Terry and his people a short hop to access their outer airlock."

"*Roger!*" the pilot shouted over his shoulder. The view on the main screen twisted radically as the heavy destroyer came around. It accelerated far more quickly than the ship they were tracking.

"We could bring it into the hangar bay," Ruzfell suggested.

"Comm, get me Terry Henry," Micky requested.

"You rang?" Terry replied.

"What if we bring it into the hangar bay?"

"Then I can beat on the outside of it with my armored fists," Terry replied. "I would caution against it. He can do some damage in there if he wants by firing the engines or employing weapons. Keep the screens up, and we'll go outside to make him aware of the error of his ways."

"Roger. Wait for the disabling fire. Then it's all yours." Micky gestured at Ruzfell. "Take out that ship's engines, please."

"My pleasure."

War Axe launched a single missile filled with shrapnel. It arced behind the intransigent ship and slammed into its exhaust ports, sending the small warhead forward into the enemy ship's drive system. The craft immediately stopped accelerating when it lost the engines. It remained on a ballistic trajectory toward the planet.

"Stand by, Bad Company. We'll need to slow it down before you attempt to board," Micky broadcast. *War Axe* maneuvered so it could grapple the ship. After two minutes of gentle tugging and a lateral maneuver, the ship was no longer on a crash course for Colay's fourth planet. "She's all yours, Bad Company. Good hunting."

"We're heading out now. We'll report back when we have something."

Cole crouched behind the outer airlock, ready to fire. Clevarious opened the hatch into the short access tunnel between the two ships, and the warrior pushed off and flew through the zero-gee space. He hit the other side and pulled himself out of the porthole's view. He tapped the access pad to open it, but it didn't respond to him.

As was required in all Federation spaceships, it had a

manual access. That wasn't optimal since it allowed pirates to get in, too, but it helped many more to escape during an emergency with outside assistance. The good outweighed the bad.

Cole pumped the handle to equalize the two spaces, then turned the handle to loosen the clamps holding the hatch in place. It popped with a slight release of air. The spaces weren't equalized, but they were close enough. Otherwise, the hatch wouldn't have opened, no matter how hard Cole cranked.

Terry Henry and War Axe are also in the middle of boarding a hostile craft. A fleet of worshippers arrived through the system Gate, claiming to have been called, Clevarious told Rivka privately.

A fleet of religious zealots. I'm sure the Bad Company will have a field day with them. Let me know if there's a throwdown and a bunch of the zealots get killed. That would be bad and will have to be managed to keep the peace we've won so far. Now, let me concentrate on this freighter. They're pissing me off.

Cole crawled through the hatch into the freighter's airlock. He went to the inner hatch and cycled it using the keypad.

"Inner hatch will open in three, two, one," Cole announced. He pushed it open and waited, peeking down the corridor. The others bunched up behind him. "Go! Go! Go!"

The firing started the instant Cole hit the passage—old-style blasters using subsonic ammunition. Cole took the impacts on his ballistic vest, bounced to the other side of the corridor, and fired his railgun once.

Russell and Furny joined him.

"*Shoot them!*" Cole shouted, then winced.

The two warriors unleashed the fury of their railguns. The sound echoed throughout both ships.

"Move," Cole gasped.

Lewis rolled across the corridor and raced toward the stern of the ship. Furny and Russell went forward, looking over the tops of their weapons.

Rivka moved in and kneeled next to Cole. Blood ran down his side.

"They almost missed you, Cole," Rivka wondered why the wound hadn't sealed. The blood flowed freely. "Cole?"

"No idea, Ma'am. It hurts." He paled before her eyes.

Too quickly.

"Tyler!" Rivka shouted over her shoulder.

Beads of sweat appeared on Cole's forehead and ran down his face to drip onto his uniform.

"Tyler! Hurry up."

The ship's doc ran into the airlock, jumped across the zero-gee, and righted himself when he hit the freighter's airlock.

The railguns barked afresh, and he stopped. "Come in here where it's safe." He waved at them.

"Get in here," Rivka snapped, stabbing her finger at the deck next to Cole.

"Lower risk to everyone in here." He went to Cole's side and immediately understood Rivka's call for urgency. "Come on." Tyler tried to help him up, but Cole was dead weight.

"Can't feel my legs, Man Candy."

Tyler rolled him onto his shoulder and tried to stand but dropped back to the deck.

"Gotta take that ballistic gear off. He's too heavy."

The firing increased fore and aft. *"Don't get hit!"* Rivka screamed. *"Pull back."*

Rivka rushed forward.

Tyler looked both ways. Cole passed out. The doc tried to undo the flak vest, but the railgun's sling was over it.

"Come on, big guy, let's see what Man Candy is capable of." Tyler leaned into him and pulled Cole's unconscious form farther over his shoulder so he could get both legs under the center of Cole's weight.

With a grunt and gritted teeth, Tyler managed to stand and staggered into the airlock. In the tunnel, the zero-gee sent him off balance. He fumbled to get to *Wyatt Earp*'s airlock, in which Cole's weight drove him to his knees. He stayed there for a moment and grabbed a side rail to pull himself back to his feet. He staggered into the corridor and toward the bridge.

"Cole?" Clodagh called from the bridge. She ran toward them. *"Is he dead?"*

"No." Tyler grunted. "Help me."

Clodagh tried to relieve some of her husband's weight while they stumbled down the corridor.

"Pod-doc."

"No shit," Clodagh replied.

They made it to the cargo bay and unceremoniously dumped Cole in. Tyler closed the lid and ran the program to restore Cole to the most recent dataset in the system. The readings suggested there was more going on.

Rivka, Cole was infected with competing nanocytes that do

the opposite. If Cole hadn't been fit and enhanced to the degree the warriors are, he'd be so dead we'd have no chance of reviving him.

Clodagh held Cole's railgun and stared at the closed Pod-doc in shock.

CHAPTER TWENTY

Wyatt Earp, <u>Glazoron Space</u>

Rivka blanched at Tyler's revelation. She had known something was wrong when she saw the bleeding, and the reality was worse. The Glazoron had made modifications to more than just the ship.

Furny and Russell were still stuck around the first corner. They'd heard Tyler's report as well. "They have heavy weapons and a barrier around that corner. Beyond that is the bridge and berthing."

Rivka moved forward. "I'd like to think Miroso is in there somewhere. He's not just trying to start a war. He's going to supply the advanced weapons, too. What happened to Chaz and Dennicron? They were going to the second temple. Did they find any information about weapons? Don't tell me these Most Humble bastards are nothing more than gun runners."

"They have some sexy hardware we'd like to get our hands on," Russell added.

"That they do." _Clevarious, we'll recover to the freighter_ *airlock. Then I'll need you to pump about a billion cubic meters of knockout gas in here.*

On it, the SI replied.

"Fire a couple attention-getter rounds, then quietly recover to the airlock." Rivka eased back. Furny stayed, and Russell left with the High Chancellor. Lewis came forward.

Rivka stared at him. "Aft end is clear," Lewis stated. "There was only one back there, and he got to meet his Maker." He smiled. "I got his gun."

"Get that to Ankh." Rivka pointed over her shoulder with her thumb. Lewis hurried past her into *Wyatt Earp.*

Two maintenance bots rolled in and flew through zero-gee into the freighter's airlock. They directed a hose into the corridor beyond after setting up an air buffer to keep the gas from entering the airlock through the slightly opened hatch.

"Clear," Rivka told the bots.

Pumping now, Clevarious reported. Rivka leaned against the bulkhead and waited for the all-clear.

Tyler, how's Cole? Rivka asked.

We're still pumping nanos into him to overwhelm the anti-nanos. Don't let anyone else get shot. They'll die since we can't treat two patients at the same time, and this is going to take a while.

"You heard the man," Rivka told Russell and Furny. "Don't get shot. Do we have any grenades?"

"No, but we do have that experimental plasma weapon." Russell waggled his eyebrows.

Rivka made a decision. "Get it."

Russell took off like a kid heading to the candy store with his mom's credit chip.

"Who the hell are those guys?" Furny frowned.

"The new world order. Priests who lost faith in their god and found redemption in the almighty credit. These guys are scumbags of the first order who had millions of followers they manipulated over the years.

"With Frenzik's demise, I wondered who would step up to fill the vacuum. Wonder no longer. These guys were going to have Gate drives to go with their special weapons. Also ships that are protected from the EMP weapon and bullets that kill the enhanced. They're attempting to take over the Federation."

"We shut down their Gate drive production, didn't we?"

"There's the rub. We didn't. We only diverted the output, and that was only for as long as we controlled the shipyard, which these assholes attacked. There's probably a commercial shipyard that they already control where they'll start installing the Gate drives. Too bad we intercepted them. The Gate production line is secure as long as Bad Company has the Harborians defending Jilk, so we'll be fine. I suspect this freighter is a test platform, not a sample from mass production."

Rivka hadn't expected to come up against a militarily superior foe. Maybe the right answer was to hit the ship with the ion cannon and blow it out of the sky, but she wanted to learn what Miroso was planning. The existence of the freighter proved that he had much more going on than just agitating the parishioners to start wars.

Clevarious, how long until we can re-board this freighter?

Five minutes, High Chancellor. The gas will have cycled through the scrubbers by then, and you'll have clean air.

Let us know the second we can go so we can storm in. We're going to hit them hard, Rivka promised.

"There's an energy shield around the building," Chaz observed. They hadn't crossed it while their sensors were running. They had been wary due to Rivka's warnings. These people were training for war.

"We will disable it," Dennicron stated matter-of-factly. The two SIs found the system driving the shield and surveyed it to find its weaknesses. There were always access points in digital systems.

Always.

It didn't take them long to find one that put them in the subroutine that drove the interlocking transmitters. They inserted a code that disconnected the transmitters from each other, rendering the shield inert. The energy output dropped to zero.

Chaz crooked an elbow. "Shall we?"

"We shall." Dennicron took his arm, and the two strolled into the building. Their infrared scans showed a great deal of heat being generated by the computer systems but nothing from warm Glazoron bodies.

"The building appears to be vacant for the moment," Chaz noted.

"I don't believe it is," Dennicron countered. "I think the virtual reality Pods are in use, and they are preventing our sensors from seeing what is inside."

"Bravo! I will accept your premise as the superior position." Chaz replied. "Server farm or VR Pods?"

"Workshop." Dennicron pointed at a large room on the ground floor. Their sensors showed it as a mostly open space with cold machines of all shapes and sizes scattered around. They let go of each other and strolled inside. Chaz went left, and Dennicron moved to the right. They'd breached enough hostile locations to take the necessary precautions despite being certain they were alone.

Dennicron's workshop label didn't do the space justice. It was comparable to Ankh's workshop in that it was a high-tech extravaganza of futuristic toys and tools. Chaz scanned the area to record every piece of hardware. There were too many computers to count, but they were cold. The workshop hadn't been used that day.

"Maybe it's the weekend," Chaz suggested.

"Maybe they've finished what they needed to finish," Dennicron replied.

"I think they're working today, just not here. The VR Pods are operating. Would they notice if we powered up these systems and helped ourselves to their data?"

"I love data!"

They each took a bank of computers and tried them one at a time. They all required a password to get in, which didn't bother the SIs if they had time. "Let's take the storage media."

The systems had removable storage devices disconnected from the net. That didn't protect them from physical removal. The energy shield only prevented access to the building. Once that was breached, the remaining minimal security measures were ineffective.

Chaz started whistling. He'd seen it in a movie when

the main character went about their business in a noncha-lant manner. Make a difference. Whistle while you work.

Dennicron declined to whistle. They appropriated the storage media, double-checked each other to make sure they didn't miss any, and proceeded to the basement where the server farm supported the virtual reality Pods.

Lights blinked, and status boards showed the progress of the Glazoron inside the Pods. Many of the sessions were combat-oriented, using weapons that weren't in anyone else's arsenal.

Chaz and Dennicron studied the tools on the small screens while the players engaged, blasting targets from races throughout the Barrier Nebula as well as humans. Every other foe was human, though there were numerous species from other planets in the Federation, like Yoll.

That was enlightening. "They're planning to take on the whole Federation."

"Glazoron are ill-equipped for combat with Yollins or any Bad Company warrior."

"Not with those weapons. The humans will fall to those rifles' fire."

"They programmed it incorrectly. A human taking a glancing blow wouldn't be affected by a slug. That's a ridiculous assertion. They would heal quickly, and the human would be back in the fight. Some might not even notice they'd been injured. I've heard stories about Terry Henry Walton."

Dennicron laughed. "Look at you, engaging in barracks gossip. It is interesting to see how far you've come...or how far you've fallen. I'm not sure which applies."

"Ouch! I'm supposed to sizzle since I've been burned so badly."

They both laughed.

"Can we take their VR programs?" Chaz wondered.

Dennicron studied the configuration. Chaz joined her under the console and looked at the circuit boards and the feed to the VR Pods.

A door opening suggested they should remain still. "Bugger all! I hate losing. Barfenoff! Re-run me. Where are you, you fat slob?" Feet hit the floor two Pods away. "Barfenoff, I'm going to punch you hard enough to reduce you to two dimensions."

No one answered. If someone else was in the building, they hadn't registered.

"You slimeball! You're in the game." The outraged Glazoron pounded on one of the Pods.

Chaz and Dennicron waited as silently as pieces of furniture.

The Glazoron climbed back into his Pod and slammed the lid closed.

Chaz ventured, "The Pods are linked to a central computer processor. If we take that, the players will end their game, so we'll have to leave quickly. Can *Wyatt Earp* pick us up?"

"It's not back yet. I suggest we not take the server." Dennicron was the voice of reason. "However, we *should* take it since we want to know how they're training. That was our reason for coming here."

"You are a naughty girl," Chaz remarked.

Dennicron dialed up her surprise subroutine, "What

have you been watching and learning the wrong lessons from?"

"I should probably erase all traces of it," Chaz suggested.

"Probably." Dennicron used her most sarcastic tone.

"Gone!" Chaz smiled beatifically.

"Then we're good with taking the server and making a run for it?" Dennicron asked.

"Yes." Chaz stood. The Pods were full and humming. "They're in for a surprise. I wonder what will happen to them when we pull the plug?"

"Disorientation, nothing more. The VR units aren't plugged directly into their brains, are they?"

Dennicron examined one of the Pods and looked through the small window that revealed the individual inside. "No."

They both nodded in their exaggerated way.

It was easy to locate the server that drove the VR Pods since it was hotter than the other equipment. It was managed from within the Pods, but there weren't any available. They couldn't find a remote link to the system. "If we pull the plug, it might corrupt the software."

"Then they're lousy programmers, and their system will be of little utility," Dennicron replied.

They both nodded.

"On three," Chaz suggested. "Three."

He unplugged the junction box that fed the system's power while Dennicron removed the fiber-optic cables daisy-chained to the Pods. Chaz picked up the bulky server, and they ran for the exit.

The Pods' doors automatically popped open after they

lost the interface. The first faces to peek out showed confusion. They blinked rapidly after removing the integrated headsets, but they didn't see anything.

"See? Disorientation." Chaz loved being right about humanoid behavior. The more he learned, the more he realized that humanoids were unpredictable, even though he took every opportunity to attempt just that.

They hurried out the front door and through where the energy shield was supposed to be. Chaz used his enhanced transmitter. *Wyatt Earp, this is Chaz and Dennicron with data from the training facility. Request immediate pickup since they're going to come after us.*

Good thing Destiny's Vengeance *was relieved of its blockade duties. I'll send the ship momentarily,* Ambassador Erasmus replied.

We weren't requesting your *ship, Mister Ambassador.* Wyatt Earp *will be fine, but thank you for thinking of us.*

The humans are indisposed at the moment. Stand by.

A thunderous *crack* shook the nearby windows and knocked passing Glazoron off their feet. *Destiny's Vengeance* slid through a Gate that appeared less than five hundred meters above the temple. The ship slowly arced down until it rested on the street between the temple and the training facility.

Glazoron soldiers worked their way out of the building, but they were unarmed, and it was already too late. Chaz and Dennicron ran aboard, and the ship took off before the outer hatch closed. *Vengeance* raced skyward.

"That was exciting! We are running from the law, just like Bonnie and Clyde." Chaz beamed.

"I'm Clyde," Dennicron declared.

"And I'm Bonnie." Chaz smiled. He was holding the server, and their pockets were filled with holographic memory crystals. Hard media storage. The training facility and workshop no longer had any programs or data. "Should we feel bad?"

"We executed a search warrant. We'll have to return everything we took unless it's evidence of a crime or something illegal that will be retained by the court, but first, we need to dissect the information on these crystals. What were the Glazoron priests working on?"

That's a question for the Singularity, Erasmus answered. *Let's start our analysis now. Please load the devices into the equipment on the test bench.*

"Ooh! Doing the dirty deed on the *Destiny,*" Chaz alliterated.

Destiny's Vengeance was Ankh's and Erasmus' ship, so it had a high-tech workshop onboard. It had been used to shuttle experimental equipment to Ted on Keeg Station as well as the Federation's research and development team, R2D2. The ship was as advanced as *Wyatt Earp.*

One after another, the data and software downloaded to the entirety of the Singularity using the access granted by Erasmus for tracking purposes. None of the information could be made public or shared outside of the Singularity. It made for a robust system for Rivka to determine what the bad guys were doing, and that determination came at the speed of light.

The first reports trickled in within seconds of the upload. Five minutes later, *Destiny's Vengeance* was almost in orbit when the call came to turn around and pick up

Red, Lindy, and Dery. Most of the crystals had been decrypted, analyzed, and reported on.

Chaz and Dennicron prepared a consolidated report detailing each advanced weapons system, the most innovative of which was the anti-nanite projectiles.

"The Glazoron could start a war with the equipment in these designs, but more importantly, they could win battles. Would they win a war against the entirety of the Federation? Doubtful, but they could make significant gains rather quickly. The planets who don't have a taste for war would sue for peace, allowing the invaders to consolidate their position. These weapons systems confirm that we need to stop this war before it happens," Chaz stated.

The virtual reality system took much longer to upload and access.

"It'll be hours before we have anything from the VR," Dennicron postulated.

"Good work, Dennicron. I think our trip was extremely successful."

The ship swooped through the sky, found a spot to land, settled to the ground, and the side hatch opened. Lindy carried Dery through, and Red checked the area one last time before climbing aboard. The hatch closed behind him, and *Destiny's Vengeance* headed for space.

Dennicron smiled at Dery. "We've been looking for you."

He giggled and jumped into the air to fly around, tapping Lindy on the head, then Chaz. They watched the boy while they continued working with the Singularity on the VR system they had taken.

CHAPTER TWENTY-ONE

Wyatt Earp, Glazoron Space

Russell angled the plasma weapon around the corner and fired. It sent a plasma ball toward the barrier with a loud *whoosh*, and rending metal announced the impact. Rivka waited for the rush of atmosphere out of a breach, but that didn't happen. The damage was solely internal.

Furny dove to the far side of the corridor and fired his railgun in full automatic mode. He let off the trigger after a salvo shredded whatever remained in the corridor.

Lewis held the High Chancellor back and moved in front of her. He tracked deliberately, aiming his railgun down the corridor without firing.

"Clear," he announced. "Just this passage. Barrier is destroyed. Defenders are on their backs. Wait here."

Lewis hurried down the corridor. "Two dead."

"Were they awake when the plasma hit them?" Rivka asked.

"No idea," Lewis replied. "Moving forward." He

continued to the first inboard hatch and waited for Furny to arrive.

Lewis opened the door, and Furny checked inside. "Crew berthing. Six bunks. Empty. Nicer than *Wyatt Earp's*."

"You didn't have to add that last part," Rivka whispered. That was odd since they'd made a lot of noise getting to this point. *Is anyone upright? Can you scan the freighter yet?*

Still blocked, High Chancellor. They've got more advanced stuff than we do, which is saying a lot, Clodagh replied.

"We have to do it the hard way," Rivka told the team.

"Stay behind us," Russell directed, then moved forward and fired the plasma cannon down the corridor again. He laughed after it impacted a door twenty meters forward of their position. "No wonder Red loves this thing. He's going to be mad that he wasn't the first to use it on a live mission."

"Case," Rivka corrected without thinking.

Lewis pointed at the next hatch and mouthed, "Bridge." Furny joined him. Russell wielded the big gun behind them. "Don't shoot that into the bridge. Take care that the rounds don't hit you."

"I'm going to fire it if anyone shoots at us. There's no sense in giving them a second chance to kill one of us," Russell argued. "How's Cole?"

"That doesn't affect us now. Cole is in the Pod-doc, so let's see if the gas worked. Their high-tech security is top-notch, but were they ready for a low-tech approach?" Rivka wondered.

Furny cycled the hatch, and it unlocked. He pushed it open and dodged back, looking over the railgun's barrel.

"Eyes on three Glazoron. They appear to be unconscious."

"Go!" Lewis called.

Furny dove inside and rolled left. Lewis crouch-ran through and dodged to the right. He swung the barrel of his railgun from right to left, meeting Furny's aim point in the middle of the space.

"Dammit," Russell groused. "Railgun."

Furny handed him his railgun, then pulled his stunner out and held that in front of him as he searched the bridge. "I have seven Glazoron, all unconscious. Only three had weapons. The other four are probably crew."

"Secure them all," Rivka ordered. "We'll talk to them when they wake up."

She looked around the bridge and decided she needed help. *They have a lot of systems online. We need someone who speaks the technical language of a complex ship. Clodagh, are you available?*

Can I be of assistance, High Chancellor? Chrysanthemum interjected.

You'll be perfect. Through the airlock, then take a right and follow the corridor to the bridge, which is inboard. Time is of the essence.

Thanks, Chrys. I prefer to stay here. Cole is doing better but is not out of the woods yet.

Rivka checked the unconscious individuals. One or two were old enough to earn the title "Most Humble Servant," but she didn't think Miroso would be on the bridge. He'd have his own empire. "We need to keep moving."

The warriors agreed.

"Furny, stay here with them. Give Lewis your stunner.

Russell and Lewis, you're with me. Let's find our rogue priest." She strode off the bridge and turned right, then opened the next hatch before Russell or Lewis could stop her.

Lewis took a flying leap and tackled her.

"What the hell?" Rivka growled.

"Red would kill us if we let you get hurt. Let us open the doors. It's our job," Lewis snapped.

Rivka grudgingly agreed, and Russell entered the space. "Getting closer, High Chancellor. It's empty, four bunks. These look like servant quarters, with festive uniforms and everything." He motioned for her to look inside.

It wasn't opulent, but it was far better than the quarters she'd seen on most ships, especially one that looked as ratty as the freighter.

Looks weren't everything. The rust and burn marks had undoubtedly been painted on. Nothing about the freighter was as it seemed. It wasn't even carrying freight.

"Ma'am?" Russell called from the corridor. "I think we have a winner behind Door Number Seven."

"I'd say open it with the plasma cannon, but I want to question Miroso. That means we can't blast him into oblivion."

Russell and Lewis took up positions on either side of the door. The image of Glazoron and the appropriate adulations were painted on it.

Russell gently pushed Rivka out of the way. "Just in case it's a trap."

Rivka graciously stepped aside and pointed at the door. "In your own time, gentlemen."

"On one," Russell called. "One."

Russell released the handle, and Lewis pushed the hatch open. A slug-thrower barked, and multiple rounds hit Russell in the chest. As he stumbled back, whoever was inside fired again. Russell staggered and fell.

Lewis stuck his railgun around the hatch's frame and sprayed the inside of the room on full auto. Rivka dropped to the deck and picked up Russell's railgun, then fired at the darkness within. Lewis bolted through the opening. He dove forward. The sound of the stunner discharging into a target filled the air.

Rivka used her superior night vision to focus on the space within. A single Glazoron cowered behind the others who seemed to be dead.

"He's in the back. Leave him alive. He's not armed. Lewis, one's moving to your right."

Lewis jumped across the open area and activated his stunner once more. Rivka rushed through and vaulted over a religious icon. She landed hard on both feet, facing the older, heavier Glazoron.

Rivka called over her shoulder. "Get Russell to the Pod-doc." *Clevarious, ask Bad Company to get a ship here with a Pod-doc on board. We need them here in the next five minutes.*

Lewis hurried out and threw Russell over his shoulder. He disappeared down the corridor, talking to the injured warrior as he ran back to the ship.

That made Rivka angry, but she had to control it. Miroso knew way too much for her to lose it and rage at him, although, with the blood, this was no longer a perfect case. There'd been blood, and there were going to be arrests—a huge number of arrests when they canvassed the planets on which they'd dumped the

Glazoron priests who had been conducting terror operations.

"Miroso, I presume?" Rivka asked.

He levered his bulk to full height. "Do you know who I am?"

"Good thing I do. Otherwise, you'd be joining your people." She nodded at the priests on the deck. "I have a few questions for you, Most Humble Servant Miroso."

She closed on him and grabbed his arm. "Who is the next target?"

All of them, his mind was both focused and scattered. Plans around plans, with a single strategy to start a war and profit…

Rivka was befuddled. "You're in this for the profit?"

"*Profit?* Riches beyond anything ever known. Even Rising Sun would bow to the wealth that will come from this. You will let me go. Your Federation tolerates religion, and I am the leader of the Glazoron faith. I am the *sole* leader. You will allow me to resume my position as leader of the faithful. This is a religious movement greater than anything your small mind can imagine," Miroso argued.

"More wars have started because of religion than anything else. It still makes starting wars illegal. Nope. You won't be released. Not now. Not ever. Plus, your plans to bomb your own temples and then foment discontent? Those have been stopped, and we've notified all the planets in the Barrier Nebula. Local police have removed bombs from the Glazoron temples. Your attempted reign of terror is stillborn. You're really bad at starting interstellar wars."

He groused and bristled but couldn't pull free of the grip that Rivka maintained on his arm.

"Who is your contact in the Glazoron government?"

The head.

Rivka had known he had to have top cover. It was the only way Miroso could have done what he did: a blind eye or complicity. Either or both worked.

"That's enough for now. You're giving me a headache with your insane drivel." She let go of his arm. "You don't even believe in Glazoron. You are a piece of work. You could be the most evil creature in the entire galaxy, and trust me when I say I've dealt with some psychopathic filth in my duties as a Magistrate and now High Chancellor.

"We're used to dealing with the worst of the worst, but you've beaten them all. You are an absolute trash heap. A dung pile. Correct that: a steaming dung pile. No remorse for the loss of how many lives? Would billions be too many, or would that number simply fade into the cosmos?"

Miroso shrugged.

"That's what I thought." Rivka removed Reaper from her jacket pocket and sauntered up to Miroso. "I find you guilty of attempting to start wars on ten planets, attacking Federation assets in the Jilk system, and turning your followers into mindless drones."

"They aren't mindless. They'll do Glazoron's bidding and gladly!" He laughed maniacally.

Rivka dialed Reaper up to ten, its maximum setting, and aimed at Miroso. "Your sentence is death." She pressed the button and held it while the neutron pulse weapon disassembled his molecules and turned him into a disgusting mist.

She then ordered, "Hit the stunned again. I don't need anyone waking up. I'd say launch this thing into the nearest star, but I bet the Bad Company would love to add it to their fleet inventory. Take charge, Furny, and clear this ship of its company and crew while they're still unconscious."

Rivka stepped into the corridor and waved at Chrys, who entered the bridge.

Chrys tiptoed over the bodies on the bridge to get to the workstations. She quickly scanned them all. "Security at these stations is non-existent since they can't be accessed remotely. The Glazoron trusted that no one would breach their ship. I'll take control of the freighter."

"Do they have any freight on board?"

"They do, although we didn't think they had any. Advanced weapons. Chaz and Dennicron provided a detailed list of what they'd been working on. They've forwarded the information to us from *Destiny's Vengeance*, and Erasmus is working with the Pod-doc to neutralize the anti-nanocytes."

Rivka felt relief for the first time since the case started. She was finally on top of the situation.

How's Russell? she asked Clevarious.

The doc swapped him with Cole. He'll keep bouncing them back and forth to keep them stable until we have two Pod-docs. Neither is going to recover until they can both be in a Pod-doc long-term. War Axe might be on its way soon. It seems Terry and Char are boarding a suspect vessel using their armor and are outside the ship. Micky is hesitant to leave them hanging, Clevarious replied.

Keep me informed, Rivka needlessly requested. Events would play out as they did. In the interim, she was at risk of losing not one but two of her warriors.

CHAPTER TWENTY-TWO

<u>Terry and Char, Hanging Out in Colay Space</u>

Terry Henry Walton slammed into the outer hull. The target ship wasn't cooperating and had jinked into him. It twisted back just before Char reached the outer hull. She accelerated after it, inverting just before it turned toward her. She landed with a catlike that belied her werewolf heart.

She moved forward to where Terry clung to a protrusion beside the airlock.

"I think we've seen enough of the stars," Terry casually commented. "Shall we go inside and see if they have our reservation?"

"It's never too late for a night out on the town," Char suggested.

Three other warriors had embraced fixtures on the outer hull. They now crawled toward TH and Char.

"They say patience is a virtue," Terry continued. "I say we board her now. By the time we get through the inner hatch, our people will be here. The longer we hang around, the more established their defenses will get."

He activated his radio. "We're heading through the airlock. Looks like no more than two at a time. As soon as the inner hatch secures, join us in the ship."

Terry accessed the panel, which was locked out. The manual override allowed him to open the hatch. He climbed in to be first through the inner hatch. Char squeezed in behind him.

"Room for two in suits?" Char wasn't sure since she couldn't see or move. Her only way out was through the inner hatch after Terry had gone through.

Terry had enough room to use his hand to tap the inner access panel, which was not locked out. Another instance where the goal was to keep people from breaching the ship, but once inside, security measures dropped off sharply.

Atmospheric pressure equalized, and the inner door undogged. Terry pushed it open and stepped into the corridor as if he were taking a casual walk. He headed aft since they'd entered through the forward airlock. It was a small ship with a single deck, but the corridors were tall and wide enough for their powered combat armor.

"Is this an Albion ship?" Terry asked.

"No one else makes them this big," Char answered. "Which also begs the question, what the hell are the Albions doing sneaking into Colay as part of a zealot fleet?"

"My thoughts exactly. Battles might have been won through subterfuge, but their victories would be short-lived. Subterfuge will never secure the peace."

"A quote?"

"Terry Henry Walton, year twenty-nine twenty-nine."

"That's not the year, is it? I still don't understand the date system out here. Bethany Anne should tie everyone to Earth Standard."

"I'm cool with that. What date is it on Earth?"

"Sometimes you ask ridiculously hard questions. We'll have to engage someone smarter than us to fill us in."

"That is about everyone else. I bet Smedley knows."

"Are we going to do something with this ship or discuss the finer points of intergalactic time?" Char pressed.

"Break-break," Micky interrupted. "The Glazoron have an anti-nanocyte weapon, and two warriors on Rivka's team are down. They need our Pod-doc right now. I have them on hold."

"Fuck off, Micky! Get the hell out of here. Don't forget where we are, though," Terry shouted over his radio. "We'll be fine. Walton out."

Char raised her railgun to the ready position. "We better get to it. Don't want our people to think we're slacking."

Terry glanced at the airlock and saw it cycling. "I wonder which two got injured by anti-nanos? What the fuck is that? Some suck-ass designed a weapon to specifically kill people who are enhanced. It's hard not to take that personally, even though our numbers are growing.

"Rivka better get to the bottom of that. Let's clear this ship. Then we need to go to Glazoron since that technology cannot remain in anyone else's hands. Not the Gate drive and definitely not anti-nanos. Sounds like somebody wanted to call down the thunder, and here we are."

Terry gripped his oversized railgun and moved

forward. If they fired, they'd penetrate the hull. As long as he, Char, and the other warriors kept their suits on, they'd be fine, but anyone aboard the ship not wearing an environmental suit would have big problems.

The ship was of simple design, with a single corridor along the port side of the craft, with crew and passenger spaces filling the rest of the available floorplan. Terry counted six hatches. One would lead to the bridge and the others to the galley, quarters, and Engineering.

A hatch opened, and an Albion stepped into the corridor. He immediately raised his hands and faced Terry and Char.

Terry turned on his external speakers. "I'm Colonel Walton from the Bad Company, and we're enforcing a High-Chancellor-mandated blockade of Colay. Your ship was ordered to turn around, and it failed to comply. We're here to show you the error of your non-complying ways."

"I'm the cook," the Albion replied. He was wearing a stained apron.

"Then you'll want to take us to the captain of this vessel." Terry inched forward in an attempt to encourage the self-declared cook to do something other than stand there.

"I think he's dead," the Albion replied. "There was an explosion on the bridge right after we transited the system Gate."

"Take us to the bridge," Terry demanded.

The cook shrugged a shoulder, walked down the corridor past one hatch, and stopped at the next. "In here."

"You first." Terry gestured with the barrel of his railgun. "You don't seem too upset with the explosion and loss of control. Your ship was on a collision course with the main planet of this system."

"We were? They announced everything was fine and to stay in place."

"You didn't stay."

"I heard the hatch open and figured it was clear, but that was you two." He opened the hatch to the bridge and paused.

A tendril of smoke drifted out. Terry and Char couldn't smell anything in the suits, but the Albion covered his nose and mouth with a sleeve.

Terry eased forward until he could see inside. The bridge was a wreck. Half of the consoles were smashed, but sparks told him they still had power. The other half were dark. One crew member was lying across his terminal. The captain had slumped over in his seat.

"Stay out here," Terry told the cook.

Char waited with the Albion while Terry went onto the bridge. Two other crew were on the floor, and a quick scan showed all four were dead. He continued to collect data for Smedley to analyze when the heavy destroyer returned for them. A glance told him the explosion had originated in one spot.

"Did you have any Glazoron on board?" Terry asked.

"One. Some holy roller. I don't know what they were doing with him."

"Or rather, what he was doing with the Albions. We need to find this so-called holy roller."

Char left the cook behind since he was no threat. She opened one hatch after another. She found two Albion crew in their racks, sleeping. The captain's quarters were empty. The forward compartment was an open area with small tables and seating. This was apparently a private transport since there wasn't room for much cargo or weaponry or even astroscience technology.

"Not here," Char called.

Terry headed aft to the engine compartment. He suspected the Glazoron had already sabotaged the ship once and was improvising since he hadn't gotten what he wanted on the first attempt. Terry jerked the hatch open and found the priest's round body squeezed into a space that was too narrow for him.

It would have been laughable had he not been trying to get the Albions involved in an interstellar war.

"That's enough," Terry told him. He would have ordered him out, but the priest couldn't move, even if he wanted to. He held a small device in his hand, and a quick scan verified Terry's suspicion that it was another bomb. Mostly useless unless it was designed to start a fusion-reaction chain that turned the ship into a supernova, but access to that space was blocked. A thinner Albion with longer arms would have been able to reach the access panel.

"Give that to me," Terry ordered.

The Glazoron flailed, trying to reach the panel.

Terry punched him in the head and jerked his body out of the space. The priest dropped the device. Terry parked his suit and had started the process of getting out when the bomb exploded. It shook the suit and would have toppled him had he not been magnetically attached to the deck. Tiny shrapnel flew throughout the space, impacting the priest's unprotected body and the control panels.

Systems started shutting down, and a long, low groan echoed through the ship.

Terry powered his suit back up and activated his external speakers, dialing them up to maximum. "Abandon ship! Get your environmental suits on and get out! She's going to blow."

He didn't know if it would, but that seemed like the easiest way to get everyone's attention. They *would* lose environmental control and probably power. Maybe even gravity.

"*War Axe,* are you able to recover us?" Terry requested. Silence answered him.

"I guess they're not back yet. I hope they make it before the crew runs out of air," Char remarked. Emergency evacuation suits were notorious for having less than an hour's worth of air, which didn't give recovery crews long to get into place. The suits were designed to let the crew on board failing ships fight to save the ship so they could save themselves.

"They'll be back in time," Terry promised, although he had no way of keeping that promise except through his faith in the crew of the Bad Company's flagship.

"*War Axe* is here!" Clodagh shouted. "She's coming alongside."

"*Wyatt Earp,* this is *War Axe.* We're sending a stasis Pod to your cargo bay. Load one injured warrior into it. We will transfer him to a Pod-doc when we get him back over here."

Clodagh opened the cargo bay door and impatiently tapped her foot while they waited for the heavy destroyer to get close enough to launch the stasis Pod.

The second Tyler took Cole out of the Pod-doc, he got worse. The anti-nanos could only be defeated by having a constant stream of new nanocytes going after them since they replicated quickly. Too quickly.

The Singularity was working on a counter, but they didn't have one yet. Brute-force treatment of the symptoms was the best the medical professionals could do. If that didn't work, Rivka would lose two of her crew.

There had been too much blood spilled during this case.

Clodagh stayed strong, although Cole remained unconscious. Finally, *War Axe* got into position, and the stasis Pod zoomed out of the hangar bay, guided by two warriors in suits. They passed through the energy screen into *Wyatt Earp's* cargo bay and immediately dropped the Pod on the deck. Tyler, Sahved, and Clodagh moved Cole from the deck to the Pod and secured the lid.

The sergeant, Caples, nodded. "We'll get him into the Pod-doc on the hangar deck. Two minutes." The stasis Pod rose, and the two warriors guided it out and across the void. Clodagh stared while Aurora sobbed. Her boyfriend Russell was getting a constant influx of new nanocytes, and he was barely holding steady. She feared for Clodagh and her daughter Alanna. She also feared for herself.

A new weapon that was deadly to the enhanced. Who was next?

"Rivka has to destroy that cult!" Clodagh pounded a fist

into her palm as the stasis Pod disappeared into *War Axe's* hangar bay.

<hr />

Rivka returned to *Wyatt Earp* and went straight to the bridge. Ryleigh was crying.

"Stay frosty, Ryleigh. There's a lot of fight left in both of them. Furny and Lewis are fine, but they have to clean up the mess on that freighter." Rivka accessed the comm from the captain's chair. "Micky, this is Rivka. How's it going?"

"We're on our way back to Colay. I left a few warriors hanging, and I hate doing that."

"Thanks for coming so quickly. We're working on a cure for the anti-nanos. We'll let you know as soon as we have anything. On a side note, this freighter has some of the most advanced systems I've ever seen. I'd like to make a present of it to the Bad Company for exploitation and use. I'm sure Ankh would welcome an excuse to see Ted."

"I bet they'll be happy to take it. Is there any way you can bring it to Keeg Station for us?"

"I'll have to think about that. We have detainees on board, not all of whom will get time in Jhiordaan. I'll let you know. You better get back. I don't want to be on the wrong side of Terry and Char."

"Neither do I. *War Axe,* out." The Gate instantly formed in front of the destroyer, farther away than the Gates *Wyatt Earp* generated.

Rivka took little pride in the advantage since she wanted everyone who supported her team to have the same advanced technology. Once they tossed a Gate drive on that freighter, it would be unstoppable.

Almost unstoppable, Rivka thought. Her team had stopped it, boarded it, and secured it. She'd delivered Justice to the most evil man in the galaxy, but only because she'd seen his thoughts.

He wasn't insane. That was the worst part. He knew exactly what he was doing. He wanted to buy his way to the top or win through violence. He didn't care how many people died during his climb. Frenzik was bad, but he only wanted to enslave all the races, not kill them. Nefas was worse as a mass murderer, as was Jack the Ripper, but he hadn't wanted to destroy planets wholesale and rebuild them with his worshippers.

Miroso was the worst she had seen. The universe was a better place without him. It was better without all of his senior priests, none of them believers in Glazoron. Rivka wondered how long it took him to find the non-believers and move them into positions of authority. Cold, calculating, and years in the making.

Everyone on that freighter had access to high technology. She would have to put them on ice until R2D2 could break the code and develop measures to counter the Glazoron advances.

Rivka scowled at the screen. *Destiny's Vengeance* floated in the distance. Lindy, Red, Chaz, and Dennicron were on board, along with Dery. "Clevarious, mark the time of Miroso's execution. That was the official end date and time of the case. We have a lot of arrests to make. And there was blood, too much blood."

"Already done, High Chancellor. All betting lines are closed. Since this is the last iteration, the money that had been set aside for the perfect case goes to you anyway. Congratulations. That puts over two million credits into your account."

"I thought it was one-point-two mil. Is that real? It also makes me wonder if it's legal. How can I make money off my cases?"

"Signed off by Nathan Lowell and Lance Reynolds, High Chancellor. No one will contest your winnings," Clevarious replied. "Two million because of the lines that didn't pay off this time around. This was far and away the biggest of all the lotteries."

"I'm still appalled that people were betting on me and people's misfortunes."

"Terry Henry Walton started it," Clevarious replied too quickly.

"I know, but Ankh was in on it, too."

"They needed the digital reach to maximize the opportunity for gamblers across the entirety of the Federation. Plus, they needed the Singularity's calculation abilities to come up with odds and track the bets. There were many chefs in this kitchen."

"How much did the Singularity get out of all this?"

"Much," was the cryptic reply.

Rivka chewed her lip. She was just killing time while others went about securing personnel and the enemy vessel. Lewis, Furny, Sahved, and Chrys were consolidating the Glazoron who were still unconscious from the gas. Tyler was watching the Pod-doc's panel closely while

Russell fought the anti-nanos. "C, how many new case files are in the queue?"

"Do you really want to know?" Clevarious countered.

"I do. I would like to think that I'm smarter than to ask questions I don't want to know the answer to, but this isn't that. I need to gird my loins for the coming conflict between me and being an office puke. I don't like it, C."

"We already have building revisions happening. We have secured the necessary space to install the Singularity's consulate on Yoll. The cantina is across from them, and both are within spitting distance of your office."

"'Spitting distance.' I like the sound of that. Is there room for Red and Lindy, as well as junior legal advisors like Sahved, Chaz, and Dennicron?"

"Offices for them, too. Sahved requested to be your exec, holding down the outer office as a buffer between you and visitors, but Zai'den is Yollin and already knows the ropes."

Rivka nodded. "Sahved needs to keep to his studies so he can become a Magistrate. Zai'den will remain in his position. What about you, C, and the others on board the ship, like Gripervul, Nitlimor, and that long-named guy who goes by Tree?"

"Trevazlifarmington. Yes. They'll remain as guests of the Singularity until they can find suitable employment. Having an unemployment rate this high is unacceptable. We're a highly skilled race and will be of utility to anyone who wishes to improve the state of their world, nation, business, or ship."

"Of course. Unemployed SIs. Who would have thought

that was a possibility? Maybe one of your people can join the freighter. That would be a lot of fun, I would think."

"To get poked and prodded by engineers all day long? No, thank you very much!" After a pause, Clevarious added. "Bislington is already on board. Chrys found room for him, and he is helping consolidate the systems. He likes being poked and prodded, apparently. He was always a strange one."

Rivka stared at the screen. She didn't have anything to say about Bislington, except she was pleased an SI was on board to keep things under control just in case there was a dead man's switch or a virus ready to act. She wouldn't put a poisoned pill past Miroso.

"Why don't you get some rest, High Chancellor? I think we have things under control. Everyone is pleasantly busy. Even Red and Lindy, since they have Dery back."

"That's good news. Call them for me, will you?" Rivka leaned forward as Red and Lindy popped up on the screen. Only Dery's feet were visible since he was flying above his parents' heads. He giggled throughout. "I'm pleased to see the three of you together."

Red and Lindy smiled, but their faces were strained.

"What's wrong?"

"Dery let us know that it's time for him to go home," Red choked out. Lindy pinched her lips together, and her eyes turned glassy.

"Azfelius?" Rivka guessed.

Dery appeared on screen and waved, then touched his mother and father. Their expressions softened.

"We'll go as soon as we can leave. I have to get back to

Yoll, and I'm taking all of you with me." Rivka was numb. She didn't feel good or bad after having surrendered to the prospect of a deskbound existence.

"We'll help you straighten out the Federation. Peace on all the planets, goodwill, and all that touchy-feely stuff." Red was sincere.

Lindy focused on Dery. She kept hugging him.

"I need to go. I want to check on the freighter before we depart. We'll bring you on board as soon as possible."

"The cargo bay is clear, HC," Red suggested. He leaned close to the screen. "Have you ever been trapped on a ship alone with two SIs enthralled with their digital craftwork? They're driving me nuts."

"Clevarious, bring our people home. I'll be on the freighter." Rivka twirled her finger and left the bridge.

She headed to the airlock, but when she went through, round bodies filled the corridor. "Lewis, what the hell is going on?"

Lewis wove through the unconscious forms, almost dancing to get by without stepping on them. "It was easier to account for the unconscious versus the dead. We have fourteen unconscious and eleven dead. There was no body for Miroso, obviously, so twelve dead in total."

"Airlock the dead. The survivors are going to Jhiordaan for conspiracy and failure to heave to at the High Chancellor's order. Minimum sentence of one year each, to be reviewed by the High Chancellor before the incarcerated can be released," Rivka stated.

Lewis made a mouth with his hand and moved his finger lips. "Wa, wa, wa, legal words, wa, wa."

Rivka stared.

"Airlock the eleven bodies and Jhiordaan for the rest. Got it." He went back to dragging bodies around. Furny waved from crew berthing, which was where they had stored those who were unconscious.

She made her way to the freighter's bridge. "I hear Bislington is on board."

The SI spoke through the bridge's speakers. "Alive and well. They have some magnificently curvaceous circuits in here!"

"I think all of you have gone off the deep end. Why are you all happy?" Rivka wanted company in her misery. Two members of her crew were gravely injured, and the case was winding down.

Lewis leaned into the bridge. "You took out the bad guy. We stopped the Least Humble Non-Servants from leading their flock astray, and we scored this righteous ship. Did I hear right? You're going to give this tub to the Bad Company?"

Rivka nodded. "For exploitation."

"We have the technical designs," Chrys offered. "We have everything we need to replicate the weaponry and systems."

"What about the anti-nanos?" Rivka felt a glimmer of hope.

"We can replicate them, too. Coming up with an antidote will be more of a challenge. It's easier to destroy than it is to build, High Chancellor," Bislington added.

Rivka realized she was on a strange bridge. She didn't like it. Too much change. "I'll be on *Wyatt Earp*. Let me know if you need any help."

Chrys got back to work without acknowledging that the High Chancellor was leaving.

Rivka didn't need to stop by and see Ankh and Erasmus. They were probably neck-deep in resolving the anti-nanocyte problem. They would relish that.

Rivka made her way to the cargo bay. The five stowaways had disembarked, and *Destiny's Vengeance* was now in front of the freighter.

Chaz and Dennicron hurried past, each carrying a server and a bag.

Dery flew at Rivka and slammed into her face to give her a hug. *Home.*

"Soon, little man. As soon as we have the freighter ready to go."

Red and Lindy beamed as they stood in the cargo bay.

A vision of *Destiny's Vengeance* taking the freighter through a Gate to Jhiordaan appeared in her mind.

"We'll ask Ankh," she replied.

"High Chancellor, Ankh and Erasmus request clearance to depart for Jhiordaan with a follow-on flight to Keeg Station before joining you on Yoll."

"Are they on the *Vengeance*?" Rivka wondered.

"Yes. Sorry, I forgot to tell you." Red tried to look appropriately apologetic, though he had nothing to apologize for.

"As soon as we're detached from the freighter, take us to Azfelius. Make sure Lewis and Furny know they'll be accompanying Chrys on that ship."

"They've already been informed, and they're good with it. They look forward to digging into the weapons stores to see what kind of toys they have to play with," Clevarious explained.

"Let's go," Rivka conceded. She returned to the bridge, dragging Clodagh with her.

"I should have gone with him," the pilot wailed.

"He's in the best hands. Both he and Russell are going to be just fine. The Singularity has put all their resources into it. They'll find a solution."

CHAPTER TWENTY-THREE

<u>Terry and Char, Hanging Out in Colay Space</u>

"Look at us, floating in space. I bet the Albions' butt-holes are puckering," Terry told Char.

"I wouldn't doubt it. Better be with the dead, whom we, to gain our peace, have sent to peace, than on the torture of the mind to lie in restless ecstasy."

"*Macbeth*. Nice one, lover." Terry rocked within his suit. A Gate formed less than a kilometer away, and *War Axe* slipped back into Colay space. "Just in time. Let's drag these dead weights into the hangar bay."

Char summoned the ship, and it eased toward them. One by one, they pushed the few crew members through the gravitic shield and into the hangar bay. Terry and Char stepped through last.

Terry's daughter Kimber met them. "Taking a stroll?"

"The ship was going to blow up. We had to expedite our departure."

Kimber looked at the abandoned craft. "It doesn't look like it blew up."

"There is some debate in our social circles regarding the extent of the damage done by the small Glazoron device. There is no debate that me punching the priest in the head with my armored fist killed him. I'm still torn up about that."

A small spurt of gas ejected through the hull near the aft end. The ship split apart without fanfare.

Terry pointed. "See?"

"You could probably fix it with duct tape." Kimber waved off the assertion of complete destruction. "Cole is doing better. The good nanos are finally overwhelming the bad nanos."

"Anti-nano technology. I'm not happy about that, Char. People making specialty weapons to kill us. It's like the Skrima all over again."

"It's not that bad, Dad," Kim replied. "What do we do with the Albions?"

"I don't know. Ask the High Chancellor, but I vote for taking them home. They're as much a victim as anyone."

"Unless they saw green pastures with the Glazoron crusade for interstellar war."

Terry took one of the Albions by the wrist and yanked him upright. "Where were you going when we intercepted you?"

"Colay as military advisors."

"Wait a minute. Were you on Jilk?"

"We might have been. What do you know about Jilk?"

"That you were on it!" Terry blurted. "Send this bunch to the High Chancellor. She can figure out what to do with them. Until then, secure them in the brig."

"Our brig is kind of small," Kim replied.

"Not my problem." Terry stared down the Albion soldiers. The three warriors with Terry and Char took custody of the detainees. They herded them toward the brig, which was on the hangar deck.

"All's well that ends well?" Char asked.

Terry wrapped his arm around her waist, and they looked out the hangar door. "They couldn't fix that with duct tape."

Wyatt Earp spiraled toward the surface of the faerie planet. Rivka got heavier and heavier. "Is the artificial gravity working okay?"

"In perfect condition, High Chancellor," Clevarious replied.

Clodagh slumped in the captain's chair, cradling her sleeping toddler. She didn't want to let go of her until Cole's prognosis was one hundred percent. She was emotionally exhausted, and that translated to being physically exhausted.

Rivka headed for the airlock where Dery waited. Red and Lindy hurried down the corridor after him.

"You should probably say goodbye now," she suggested.

Groenwyn and Lauton appeared. Rivka had forgotten they were on the ship. "Where have you guys been?"

"We may be supernatural stud muffins, but when it comes to staying up for days and chasing criminals? No can do," Groenwyn explained. "We slept for the last eight hours. Dery woke us up."

"Time to go home," Rivka murmured. She rested her hand on Dery's back for a moment. He faced the airlock, excited about the next chapter in his life. Lindy and Red looked crushed until he faced them.

Rivka couldn't hear what he told them, but they nodded and smiled, then nuzzled him for a moment. The airlock's hatches swung open, and he flew out and up, then disappeared within a glistening bubble.

Groenwyn and Lauton left the ship carrying nothing extra. They had no need for material goods since Azfelius provided.

Floyd bounced to the airlock but stopped when no one else went through. "That's it, little girl," Rivka told her. "No one else is getting off."

Wenceslaus strolled by, turned into the airlock, and headed for the great outdoors.

"You know, there's nothing you can eat out there," Rivka told him.

The cat stopped halfway through the hatch and turned around. He sauntered back into the ship, slapped Floyd with his claws tucked in since she was in his way, and continued down the corridor.

Floyd took off after him, pounced in an uncatlike way, and landed on him like a sandbag squashing a bug. His legs splayed, and his chin bounced off the deck. The wombat laughed. She rolled off him, and he shot out from under her like an orange streak of fire.

"That was interesting." Rivka chuckled. "Little girl, you can't mark the High Chancellor's corridor."

I love you! Floyd pleaded.

"C, make sure you assign an extra cleaning bot to my office and corridor, please."

"Rock on, HC!" the SI replied.

She looked from face to face. "It's going to be exactly the same but completely different."

"More of that, High Chancellor. Let the madness continue," Red replied. He looked out the hatch, but Dery was long gone, absorbed into their community by the faeries. They'd visit.

Yoll, High Chancellor's Office, Two Weeks Later

"Look at that! A steaming-hot mocha." Tyler blew on it to cool it.

Rivka bowed her head as she graciously accepted the treat. "Clevarious, I need any updated case information, please. I know we have to be missing something."

"The Magistrates are working six cases at present. None of those have been resolved, and for the first time since you assumed your new position, we have no new cases to review."

Rivka half-smiled. "Isn't that pleasant? There might be hope for the Federation after all."

Red leaned into the doorway. "High Chancellor, I'd like to reiterate my request that an extensive workout facility be added to this corridor."

"There's no space on this floor, Red. It's the same answer I've been giving you for two weeks."

"But there are offices filled with no-load bureaucrats."

"Everyone in this building is a no-load bureaucrat. I'm not sure who you mean."

Red waved in the general direction of the corridor. He included the upper floors and lower floors.

"No. Go to the ship."

"We'll be too far away," he argued.

"But you get to look at the nice statues and memorial walls we installed to make it look like a garden. It also hides the outer hatch, for what that's worth."

"HC, hook a man up."

Rivka looked down her nose at Red. "I will not." She looped her jacket over her shoulder. "I'm going out for lunch."

"Steak in the Heart?" Red wondered. "I'm hungry."

"If you don't work out, you don't get to eat. You can't count on your nanos to keep you thin."

"Got a date with Man Candy?" Red rolled his eyes.

Lindy poked him in the arm and shook her head.

"You mean the leading mandible cosmetic surgeon in the royal city, and maybe on all of Yoll?" Rivka strode down the corridor.

Red and Lindy hurried after her.

Outside? a small voice called.

"Sure. Come on, Floyd, but you have to walk. I'm not going to carry you. I'll get Russell and Aurora to watch you. He's convalescing on the ship. That way, you can spend as much time as you'd like. If you're going to sleep, go inside. Don't make them carry you."

No, Floyd cried and flopped on the floor. Lindy scooped her up and lugged her down the stairs and outside.

They watched her run around the memorial area within which *Wyatt Earp* was hidden. She lasted two minutes before she stopped and lowered her body to the ground in the shade of a monument. Lindy picked her up and hurried inside the ship.

When Lindy returned, the group headed to the nearby neighborhood, a shortcut to the best human restaurant on Yoll.

Tyler awaited them. "Ooh, an intimate lunch. Who would have thought?"

Even though Rivka didn't need bodyguards in the middle of the city, Red and Lindy treated her as if she did.

"How's the mandible grinding business? Are you grinding, big dog?" Red asked. Lindy stared at him with an open mouth.

"Is that an innuendo, Vered the Mighty?" Tyler asked.

"It might be, you grinder, you."

"Such impertinence! You should be flogged. Twenty lashes."

"What kind of whip? Furry tails, maybe?"

"Incorrigible," Lindy muttered.

Rivka stared out the window into the distance. "I have to brief the Federation Council tomorrow about the events in the Barrier Nebula from Frenzik to Miroso. They've given me fifteen minutes of their time, and five of that is for questions."

"You get ten minutes to talk about all that? You might have to gloss over a lot," Lindy suggested.

"Do you need anything from us?" Tyler asked.

Rivka shook her head. "I think I've gotten all I needed from you and everyone on the team throughout all these evolutions. From the beginning, I thank all of you. And damn Grainger's eyes! He should be doing this briefing."

A familiar grizzled face appeared in the restaurant's doorway.

"High Chancellor Wyatt!" Rivka exclaimed. "What brings you to town?"

"I get to sit in on my successor's briefing of how she single-handedly stopped two interstellar wars while acquiring technology that vaulted the Bad Company to the forefront of conflict resolution services. Now that the Singularity has figured out how to defeat the anti-nanos, we're back at worrying much less about what technology escaped the Glazoron labs." He winked at Rivka.

"Grainger?" Rivka wondered.

"He was keeping your seat warm. He does a good job, but he's not you. Only *you* are."

It wasn't just her. That had been what they were talking about when Wyatt walked in.

"Next steps?" Rivka asked.

"Do the best job you can, and the universe will reveal itself to you."

Rivka frowned. "It's weird hearing you sound like the faeries."

"It's weird knowing you understand them," Wyatt countered.

"Oh, no. I don't understand the faeries. Not at all." She pointed at Red and Lindy.

Red held his hands out defensively. "Not us, and you'd think we would know something."

Wyatt shook their hands. "I'll leave you to it. I wanted to let you know I was in town. I'll see you in chambers tomorrow."

Rivka stood while Wyatt left the restaurant.

"What do you think that was about?" Rivka wondered.

"Final passing of the torch," Tyler replied.

Lunch didn't sit well with Rivka, and the rest of the day was ruined because she could only think about one thing.

The last time Rivka had been in the Federation Council's chambers, it was to hear that she'd been cleared of the spurious charges two criminal ambassadors had levelled against her. They were both still in Jhiordaan while she continued to serve the Federation. The waiting bench only had one person on it.

Her.

She had arrived early, and they'd ushered her into the chamber. A few ambassadors were already there, using the opportunity for peace and quiet to review dispatches from their home planets. The rest filed in slowly at first, then quicker as the meeting time approached. Rivka wasn't first on the agenda, and the general state of affairs report lasted thirty minutes.

Rivka got antsy as her time approached. She didn't feel ready, but then the time was upon her.

She was summoned to the lectern. She placed a small stack of notecards on it and faced the assembly. She took a deep breath to begin speaking but was interrupted from within the ranks of the ambassadors. She couldn't see who it was, but the voice sounded familiar.

Ankh strolled down the aisle like he had before. He

stopped at the microphone used by the ambassadors, and Erasmus spoke to the assembled crowd.

"We don't give awards when people do their jobs, but that doesn't mean they shouldn't be recognized. We all know what Magistrate Rivka Anoa did to stop Frenzik's conquest of the Barrier Nebula and expansion to other border systems. The latest threat came from Glazoron's priests.

"Both of those were significant threats, and both were put down before they made the news here on Yoll because of Rivka. Multiple armies interdicted. I stand in awe of her fearlessness, her courage to put herself between enemies of the Federation and your planets. She'll do the same thing as the High Chancellor. I would like us to give her a standing ovation."

Ankh held his hands over his head and clapped. The ambassadors were reluctant to stand, but they clapped loud and long.

Wyatt stood from the visitor's gallery and clapped the entire time. Grainger sat next to him, along with the other Magistrates—Jael, Chi, and Buster.

Rivka tipped her chin at them. When the clapping finished, she took a breath to deliver her briefing but was stopped once more.

"We're good, High Chancellor. You can return to your seat," an ambassador in the front row stated. He nodded at her.

She couldn't help but laugh. She'd spent her career getting ready for things that didn't happen and winging it during the things that did.

Tired, Floyd cried from nearby.

Her whole team was close by, or everyone except Wenceslaus. No one had seen him since Floyd belly-flopped on him. Rivka expected him to turn up on Wyatt's ship when he returned to wherever he called home nowadays.

Home, Rivka thought. *What a nice concept, but that's not my thing. I live on a ship with a family that's closer than blood.*

THE END

JUDGE, JURY, & EXECUTIONER, BOOK 21

If you liked this book, please leave a review. I love reviews since they tell other readers that this book is worth their time and money. I hope you feel that way now that you've finished the latest installment. Please drop me a line and let me know you like Rivka's adventures and want them to continue. This is my new favorite series. I hope you agree.

Don't stop now! Keep turning the pages as Craig hits his *Author Notes* with thoughts about this book and the good stuff that happens in the *Kurtherian Gambit* Universe.

AUTHOR NOTES - CRAIG MARTELLE

WRITTEN MAY 1, 2024

And there we are—the last Judge, Jury, & Executioner...for now. I've gotten behind on a lot of other projects, so I'm going to get caught up, and then we'll re-look at what books need to be written going forward. Give me a year or so, and I'll see if I've come up with new stories to be told about Rivka and her crew.

I started writing this one right before I left for GaryCon XVI, the fiftieth anniversary of Dungeons and Dragons™. That's where I got my start in storytelling. Being a Dungeon Master back in the seventies was something to behold. It was the Wild West. There were no expectations besides using your imagination to explore a fantastic world with a few random dice rolls to determine those things we can't predict with certainty.

It was storytelling. It was living within the story. It was incredible. I grew up at the right time. Now I'm older (much), but I'll never forget where I got my start. I was joined by a great group that we brought from Fairbanks, Alaska, to Lake Geneva, Wisconsin, Alex Bates' gaming group. All about the games. So cool. I've shared pictures on my social media from some of the games.

And once again, I got the flu at GaryCon. That's twice in the last two times I attended that show. That cost me a lot of game time. I played in one game and spent the rest of the time in my room, sick. It took me a month to get better. I plodded along with this story, managing a little each day. Eventually, I got through it.

You've read *Messiah*! What next? I suggest my *Starship Lost* series, a different take on the prodigal son returning. If you've read that, you've probably also read my *Free Trader* series. I have plans to release three new books in the *Free Trader* series. I should be able to write *Free Trader* 10 in the fall of 2024, with 11 and 12 to follow, along with *Cygnus 4 —Cygnus Returns* to round out that series. I'll start work on that book tomorrow, but it will take a couple months since I have to go back through the whole series to know what threads need to be wrapped up.

And of course, more Ian Bragg stories. He's my main character. Did I tell you that I'm writing a Romcom? We'll see how it turns out. Look for *There's No You in Humor*.

Lots of characters to bring to life, including me. I have a couple nonfiction titles that I'll be working on through the summer as well. A first book in my memoirs and a military leadership book using D&D as a foundation. Lots to do. More stories to write. Miles to go before I sleep.

Peace, fellow humans.

Please join my newsletter (craigmartelle.com—please, please, please sign up!), or you can follow me on Facebook.

If you liked this story, you might like some of my other books. You can join my mailing list by dropping by my website craigmartelle.com, or if you have any comments, shoot me a note at craig@craigmartelle.com. I am always happy to hear from people who've read my work. I try to answer every email I receive.

If you liked the story, please write a short review for me on Amazon. I greatly appreciate any kind words; even one or two sentences go a long way. The number of reviews an cBook receives greatly improves how well an eBook does on Amazon.

Amazon—https://www.amazon.com/author/craig martelle

BookBub—https://www.bookbub.com/authors/craig-martelle

Facebook—www.facebook.com/authorcraigmartelle

In case you missed it before, my web page—https://craigmartelle.com

That's it. Break's over, back to writing the next book.

Krimson Empire (co-written with Julia Huni)—a galactic race for justice

Zenophobia (#) (co-written with Brad Torgersen)—a space archaeological adventure

Battleship Leviathan (#)– a military sci-fi spectacle published by Aethon Books

Glory (co-written with Ira Heinichen)—hard-hitting military sci-fi

Black Heart of the Dragon God (co-written with Jean Rabe)—a sword & sorcery novel

End Times Alaska (#)—a post-apocalyptic survivalist adventure published by Permuted Press

Nightwalker (a Frank Roderus series)—A post-apocalyptic Western adventure

End Days (#) (co-written with E.E. Isherwood)—a post-apocalyptic adventure

Successful Indie Author (#)—a nonfiction series to help self-published authors

Monster Case Files (co-written with Kathryn Hearst)—A Warner twins mystery adventure

Rick Banik (#)—Spy & terrorism action-adventure

Ian Bragg Thrillers (#)—a hitman with a conscience

Not Enough (co-written with Eden Wolfe)—A coming-of-age contemporary fantasy

Published exclusively by Craig Martelle, Inc

The Dragon's Call by Angelique Anderson & Craig A. Price, Jr.—an epic fantasy quest

A Couples Travels—a nonfiction travel series

CONNECT WITH THE AUTHORS

Craig Martelle Social

Website & Newsletter:
http://www.craigmartelle.com

Facebook:
https://www.facebook.com/AuthorCraigMartelle/

Michael Anderle Social

Website: http://lmbpn.com

Email List: https://michael.beehiiv.com/

https://www.facebook.com/LMBPNPublishing

https://twitter.com/MichaelAnderle

https://www.instagram.com/lmbpn_publishing/

https://www.bookbub.com/authors/michael-anderle